Fiona Leitch is a nove chequered past. She's motoring magazines, childbirth videos and mail order catalogues; DJ'ed at illegal raves in London, been told off by a children's TV presenter during a studio debate; and was the Australasian face of a series of TV commercials for a cleaning product. All of which has given her a thorough grounding in the ridiculous, and helped her to write funny stuff. She writes the Jodie 'Nosey' Parker series for HarperCollins because she loves thinking about Cornwall, food, and murdering people (but not necessarily in that order).

 twitter.com/fkleitch
 facebook.com/fionakleitch

Also by Fiona Leitch

The Nosey Parker Cozy Mysteries

The Cornish Wedding Murder

The Cornish Village Murder

The Perfect Cornish Murder

A Cornish Christmas Murder

A CORNISH RECIPE FOR MURDER

A Nosey Parker Cozy Mystery

FIONA LEITCH

One More Chapter
a division of HarperCollins*Publishers* Ltd
1 London Bridge Street
London SE1 9GF
www.harpercollins.co.uk
HarperCollins*Publishers*
1st Floor, Watermarque Building, Ringsend Road
Dublin 4, Ireland

This paperback edition 2022
1
First published in Great Britain in ebook format
by HarperCollins*Publishers* 2022
Copyright © Fiona Leitch 2022
Fiona Leitch asserts the moral right to be identified
as the author of this work
A catalogue record of this book is available from the British Library

ISBN: 978-0-00-852537-8

This novel is entirely a work of fiction. The names, characters and
incidents portrayed in it are the work of the author's imagination.
Any resemblance to actual persons, living or dead, events or localities
is entirely coincidental.

Printed and bound in the UK using 100% Renewable Electricity
by CPI Group (UK) Ltd

All rights reserved. No part of this publication may be reproduced,
stored in a retrieval system, or transmitted, in any form or by any
means, electronic, mechanical, photocopying, recording or otherwise,
without the prior permission of the publishers.

Prologue

'**B**efore I say anything, you have to promise not to get annoyed.'

That's never a good way to start a conversation, is it? And accompanied by the guilty expression that was currently occupying Nathan's face, it was doubly concerning. DCI Nathan Withers, lifetime holder of the 'Cornwall's Dishiest Detective' title, stood on my doorstep, holding an envelope in one hand.

I stood back to let him in. 'Oh no, that's not going to work. I'm not promising anything until I know what you've been up to…'

Nathan looked up as, behind me, my daughter Daisy came bounding down the stairs.

'Hi, Nath—' she began, then stopped. I turned round just in time to see the two of them share a conspiratorial look. I wasn't sure at first if I was imagining it, but a guilty expression crossed her face too before she could wipe it off. She looked at the envelope in Nathan's hand. 'Is that…? I was just – I'd better—' She turned back up the stairs to make her escape.

'Oh no you don't,' he said. 'This is on you, too.'

'What on earth is going on?' I said, beginning to get seriously irritated.

'It was all Daisy's idea,' said Nathan quickly. She snorted.

'Oh *thanks*, Nathan. I knew I could rely on you not to crack under pressure…'

Mum came out of the living room, Germaine the dog yapping at her heels. 'What's going on? Oooh, is that…?'

'OH MY GOD!' I snapped. Germaine plopped herself down on my foot and looked up at me, but I ignored her. 'WHAT IS GOING ON? Why has my hallway suddenly turned into Clapham Junction? Somebody had better tell me what this is all about within the next thirty seconds or else I swear to God—'

'We entered you for the Best of British Baking Roadshow,' blurted Nathan. He held out the envelope – addressed to me but at his cottage, and already opened – and I took it from him. 'We got you a spot. You're going to be on the telly.'

Chapter One

'I still haven't forgiven you. Any of you.'

Mum carried on studying the menu, looking completely unconcerned, as Daisy snorted and rolled her eyes; no guilty consciences there. At least Nathan tried to look contrite, gazing at me beseechingly across the table. Under it my faithful canine companion whined pitifully. I laughed.

'Oh my God, your puppy dog eyes are worse than Germaine's,' I said. 'All right, I forgive you, but I'm still not sure this was a good idea. I keep telling everyone, I'm a chef, not a baker.'

It was just under a year since I'd moved back to Penstowan, the small Cornish town I'd grown up in, with Daisy in tow. We'd left the noise, pollution and dangers of my career in the Metropolitan Police in London for a safer, more peaceful life, with none of the risks my previous line of work had made my daughter worry about. It had definitely been a move for the better; I'd swapped a life of trying to avoid my useless, unfaithful ex to one of genuine love, affection and respect with Nathan, and my catering business, after a few (murderous) hiccups, had slowly picked up. But it was a good job there were no wolves in Cornwall, as it still wasn't earning me enough to keep them permanently from my door…

We were sitting in the Cavalier, a rather nice country pub with bistro pretensions near Canworthy Water. Nathan and the rest of the family had come to pick me up after my first day of filming (I'd been too het up to drive myself that morning) and had suggested we stop for dinner on the way home. The pub sign – a furry-faced Cavalier King Charles spaniel, in a Three Musketeers-style hat with a floppy feather in it – reassured me that all five of us would be welcome inside.

'It'll be really good publicity for Banquets and Bakes —' started Nathan.

'Yeah, if I don't go out in the first elimination round,' I said. Mum huffed and put down the menu.

'Oh for goodness' sake! Your cakes are always proper tasty, even if they do look like something the dog's dug up.'

'Not helping, Nana,' muttered Daisy under her breath.

'And you are a trained chef,' Nathan pointed out, reasonably enough. 'I was surprised when they let you in. You must have an advantage over the other contestants.'

'Exactly!' Mum was looking around impatiently for a waiter. 'It's not like you're competing against Fanny Craddock or someone. More like a bunch of housewives and accountants. Are we ordering or what?' She always got a bit stroppy when she was hungry.

I found out what Mum and Daisy wanted, then Nathan and I headed to the bar to order. Before we got there he pulled me into a quiet corner, and into his arms.

'You do forgive me, don't you?' he said, gazing into my eyes in a way that meant I would have forgiven him anything — stinky armpits, farting during sexual intercourse (I hasten to add he never did either). Anything, in fact, except maybe eating the last of the Christmas chocolate without me, which a) he knew better than to do, and b) there was rarely any chocolate left past 27th December anyway, so he would probably never get the chance.

'I'm not letting you off that easily,' I said, although I totally was. He laughed and leaned down to kiss me.

'You'll thank me for it. Eventually.'

'Yeah... No, I do thank you for it, but you know what

my cake-decorating is like. When I left the Force I did think about setting myself up to make people's wedding cakes and that, but I was so useless at all the fancy stuff I gave up on the idea. I'm just worried I'll look like a right muppet.'

'Of course you won't!' said Nathan, giving me a squeeze. 'No more so than usual, anyway.'

'Oh, ha ha.'

We ordered at the bar, and very soon we were tucking into some seriously good food: a spicy chicken burger for Daisy, with a ridiculous amount of crispy, golden chips; lasagne for Mum (who had said she wanted 'something light' and then gone for a massive plate of meat, pasta and bubbling cheesy topping – with garlic bread); a chicken pot pie for Nathan, which looked so amazing that I immediately wished I'd ordered it; and a Thai chicken salad for me, which *was* very tasty, but compared to the other meals it was decidedly lacking in chips, molten cheese and flaky pastry. I sat and ate my lettuce and tried to convince myself that I was feeling smug and virtuous for having chosen such a healthy option instead of one of the grease-laden, calorific and fattening dishes my companions were shovelling in with great gusto (and better table manners than that suggests).

It didn't really work.

'So come on then,' said Nathan. 'Tell us about your day.'

• • •

The Best of British Baking Roadshow had only been going for about six years, but it was already something of an institution, as much a part of the British springtime as complaining about Easter being early/late this year, unpredictable heatwaves and equally unexpected snow storms, and daffodils.

The roadshow did exactly what the title suggested. It travelled around Britain, stopping in every county (or most of them, anyway; some of the smaller ones were combined with their larger neighbours) and choosing five of the best local cooks to compete against each other, whittling them down to each county's top baker. In the finale, the last cooks standing would compete against each other for the title of Best of British Baker. The nation would be united every Sunday night during Roadshow season, glued to their screens to see if Dave from Doncaster would manage to get his croquembouche to stand up straight, or if Bella from Brighton had bitten off more than anyone could chew with her Earl Grey-infused sponge and lemon cream frosting. But it wasn't just about the baking, it was about the camaraderie of the bakers, the way they all supported each other and played fair, despite wanting to win. It was somehow very British, very 'spirit of the (baking) blitz'.

The roadshow had rolled into Cornwall and set up

7

camp in the grounds of Boskern House, a beautiful fifteenth-century manor house just outside Launceston. A big marquee took up most of the striped lawn in front of the house, filled with a mobile but better-equipped (and prettier) kitchen than my one at home. Long work benches in pastel colours, with ovens underneath; all sorts of mixers and blenders, bowls, whisks, scales, every kind of utensil you could think of and probably several you couldn't. There was everything a baker could want.

Every week, five new bakers were given a series of five challenges, usually with five to six hours to work on each one. They could be anything. Complicated technical bakes, with lots of different steps in the process, any one of which could trip you up; delicate, time-consuming decorative techniques, which would rely on your artistry as much as your baking know-how; and recipe challenges which tested your knowledge of which flavours, textures and ingredients worked together, with an emphasis on not sticking to the traditional. The assorted cakes, breads and pastries were given the once-over by judges Pete Banks and Esme Davies.

Banks had been one of the first celebrity bakers, if not *the* first. He'd begun baking for the rich and famous in the late nineties/early noughties, including a cake for Mick Jagger's sixtieth birthday bash in 2003. That had catapulted him into the public eye, with celebrities clamouring for a 'Banks' for their own birthday, wedding, album launch, end of tour party, whatever. He'd become a legend, even making a cake buffet for Elton John's engagement party in 2013.

But the rockstar lifestyle took its toll. His marriage failed. His chain of patisseries, launched at the height of his success, went to the wall. After Elton chose someone else to make his wedding cake in 2014, Pete had hung up his piping bag and semi-retired. But you can't keep a good baker down, and soon he'd scored a publishing deal for a series of cookbooks. The first couple were basically food porn, recreating some of his most famous (and intricate) bakes; not the sort of thing a home cook could ever achieve. His later books, however, had been more accessible and, as a result, more successful. He was back!

Esme Davis was a contemporary of Delia Smith. They'd begun their respective careers in similar ways, both writing cookery columns for newspapers and appearing on TV magazine shows before each being offered their own series. It being the seventies, much was made of both women's appearance, and it wasn't long before the tabloid newspapers were heralding 'the battle of the baking beauties'. Because up to this point, the only female chef on TV had been Fanny Craddock, who was frankly a bit scary both in looks and temperament. Rumours circulated of a ferocious rivalry between the two young women, a bitter animosity as they competed for ratings glory. Because as far as the press were concerned, much like in the movie *Highlander*, there could be only one.

Someone high up in the BBC even went so far as to suggest their very own bake off, before bake offs were even a thing in the UK. Esme and Delia would both appear (beautifully made up, hair coiffed, and dressed up to the nines no doubt) and be judged not just on their cooking skills, which were undeniable, but also on their poise, elegance and confidence in front of the camera... It would be like the Miss World of the TV cookery industry.

Delia had never commented publicly on this proposed TV special, but Esme had. Boy, had she. She had loudly denounced the BBC for their sexism and had quit in spectacular fashion, right in the middle of being interviewed on Michael Parkinson's prime-time TV show. There had never been any rivalry; she and Delia had been friends, and had seen themselves as pioneers, both attempting to blaze a trail for other women on TV. But no more. Esme had stepped away from the cameras and, like Pete, began to write cookery books. She was also given a weekly cookery slot on Radio 4, who had carefully positioned themselves above the terribly crass commercialism of BBC 1.

Esme sank slowly into obscurity, apart from amongst keen cooks; her books were looked upon with the kind of reverence normally reserved for religious works. And in obscurity was where she had stayed, until ten years ago when Channel Four had commissioned a bunch of students to make a cookery show. Esme, by this point, was approaching seventy years old, and the students had thought it would be funny to have an older, grandmother substitute helping them out. They had probably expected to make her the butt of their jokes, but the joke had been on them. Esme had blown everyone away with her sense of humour and her still very strong sense of justice. She released a new book, *Cake Is a Feminist Issue*, off the back of the TV show, and suddenly everyone wanted to know her again. When the idea for the roadshow came up, there was only one person they absolutely *had* to have on board: Esme Davies.

She and Pete were joined for the final judging each time by a trio of guests: celebrities with links to the county, or a local bigwig or two. The bakers' whole stressful (but fun) week of baking would be condensed down into just one ninety-minute episode. And then the roadshow would move on to the next region.

The show was hosted by the softly spoken comedian Russell Lang, or, more accurately, by his alter ego Barbara Strident, a mouthy Essex karaoke queen who told us she was using the show as an audition piece for *Real Housewives of Clacton-on-Sea*. Barbara was *so* different from Russell that it was difficult to think of them as the same person; but he was still there, hidden under layers of make-up, wigs that would have made Dolly Parton green with envy, and the kind of wardrobe that would have had Elton John sacking his costume designer and poaching Barbara's instead. She was also hilarious, in a slightly-bitchy-but-not-enough-to-really-offend-you kind of way.

At least, that's what I thought. Not all of my fellow bakers found Barbara quite that funny…

'So what was the challenge today?' asked Nathan, swallowing a chunk of chicken pie and dabbing gravy off his chin. 'I know it was a celebration cake, but they always throw in something unexpected, don't they?'

'Yes. Good job it was a non-elimination round, just to settle everyone in,' I said. 'You know how they got us to write out a step-by-step plan of what we were going to bake today, and how we were going to decorate?'

'To help you get it all done within the time, yeah,' said Mum. I shook my head.

'They lied…'

It had all started so well. My fellow bakers and I had been working for about an hour, long enough to get cakes in ovens and relax slightly. We'd exchanged a few words before the contest (and filming) had started, but not enough to get to know each other or psych each other out. But with the first stage over, we all had a few moments to breathe and chat to the bakers nearest us.

On the next bench along was Elaine, a smiley, friendly woman in her thirties from Redruth. She had hummed a little tune under her breath as she whisked up her cake batter, which could have been annoying but was actually quite nice; it was certainly better than the awkward, nervous silence that would have pervaded the tent at times otherwise. She giggled self-consciously when she realised that she was doing it, which made me laugh as well, and we'd shared a grin. She'd made an effort to keep quiet after that, but it had only been a couple of minutes before the humming returned. Elaine had a gorgeous, glossy mop of curly auburn hair, tied back in a high pony-tail, which made me feel quite envious. My own hair was scraped away from my face under a wide sweatband like a tennis player, as my unruly mane had a habit of escaping from hairbands, and my pony-tail always ended up sinking lower and lower as the day went on, with less and less hair caught in it. The last thing I wanted was for Esme Davies to bite into my sponge and choke on a hairball. She was a National Treasure, and I probably would have been deported.

The bench in front of me was occupied by Ravi, a young Indian guy who had taken leave from his job as an anaesthetist at Truro Hospital in order to show off his baking skills to the country. He was making *gajar ka halwa*

– an Indian-style carrot cake – which was already fragrant with spices and smelling fabulous. He had measured everything out very precisely, with host Barbara standing over him all the time, flirting, making jokes and trying to make him spill his ingredients; he was well-groomed and nice-looking, and she obviously had a bit of a soft spot for him. He had taken it in his stride and laughed all the way through. I had a soft spot for him, too.

One person I did NOT have a soft spot for was the bloke at the back of the tent. Martin was also a chef (but not a baker), who worked in a café in Bodmin. He looked to be in his forties, but he was one of those people who could have been much older or even much younger than he appeared. He wore a tie-dye T-shirt and had a crystal pendant on a leather thong around his neck. He was bald at the front, but rather than admit to it and shave off the rest of his hair (much the best way to deal with it, to my mind), he had steadfastly continued to grow what was left, so at the back of his head he had a long, straggly blond pony-tail. Basically, if you Googled 'Humourless New Age Hippy', a picture of Martin would be top of the results. It didn't suit him, but then it wouldn't have suited anyone. But his looks weren't the problem (I'm not *that* shallow); his attitude was. He was far too serious. He was obviously nervous, we all were; but the rest of us weren't looking around furtively at what everyone else was doing (we were openly being nosey and talking to each other). He was super-serious, even bringing in his own set of utensils – nothing fancy, just the usual measuring spoons and whisks and so on. He'd not cracked a smile at any of Barbara's jokes, or even really acknowledged the other people in the room. Maybe I was being mean. Maybe he was just really nervous.

But whatever the reason, he was forced to abruptly snap out of it, along with the rest of us, when Barbara called a halt to proceedings after an hour.

'OK, my lovely lads —' accompanied by a lascivious glance at Ravi which made us all giggle — 'and lassies! Please stop what you're doing and move over to the work bench to your rear.' Another bawdy wink at Ravi. 'Don't ya know where your rear is, Ravi babes? I'll help you find it...' We all laughed again as Ravi jokingly put up his hands to ward our amorous hostess off and practically ran to the next bench.

We all moved along, murmuring to each other, wondering what was going on. All of us, that is, except Martin, who obviously didn't want to move. I stood in front of him and smiled.

'I'm assuming you'll have to go to the one down the front,' I said, pleasantly enough. He frowned.

'What's going on?'

Barbara did a massive, over-the-top eye roll (it was on

a par with one of Daisy's most stroppy teenage gestures). She clicked her fingers in the air impatiently.

'Come on! Come on! Get yer under-crackers in gear, Martin! Down the front here with me, babes!' Martin reluctantly abandoned his cake and headed down to the work bench recently vacated by the fifth contestant, Lynda from St Ives.

Pete Banks stepped forward. 'Now I expect you're all wondering what's going on,' he said, with a friendly smile that seemed to me to be actually bordering on evil.

'You could say that,' said Elaine, and we all nodded in agreement.

'On the worktop in front of you, you should all have the instructions your fellow contestants have written out,' he continued. 'The challenge is to complete your rivals' cakes, following their instructions.'

A loud groan rang out around the tent. The judges and Barbara all smiled. They were enjoying our suffering.

'Now, this isn't an elimination challenge,' said Esme. Lovely Esme, everyone's favourite granny. Not any more she wasn't. 'But there will be points for the best cake, which will get carried over to tomorrow. The points will be awarded to the baker whose cake it was originally, NOT to the baker completing it.' There were more groans. Pete grinned and looked at each one of us meaningfully.

'So you have a choice,' he said. 'You can either do your best, follow the instructions in front of you and complete it to the best of your ability, gaining points for your opponent, or—'

'Or you can sabotage it,' finished Esme. 'So the question is: do you nobble the opposition, or do you play fair and risk being sabotaged yourself?'

'Oh that is EVIL,' I murmured. Barbara nodded.

'Yeah, babes, it is,' she said. 'All's fair in love and cake, innit.'

Mum, Nathan and Daisy were all staring at me, open-mouthed. I laughed.

'Your faces! You all look as outraged as we were.'

Nathan pulled himself together. 'I bet that went down well. Who got your cake?'

'Ravi,' I said. 'He's good. He did a better job of it than I would have done.'

'And you got that Rent-A-Hippy wazzock's cake?' said Mum. Nathan had just taken a sip of his drink and coughed with laughter.

'Shirley, I can't believe you never made Poet Laureate.'

'I didn't like the hours,' she said, which made him laugh even more.

'Yes,' I said. 'Proper complicated it was and all.'

'Did you sabotage him?' asked Daisy, eagerly. She looked disappointed when I shook my head.

'No, but I blooming wish I had done…' I remembered the look on Martin's face when he'd seen the finished cake. It's not like I hadn't tried; it was obvious that I hadn't mucked it up on purpose. Or maybe I was kidding myself; maybe my best efforts really were that crap. Either way, he had been furious. He had looked like he was going to explode, but he remembered just in time that the cameras were filming our reactions and held himself back, his face turning bright red.

The judges had come round and inspected each cake, judging it not just on presentation and taste, but against the written instructions. Mine, thanks to Ravi's extremely precise decorating techniques (the way he cut out sugar paste stars and flowers made me think that he should have been a surgeon, not an anaesthetist), and my ability to knock up a really good moist, fudgy, chocolate cake, meant I got much higher marks than I was expecting. Elaine had taken over Ravi's, and her decorating was next-level stuff; but sadly, the carrot cake itself was a bit of a let-down, which surprised me. Lynda had taken over Elaine's Victoria sponge, and even from this distance I could see that I wasn't the worst decorator in the tent… Luckily the sponge itself was declared one of the best Esme had ever tasted, and Pete even stuck up his hand to high-five Elaine, which hardly ever happened. Martin had done a perfunctory job on Lynda's cake; he was obviously extremely skilled, though, so even his poorest effort was better than most. The cake inside was not declared a hit, unfortunately, and I thought it was a good job that today was not an elimination round, otherwise she would have been heading back down the A303 to St Ives.

And then they got to Martin's cake. Like I said, I had tried. It wasn't a *bad* attempt; but his instructions had not been very clear – like the rest of us, he'd not expected anyone else to even see them, let alone try to follow them – and I'd had a hard time working out what he wanted it to look like at the end. So I'd gone with what I was good at. Which, according to Martin, wasn't cake-decorating.

The judges had taken one look at his cake and laughed, albeit sympathetically after reading his complex instructions. He hadn't been happy. But Barbara had made things ten times worse.

'Ooh, you've made a Disney cake!' she cried. Martin looked confused. Barbara laughed and her voice dropped several octaves and she put on a slightly random Scottish accent. She sounded more like a Glaswegian football supporter than a heavily made up housewife disco diva. 'It disnae look very good, ya know what I mean, pal?'

Martin had stared at her with murder in his eyes. His expression was so hostile that Barbara had been momentarily discombobulated, which I couldn't imagine happened very often. But then Esme had tasted his cake — a layered lemon, raspberry and pistachio sponge — and had moaned almost orgasmically at the taste. Which thankfully (if slightly inappropriately — she was no spring chicken) shattered the icy atmosphere.

'So he's a bit of a dick, then?' said Daisy, and we all laughed and then told her off for using the D word (she seemed to forget sometimes that she was only thirteen). But she was right. He was.

We finished our meal and headed for the door, stopping for a moment to let Mum go and 'use the facilities', as she euphemistically put it in front of Nathan. As we waited, Daisy nudged me and nodded over to a couple of guys sitting in a corner booth.

'Mum, isn't that Russell Lang?' she whispered. I squinted, trying to get a good look while remaining discreet, just in case it wasn't him.

'I think so... He's difficult to recognise without the wig and the fake boobs,' I said.

'Can we go and say hello?' Daisy would have been halfway there if Nathan hadn't put out his arm to stop her.

'I wouldn't,' he said. 'It looks like they're having an argument.' And now that I looked more closely, it was obvious they were. Russell's companion reached out a hand to touch his arm, trying to plead with him, but Russell shrugged him off angrily.

'What we looking at?' said Mum, joining us. 'Ooh, a lover's tiff. Can we go home now? Me underwire's killing me and I can't wait to get me bra off.'

Chapter Two

The next day I was up and about early. I took Germaine out for her early morning constitutional, my cute, fluffy, harmless baby snarling in what she obviously intended to be a vicious manner at the fat old Labrador in our neighbour's garden, who had looked at her hopefully, tongue lolling, tail wagging, as we passed his gate.

'He just wants to be friends,' I said, but Germaine was having none of it. This was *her* manor.

Back home, dog bladder duly drained, I got Daisy out of bed and made sure Mum took all her pills. Daisy bustled about, moaning in a good-natured way about having to go to school while I had all the fun at the baking roadshow. I was half tempted to let her come with me (I'm a great believer in school not being the only educator; experience is too, and the more varied experiences I could give Daisy, the better), but the schools would be breaking up for Easter soon, so I couldn't really.

Nathan hadn't stayed the night before. He did stay over now a couple of times a week, and it was starting to become obvious that the current situation, with him shelling out rent on his own cottage, was getting a bit daft, but neither of us had dared broach the subject of him moving in permanently. I'd been cautious about him staying over at first, because it wasn't like I had the house to myself, but Mum and (more to the point) Daisy had both really taken to him, and they seemed to like having him around almost as much as I did. But he'd had an early start this morning — paperwork to catch up on, best done when the station was quiet — so I would have to drive myself to Boskern House today.

I packed Daisy off to her friend Jade's house, a few doors down. The girls usually walked to and from school together, unless the weather was bad, and Jade's mum Nancy and I had a reciprocal agreement about after school; if one of us was caught up with work or whatever, the other would take both girls in and feed them if it was near a meal time. It had proved very handy for both of us in the past, and it would prove so again today, because I had no idea what time filming would end.

It was only after Daisy was gone and I was about to leave that I realised that Mum was not her usual chirpy (slightly barmy and irritating) self. She was sitting at the kitchen table, staring off into space.

'Mum?' I asked, and she jumped slightly, as if she'd been miles away. 'You okay? What you doing today?'

'I don't know,' she said vaguely. 'Brenda and Malcolm invited me to theirs, but I don't know if I feel like it…'

Brenda and Malcolm Penhaligon had been close to my mum and dad for years. Brenda had been convinced that one day we'd actually end up related (by marriage); and that their son Tony, my oldest friend in the world, and I would get married. We had gone out for two weeks in 1994, and then not kissed again until just last October, when I'd thought Nathan had been planning to go back to Liverpool; and despite the fact that Tony was actually a lot more attractive now than he had been in 1994, it had been weird, and we'd decided that we would remain very close but completely platonic friends.

I wondered why Mum would turn down an invite from the Penhaligons. Had they fallen out? And then I looked at her and, with a sudden rush of guilty comprehension, I realised what day it was.

'Oh Mum!' I said, sitting down next to her and

putting my arm around her. 'I'm so sorry. I can't believe I forgot.'

'Don't be daft,' she said, sniffing slightly. 'Dad wouldn't expect you to mark the day every year. It's not like you've forgotten him. You're busy, you've got Daisy, and Nathan, and now this baking malarkey…'

'Even so,' I said, feeling like the worst daughter in the world. It was the anniversary of the crash that had taken my dad's life, eight years ago. He'd been following a couple of stupid teenagers in a stolen car, sedately enough to start, but it had grown into a car chase and ended with a bang on a blind corner on the A39. I had made sure to come down and spend the day with my mum in the years that followed, not necessarily doing anything, but just remembering my dad, talking about him, going to his favourite cafe in Penstowan. And this year I was already here, on the spot, and I'd forgotten.

'It's fine,' said Mum, and although she smiled, I still felt guilty. There was no way I could leave her home alone.

'It's fine,' said Camilla. The director was in her late thirties and *terribly* well spoken. She had the sort of voice that made me visualise her in a twin set and pearls, even when she wasn't wearing them, like today. Or yesterday, for that matter. She may have been achingly posh, but she was nice. When I'd rolled up (late) with Mum in tow, and had taken her off to explain the situation, leaving Mum sitting on a stool at the back of the tent, she'd nodded her head and made soothing noises.

'It's fine,' she said again. 'It might get a bit boring for her, but at least she won't be on her own. Let me see if I can find something more comfortable for her to sit on.'

Camilla gestured to one of the production assistants, a guy who looked to be around twenty-eight to thirty, short dark hair, about five foot eight... An automatic throwback to my police officer days is taking note of people's appearance, in case I ever need to bring it up in a witness statement. I hadn't needed to so far, but it was nice to feel that my mind and my instincts were still fresh.

'Harry, be a love and find that lady somewhere to sit off-camera,' she said. Harry looked me up and down, then did the same to my mum across the tent. I wasn't sure I liked being under his close, almost mocking scrutiny. It was fine for me to do it — it wasn't like I was passing judgement, just committing identifying marks and features to memory — but there was something about this Harry that immediately got my back up. And then he smiled, and I told myself I was being daft.

'Sure,' he said, and went off to find a better chair for a

seventy-one-year-old to sit on. I just hoped it wouldn't be so comfy she'd fall asleep. Her snoring put me in mind of a rhinoceros with sinus trouble (or possibly one wielding a chainsaw), and it would be sure to disrupt filming. At least I'd found someone to look after Germaine, as I could hardly take a dog to a cooking contest. My friend Debbie had spent the last three months trying to persuade her husband, Callum, to get a dog, and she had agreed to take Germaine in the hope that she would melt his heart. He didn't know it yet, but when he got home from work that night my fur baby would be relaxing on their sofa, no doubt being spoilt rotten by their kids Matilda and George, who were firmly on their mum's side. The poor bugger had no chance. I confidently predicted they'd be visiting the RSPCA branch in Bideford at the weekend.

I left Mum in the production crew's capable hands for five minutes and headed for the contestants' toilets. Goodness knows, I'd been in more terrifying situations in the past than having to ice a cake on national TV, but my tummy wasn't in agreement this morning; I would almost rather be facing an angry mob than a camera crew. The toilets weren't exactly plush – a row of Portaloos in the car park – and I hoped my nervous tummy would settle down once we got further into the contest, as the facilities didn't feel very private or soundproof. I was proved right in that assumption, when (as I sat contemplating the day ahead) I heard the sound of raised voices, one female with a hint of a South West accent, one male and more posh Surrey. Russell was arguing with someone.

I strained on the toilet (my ears, that is), trying to hear what they were arguing about, but I couldn't make out the words. I could just hear that she was very, VERY annoyed with him. I stood, pulling up my jeans; should I flush? I mean, I hadn't actually managed to – you know – despite my tummy hurting (it was definitely just nerves). I normally wouldn't question it in someone else's lav, but if I did, would the arguers realise that there was someone nearby, eavesdropping?

I wrestled with my conscience and then decided I would follow the old water-saving adage – if it's yellow, let it mellow, if it's brown, flush it down – and crept out of the toilet, promising whatever gods were looking down at me (probably frowning) that I would come back and flush it in a minute but, you know, I didn't want Russell and whoever he was arguing with to know that I was there in case it embarrassed them. *In case it scares them off before you've found out what's going on, more like*, said a little voice in my head, but I ignored it. I crept around to the edge of the Portaloos, where a row of wheelie bins offered me some shelter, and peered around the corner.

Russell – or half Russell, half Barbara as he was at

that point, being dressed in Barbara's clothes but *sans* wig – stood behind the toilets with a blonde-haired woman who looked so furious that for a minute I thought she might do a Rumpelstiltskin and stamp her foot so hard she tore herself in two.

'It wasn't like that!' cried Russell, looking quite distraught. 'It was your choice—'

'Might have known I'd find you lurking out here,' said a familiar voice behind me. Russell and his companion looked over in my direction, but I was well camouflaged behind the bins. I quickly took a step backwards and whirled around.

'Tony! What the bloody hell are you doing here?' I gasped, my heart beating. I'd been so intent on my nosiness – I mean my observations – that I hadn't heard my old friend come up behind me.

'I could ask you the same thing,' he said, grinning. 'You're supposed to be baking, not spying.'

'Shh!!' I pushed him away from the edge of the toilets and back towards the tent. The last thing I wanted was for Russell to know that I'd been eavesdropping on his conversation. 'I just had an attack of last-minute nerves. Come on, I was already late this morning, I don't want to hold them up.'

We headed back to the tent.

'Anyway, what *are* you doing here?' I asked Tony.

'You're not baking, are you? The hospitals down here are full enough as it is.'

He laughed. 'Yeah, I ain't the best at cooking. Although I do a mean spag bol.'

I rolled my eyes. 'Tone, *everyone* does a mean spag bol, it's meat and pasta, it's not rocket science.'

'Cheek! But nah, I'm not baking, it's my day off and I just thought I'd pop in and have a look. I'm going to be one of the guest judges at the end.'

'Really?' I was surprised, but pleased. Tony had always been a fan of my saffron buns (not a euphemism) and he was a sucker for a lemon drizzle cake, so suddenly my chances of winning were looking better. Not that I would ever condone nepotism or the judges playing favourites or anything, but ... it was probably the only way I'd beat Martin.

Indira, a young production assistant who I'd spoken to the day before, rushed over to us.

'There you are!' she said. 'We need you in the tent. Are you ready?' I apologised for taking so long – although of course I didn't say why – and we left Tony to have a mooch around.

I quickly scooted behind my counter as Russell (now fully Barbara'd up in a big blonde wig), Pete and Esme entered the tent, chatting to each other. At least, the two cookery experts were chatting to each other, looking happy and relaxed, but Barbara seemed tense; nervy and on edge. Then she looked up and saw that all eyes were on her, and immediately flashed up a big smile. Of course the whole point about Barbara was that she wasn't real, she was a larger-than-life character with larger-than-life emotions and reactions, but that smile looked really, really strained to me. It looked like the man underneath the make-up was having a hard time hiding himself today, and Barbara was struggling to assert herself. The wig hadn't been enough for Barbara to shake off the argument Russell had just been having, defending himself against the angry woman outside. My mind flashed back to the scene in the pub the night before; what with his lovers' tiff, he obviously wasn't having a great time of it lately.

The three presenters stood at the front of the tent while the crew miked them up. Harry was there, struggling to clip the battery pack for Barbara's mike onto the back of her dress. I saw her scowl and grab it from him as he jabbed it into her, reaching around and clipping it on herself. That was very different to the Barbara of yesterday, who had had a smile and a joke for every member of the crew, no matter how lowly. Not that it seemed to bother Harry, who just turned away, a smirk crossing his face before he hurriedly wiped it off.

Filming began. Barbara made a few jokes, which were hilarious (as usual), but her delivery just felt a bit flat, like she was going through the motions. It seemed to me like Barbara just wanted to rush through the day so she could get back to being Russell and go and hide somewhere. I felt a rush of sympathy for her. And him.

The other two presenters announced the challenge, and day two of the contest began in earnest...

Chapter Three

Today's challenge was to cook twelve identical small cakes or bars, containing an unlikely or unusual cake ingredient. I was glad we'd been given plenty of advance notice of each challenge, because it meant that I'd had lots of time to plan (otherwise known as panicking, spending hours on the internet searching for inspiration, days working out the recipes, then stressing out because they weren't fancy enough and going back on Google to try and get more ideas. And then, more often than not, going back to the first one). I had decided to use sweet potatoes as my star ingredient, because I'd first discovered them while pregnant with Daisy and had become completely addicted to them. Daisy, however, didn't like them, so I hadn't had an opportunity to eat them much over the last few years, and I was hoping this recipe for a vegan chocolate and raspberry brownie would fool her into eating them.

I stood at the work bench, fumbling with two boiling hot orange sweet potatoes I'd just taken out of the microwave (I'd toyed with using a purple one, but thought my cakes might end up a weird and unappetising colour), and watched Mum relaxing in her chair. I might not have warmed to Harry, but he'd come up trumps and had borrowed an actual armchair from somewhere, and Mum sat there looking very regal and just a bit smug as the rest of us ran around like headless chickens, worrying about oven temperatures and timings. I caught her eye and she actually raised a hand to me and gave me a royal wave. I cringed as I watched her imperiously look Barbara up and down, really obviously, like the blooming Queen of Sheba giving the Queen of Drag the once-over; and when Barbara saw her, I cringed even harder, hoping Mum hadn't offended her. But she just pointed at Barbara's high-heeled boots and said something that made both of them roar with laughter. After that, every time I looked up from my work, Mum and Barbara were chatting away like they were besties. I felt a huge wave of relief sweep over me. I'd been feeling bad about not remembering the anniversary of Dad's death, and worried that, left to just sit there, Mum would become melancholy and sad thinking about it. But she was having a whale of a time.

And Barbara seemed happier too, although every now and then she'd look at the clock, like she was waiting for (and dreading) something to happen.

So, back to my sweet potatoes, which were finally just about cool enough to handle... I cut them in half, and then scooped out all the soft, cooked flesh into a bowl. I added a cup of crunchy peanut butter (another ingredient I love) and mashed it all together until it was smooth. Or as smooth as it was going to get, anyway. In went another cup, cocoa powder this time, with the same again of ground almonds, then one and a half cups of brown sugar. I mixed everything in, ending up with a very stiff mixture; I had to get my hands in there and smoosh it, until it came together in one big, unpromising-looking lump. If I hadn't already tried (and loved) this recipe at home, I'd have been feeling very nervous about now.

I divided the thick mixture into two, then dumped it in a couple of brownie pans, lined with baking paper, pushing the dough out into the corners then smoothing it down with the flat of my hand. I took a block of raspberry-flavoured dark chocolate, which had been in the fridge, and smashed it into rough pieces with the end of a rolling pin, then pushed shards of it into the brownie mix, randomly but not so haphazardly that it risked the judges getting a piece without some in it. Then into the oven, 180°c for half an hour.

And breathe... The camera operator had been roaming around, filming us cook, while Camilla stood behind him and asked us a few questions about why we'd chosen this recipe, what we normally did in our day-to-day lives, that sort of thing. Now and again Barbara would also walk amongst us, stalking about in the high-heeled boots that I hadn't even really noticed until Mum had pointed them out, but which were leopard print and absolutely magnificent. She joked with everybody but gave Martin (who, after doing a few deep breathing exercises and giving his crystal a rub – not a euphemism – seemed super-focused today, to the point I'd almost forgotten he was there) a wide berth. But they left us alone for a few moments now, the camera operator going off and fiddling with the lens, doing something technical. It was nice to just stand there for a few minutes without worrying about what I looked like on camera (I will neither confirm nor deny that I had been holding my stomach in for most of the morning). The sound guy – a strapping young man in spectacles, wearing headphones, carrying a boom and some recording monitor thing slung across his hip – looked down and said something to Camilla, who frowned. She waved Harry over to where she stood with Barbara who, away from her new bestie, my mum, was looking a bit pensive again. I wandered along to the end of my counter, where my freeze-dried raspberries were waiting, which *just happened* to be within earshot of the group.

'You really must check the battery packs before we start filming.' Camilla was remonstrating with Harry, who looked like he couldn't care less. 'It's a good job Josh noticed before Barbara's pack completely ran out, otherwise we'd have had to reshoot all her pieces to camera.'

'Sorry,' said Harry, but he didn't look particularly sorry. 'I'll change *his* batteries now, shall I?'

Was it just me, or was there an emphasis on 'his'? Was it a slip of the tongue – everyone referred to Barbara as 'she', and Russell as 'he' – or was Harry making a point of some sort? Hmm. Barbara didn't say anything, but held out her battery pack. I edged closer and loitered by the fridge as Harry changed the batteries and tried again to clip the pack to the back of Barbara's dress.

'What the hell are you doing?' hissed Barbara, snatching her dress away from him and looking down at it. There was a rip in the seam. Like earlier, a quick smirk flashed across Harry's face, so quickly that I doubted anyone but me had spotted it.

'I am so sorry…' he said. Barbara grabbed the battery pack from him and stormed off. Camilla glared at him.

'You need to be more careful!' she snapped. 'You're lucky it's probably a small enough rip for Wardrobe to just patch it up with safety pins. Remember, we don't necessarily film everything in order, so we can't have Barbara changing outfits left, right and centre because of some cack-handed PA. Think about continuity.' She was clearly pretty annoyed, and I couldn't blame her. 'Remember, you only got this job because we were short-handed and Indira asked for a favour. Don't make her regret that.'

Mum, sitting nearby, had heard most of the exchange – I'm not the only one in the family who's nosey – and she looked over at me with an *oooh, get them!* expression on her face. She was obviously enjoying herself immensely. I smothered a laugh and headed back to my bench.

An hour later Camilla announced that it was lunchtime for the crew. Barbara immediately shot out of the tent, first off the blocks in her high heels, for all the world like a drag version of Usain Bolt. Most of the crew wandered off in search of food, just leaving one of the camera operators, Indira and the sound guy behind. He was trying really hard, bless him, to be a bit flirty with her, but she was either completely unaware of his intentions or didn't share them and was trying to be gently discouraging. I was at that stage in my baking where I couldn't really do much more until my brownies, which I'd not long taken out of the oven, had cooled down completely – if you try to ice a hot cake the icing will just melt and run off of it – so I hauled Mum out of her chair. Her eyelids had started to flutter, and she'd done a couple of those big nods people do when they're falling asleep in the chair, waking herself up with a jolt every time her head drooped.

'Come on,' I said, 'I think we both need some fresh air. I can leave that for half an hour.' A couple of the other bakers, Elaine and Lynda, also left the tent to get some air while their cakes cooled, but the two guys, Ravi and Martin, carried on faffing about with their bakes.

'Hello, Shirley!' Mum smiled warmly as Tony, who had been standing outside talking to a crew member, looked up and greeted her.

'I didn't think you'd still be here,' I said. Tony smiled.

'I got chatting, and then it was nearly lunchtime so I thought if I hung around long enough I might get some cake...'

We wandered over to another tent that was a little distance away from the big baking marquee. Inside was a table full of sandwiches, salads and cold drinks. Not quite the dizzy heights of the film set I'd catered for back in October, but then this was a baking roadshow; the crew doubtless managed to consume at least some cake at the end of each day, so the salads were probably a good idea.

'I got proper stiff sitting in there,' said Mum, doing some surprisingly energetic stretches. Tony yawned and stretched too. 'Are you stiff too, Tony love?'

'No, it's just the way I'm standing,' said Tony, giving me a cheeky wink. 'Maybe we should go for a walk to wake us all up.'

I groaned. 'Can we not? I've been standing up all morning and I'm perfectly awake, thank you. My feet are killing me.'

'Thought you'd be used to that, ex-copper on the beat and all,' said Tony.

'Yeah, I got out of that habit pretty quick.'

I grabbed a sandwich and sat down, Mum deciding that she'd had quite enough exercise with all that stretching, and sitting next to me. Tony pulled up a chair too and looked around.

'I was hoping you might introduce me to Barbara,' he said. I laughed.

'Fancy your chances with her? I didn't think she was your type,' I said. 'Anyway, you want to ask Mum for an introduction, her and Babs are best friends now.' Mum preened herself. 'What were you two talking about, anyway? Every time I looked over, both of you were giggling away.'

'She's a right scream, that one. I told her I had boots just like hers once, but they gave me terrible bunions.'

'I bet she was thrilled to hear about that.'

'She was very sympathetic, actually. At one point my big toe was so deformed the only thing I could get me foot in was me wellies. They still give me gyp now. And don't talk to me about fungal nail infections!'

'I wasn't going to. Anyway,' I said, wanting to steer the conversation away from Mum's manky feet, 'where would you get a pair of boots like that in Penstowan?'

'I didn't get them in Penstowan, did I? I got them in Chelsea.' Mum sat back in her chair. I think she was going for 'enigmatic' but she just looked constipated.

'When have you ever been shopping in Chelsea?' I asked her, incredulously. This was the woman whose idea of retail therapy was going to the hospice charity shop in Fore Street.

'August 1967,' she said promptly. I snorted. She looked defensive. 'I did! Deirdre Hurley who I was at school with, she moved up to London when she was fifteen to be a model. Proper famous, she got. Modelled with Twiggy. David Bailey took her picture and everything.'

'Proper famous? I've never heard of her.'

'No, they made her change her name. DeeDee they called her. Anyway, after a couple of years she was doing well, had her own flat just off the King's Road, so a gang of us went up there to see her. Oh my Lord, we had a right laugh! Going to nightclubs, drinking champagne, dancing on the tables...' Tony and I exchanged amazed looks, but Mum was lost in a haze of nostalgia. 'There was this rich smoothy type, said he was looking for a wife to take back to his holiday villa in St Tropez. Had a thing about blondes, he did. Deirdre was naturally fair – all the Hurleys were – but they'd turned her into a redhead for a shoot, which left Brenda as the only blonde in the group, so she—' Mum suddenly came back to the present and shot a guilty look at Tony. 'Well, we had a good time.'

'Brenda? You mean my mum Brenda?' Tony looked even more amazed now. 'What did she do?'

'Well, she – ooh, these egg sandwiches are nice, aren't they?'

'Mum! Come on, spill.'

Mum shook her head firmly. 'What happens in Chelsea stays in Chelsea.'

Tony opened his mouth to persuade her, but I could see she had that stubborn expression on her face, the one that meant her lips could only be unglued with the copious application of that chocolate and cream liqueur she was so fond of. I changed the subject.

'Where is Barbara, anyway? I saw her shoot out of the tent but I didn't see where she went,' I said. 'She's not in here.'

'Maybe she's eating in her trailer,' said Tony. I looked at my watch and bolted down the rest of my sandwich.

'I'd better get back to my baking,' I said. 'Are you hanging around or going home?'

'Going home, I think.'

I turned to Mum. 'Do you want to go home? Tony could give you a lift.' I mean, I hadn't asked him, but I knew he wouldn't dare refuse if I asked him in front of my mum.

'Would you mind, Tony love? It was fun this morning but I think I've had enough now.'

'Of course,' said Tony. 'It's on my way home.'

We all stood and I kissed Mum goodbye.

'Good luck, Nosey,' said Tony. He turned to Mum. 'Your chariot awaits, madam.'

'Thank you,' she said. 'If we could just pop into Fresh Choice on the way?'

'Sure.'

'And then I need to pick something up from the chemist.'

'Oh…OK.'

'And I got a message from the library telling me the book I reserved is in.'

'Right…'

'And if we could swing by the baker's, I could really fancy a cream horn with my tea…'

Poor Tony. I grinned at him, knowing that he'd make me pay for this at some point, and made my escape.

The other bakers were all back at work. As I whisked together whipping cream and caster sugar, I let my eyes rove around the tent. Elaine was a messy baker, with bowls and utensils scattered all over her work bench, but she was very calm and looked like she had everything under control; the personification of organised chaos, if ever I'd seen it. She had a tray of mini pastry tart cases cooling on the counter, and was busy scooping the flesh out of a couple of avocados. She dumped the flesh into a blender and pulsed it into a thick purée, leaving the discarded avocado skins lying on the work top right next to the bin. It would've been the work of two seconds to actually lift the lid and put them IN the bin, but hey-ho. That wasn't how she rolled.

Ravi, by comparison, was Mr Clean. His counter was spotless, and he was methodically chopping, measuring and whisking each ingredient before moving onto the next one. I couldn't tell yet what he was making, but as I watched he put a tray of mini tartlet cases in the fridge. I didn't see what was inside, but it was clearly something that needed to set.

I discreetly half-turned to check out the competition behind me, but Martin had set up a row of pots, pans and mixing bowls along the front of his counter. Whether he'd done it like that on purpose, to stop any of the other contestants spying on him, or if it was just done to clear space, the effect was the same; I couldn't see a blooming thing he was doing. But he was looking super-focused (again). *Someone is taking this VERY seriously,* I thought to myself. I was pretty much just there for a laugh, and the others were attempting to enjoy themselves too, but

Martin was there to win. None of this taking-part-is-its-own-reward nonsense for him.

Someone else who didn't seem to be enjoying themselves at this particular moment was Lynda. Even from back here, it was clear that she was panicking. She had written herself a to-do list, and I could see her head moving back and forth between the instructions and the mass of pots, pans and baking trays in front of her. I could tell from her body language that she was not in a good place; she looked like she was ready to flee from the marquee, possibly in tears. I looked around for Barbara, because this was kind of her job, to chat with the bakers and, if necessary, gee them along, keep them going. But she still wasn't back from lunch. I tried to get Camilla's attention, but she was talking to Indira, looking harassed. Maybe Harry could go and find Barbara? Only he wasn't back from lunch either. The crew were dropping like flies…

I looked over to Elaine, and she'd spotted Lynda's distress too. She turned off the blender – she was mixing the avocado purée with coconut cream, melted chocolate, cocoa powder and maple syrup, going by the hastily discarded packaging nearby – and went over to talk to her. I checked my watch and went to put my bowl down too, but the camera operator had already descended on the two women down the front and was filming them having a heart-to-heart. I decided to keep out of the way.

Elaine moved some stuff off Lynda's bench, giving her more room, which seemed to calm her down a bit, then gave her a hug and left her to it. I smiled at Elaine as she returned to her own baking.

'That was really nice of you,' I said, and she shrugged modestly.

'It's nerve-wracking, innit?' she said. Behind me, Martin snorted. I turned round to glare at him and he looked defensive.

'What? If you can't take the heat, stay out of the kitchen,' he said. I rolled my eyes, and I would have said something only Barbara chose that moment to make a grand entrance.

'Afternoon, baking babes! What's cooking?' She tottered across the floor and stood in front of the work benches. We all dutifully replied.

'Afternoon, Barbara...'

Behind her, Camilla said something, her voice low but her expression sharp. Barbara rolled her eyes at us and grinned, then answered without turning around.

'Can't a girl put her size nine stilettos up for a bit of a disco nap after lunch?' she said, loudly. Again, I didn't hear Camilla's reply, but she didn't look best pleased. And I could understand why.

Chapter Four

'**B**arbara's had a complete costume change,' I murmured, to myself I thought, only Elaine was still standing close to me and heard.

'You know what these drag queens are like,' she said, and I nearly asked her if there were a lot of them in Redruth, but that would have been facetious. It's a nice enough, non-touristy part of Cornwall, but the locals aren't necessarily known for their flamboyant dress sense.

'I know, but Camilla had a go at Harry earlier for ripping her dress,' I explained. 'She told him off, because if Barbara had to get changed it would be difficult to keep continuity.' But not only had Barbara changed her dress, she'd swapped her amazing boots for the highest (and largest) glittery red heels I had ever seen in my life and, more noticeably, changed her wig. This morning she'd been channelling Dolly Parton in a long, curly blonde do, the sort of style that had been inspired by the 1980s concept of 'big hair' and then been given growth hormones. Now she was a sleek redhead. And talking of Harry, where was he? He'd been hovering around all morning like a bad smell, moving cables and making sure the camera operator didn't trip over anything as they walked around the tent, but he still hadn't come back from lunch. Maybe Camilla had had enough of him and sent him off to do something outside of the tent.

'Wardrobe must've managed to repair that split earlier, because Barbara kept the dress on all the way up to lunch,' I said, 'so I wonder why she ending up getting changed after all?' I watched Barbara thoughtfully across the room, as she and Camilla got into a whispered but definitely heated debate. Elaine shrugged, demonstrating a complete lack of interest which I found both baffling and frustrating, but then not everyone is as nosey as me, I suppose. Anyway, it wasn't my place to worry about continuity. All I had to worry about was getting my twelve chocolatey treats finished and looking fabulous, ready for judging.

I looked around the tent at everyone else's work and it all looked super complicated and delicious, apart from poor Lynda's; her blueberry and courgette squares looked a bit anaemic to me. I had the feeling she would be heading back to St Ives today, but who could tell? Maybe they tasted fantastic. Maybe my vegan brownies were too simple? I was going to decorate each one with a thick drizzle of white chocolate, sprinkled with freeze-dried raspberries, with a ramekin of (non-vegan) Chantilly cream flavoured with a raspberry liqueur on the side, but none of that was technically that difficult. I was relying on the taste of my bakes to get me through at least to the next round – I really didn't want to be the first to leave – and I was pretty confident that everything I planned to bake that week would be delicious, but would my decorating let me down?

I'd just persuaded myself that I needed to do something extra to elevate my brownies when there was a commotion outside the tent. Raised voices, highly alarmed by the sound of it. Camilla glared towards the entrance and then turned to us bakers; we'd all stopped mid-whisk and were looking around nervously.

'It sounds like the zombie apocalypse has finally arrived,' said Ravi, his attempt at humour masking the real concern on his face. I snorted.

'Zombies, down here? Would anyone notice?' I said, and we all laughed, but nervously.

'No need for alarm, everyone,' said Camilla, 'just keep going and pay no attention to it. We'll find out what's going on.'

In the distance, I could hear sirens approaching. *Holy*

moly, I thought. Maybe Ravi was right, and any minute now the zombie horde would blunder in through the tent flaps. *I vote we sacrifice Lynda's courgette cakes,* I thought, *or maybe Martin.*

Camilla gave Barbara a look and made a 'keep going' motion with her hand, before rushing outside with Indira close behind her. Barbara took a deep breath and I could sense her steeling herself. Was it just me, or was a terrified-looking Russell peeping out from behind the make-up?

'OK bakers, you have thirty minutes remaining!' cried Barbara, but with none of her usual Essex *joie de vivre.* 'That means ya need to get your bottle and glass in gear!' She smiled for the camera, then made a 'cut' gesture and hobbled off to the armchair formerly occupied by my mum, where she perched nervously, looking (to me) like she was getting ready to do a runner.

I spooned my Chantilly cream into a piping bag, then piped swirls of it into twelve small ramekins. I placed them on a tray and popped them in the fridge (even though they didn't really need to go in there), then casually wandered over to the door of the tent. The camera operator followed me.

'You all right, love?' he asked. 'I don't think you should go out there. Sounds like bloody chaos.'

I know it does, I thought. *That's why I want to go out there!*

'I need some air,' I said. 'I'll just stand here for a bit...' The camera operator looked at me dubiously, but short of ordering me back to my work bench there wasn't a lot he could do.

I peered through the gap in the canvas. Outside, a group of crew members were gathered around Indira, who was sitting on a stool that must have been dragged from somewhere, looking very pale and shocked.

'Are you okay?' said a woman with a clipboard. She was using it to fan Indira, but Indira was starting to look irritated.

'I'm fine, it's just a shock,' she said. 'If only I hadn't—'

Camilla bustled up to the group, and turned to a young man wearing a blue shirt and an expression that was equal parts excitement and shock. 'The police are here. Marcus? You found him, you go down and talk to the detective.'

'Found him'? Found who? My ears had pricked up at the word 'detective', because there was only one detective on this patch – one official one, anyway – and that was Nathan.

'Ten minutes, bakers!' Barbara still looked a bit shifty, but she plastered on a smile for the camera. Lynda gave a little shriek and redoubled her efforts, and her panic along with it. Elaine and I exchanged looks, but all of us were too busy finishing our own bakes to go to her aid. I forced myself to concentrate on the job in hand, which wasn't easy when I was dying to go and find Nathan and grill him. But our time was nearly up, and today was an elimination round so I really needed to pull myself together and make my dishes look special.

I reached for the white chocolate that was I going to melt and drizzle over my brownies, then stopped. It wasn't there. It *had* to be there! I'd lined all my ingredients up on my counter in the order I was going to need them just before we went to lunch, and I hadn't moved them since. My brownies would still taste great without the drizzle, but they wouldn't look like much. And I wouldn't be able to get my freeze-dried raspberries to stick on them, either.

'No, no, no....' I groaned. Ravi looked up.

'What's the matter?'

'Did you see anyone at my bench earlier? I left some stuff here but it's been moved.'

Ravi shook his head. 'No, but to be honest I was panicking about my cheesecakes having enough time to set, so I wasn't really looking. What do you need?'

'Some white chocolate, not much, just enough for a drizzle.'

'You're in luck. My cheesecakes are white chocolate and lavender, and I've got a little bit left if you want it?'

'Ravi, my 'andsome, you are a STAR!'

I whacked Ravi's leftover white chocolate into the microwave to melt it, drumming my fingers on the bench impatiently. Honestly, I'd had *loads* of time, but it had run away from me and now the race was on.

Camilla came back into the tent, with a wide and obviously fake smile on her face, followed by the two judges, Pete and Esme.

'Bakers, you have one minute left!' called Barbara. 'Don't waste it!'

Chocolate melted, I carried it over to my brownies, which were now cool and cut into twelve more or less equal squares. I drizzled the chocolate over, then, while it was still warm, sprinkled on the freeze-dried raspberries so they would stick. I would've liked another half hour, just to let the chocolate set, but it wasn't to be. I rushed over to the fridge and retrieved my ramekins of cream, then arranged everything on the serving platter. As I allowed myself to relax for a second there was another commotion outside the tent, and I heard Nathan's voice. We'd been together for nearly six months now, but that voice still did things to my insides.

Everyone looked up as Camilla bustled over to the entrance of the tent and stood guard. I could hear her telling Nathan he would just have to wait, as we were at a crucial point in filming and would be done in half an hour or so. I grinned to myself as I imagined Nathan's response. He would be polite but firm, insistent but not unreasonable; he was very good at dealing with difficult people. *He deals with you*, that sarky little voice in my head piped up. It had a point.

Camilla came back over and made a 'winding up' motion to Barbara and the judges.

'Time's up, step away from your bakes!' said Barbara, looking around the room. We all stopped and the judges began their tasting.

They started at the front. As expected, Lynda's blueberry and courgette squares were underwhelming; the judges were polite enough, but they weren't falling over themselves to eat a whole square. Ravi's lavender cheesecakes looked gorgeous and Esme loved them, but Pete made a comment about them tasting like an old lady's underwear drawer, which made Esme cackle and proclaim that not all old ladies wore underwear, and prompted Barbara to ask him exactly when he'd eaten a geriatric's knickers for comparison.

Elaine's avocado mousse cake was definitely a hit, although Pete (definitely the bad cop in the judges' partnership) pointed out that avocado and chocolate mousse was so trendy these days that it wasn't a particularly surprising ingredient. I trembled slightly as they reached my counter and helped themselves to a brownie, but I needn't have worried as they were declared rich, fudgy and chocolatey, with enough of a raspberry kick to cut through the sweetness. And Esme (who Barbara accused of being a secret drinker) loved the raspberry liqueur in my Chantilly cream.

Martin's cakes were (of course, annoyingly) amazing, and far more unusual than the rest.

'What are these?' asked Pete, raising an eyebrow. Martin looked smug.

'Mpanatigghi,' he said, in a terrible attempt at an Italian accent. 'Sicilian chocolate and beef pastries. I discovered them when I was on a yoga retreat in Castiglione di Sicilia.'

I could feel the entire tent thinking, *ooh, get you*, but he just smiled and watched as Pete and Esme tried them.

'Bellissimo!' said Pete, with a wink. *Bugger*, I thought. It looked like Martin was going to go all the way. The judges went off into a huddle, but not for long because it was obvious to everyone who was leaving.

'And the baker going home today is...' said Barbara, and I thought, *Yes, yes, get on with it, will you?* before feeling really bad, because she would no doubt be really disappointed. '... Lynda.'

We all gathered around Lynda, who looked fifty-fifty upset/relieved to be out of it. *So sorry, you gave it your best shot, we'll miss you, now WHAT THE HELL IS GOING ON OUTSIDE?!*

No sooner had Camilla called 'cut!' than Nathan entered the tent, followed by his trusty detective sergeant Matt Turner. Nathan ignored me – he was being professional, which of course just made him all the more sexy – but Matt looked over and winked at me. Martin saw and turned to me.

'What's going on?' he demanded.

'How would I know?'

Nathan's eyes rested on me fleetingly, then he addressed everyone in the tent. 'Ladies and gentlemen,' he said. 'It's my duty to inform you that a death has occurred.'

Chapter Five

For a moment, nobody moved or even spoke.

'Who's dead?' I asked. Behind Nathan, Matt quickly looked down, trying to smother a grin. Camilla glanced round at the assembled bakers and judges.

'Harry,' she said. Barbara wobbled and then sat down heavily.

'Sorry,' said Barbara, although the voice was pure Russell now, 'High heels and shocking news don't mix.' But to my eyes she looked surprised rather than shocked. I looked at Nathan to see if he'd noticed anything untoward, but he avoided my eyes.

'Who's Harry?' Martin sounded confused.

'The production assistant,' said Ravi. 'The guy who helped us with our mikes this morning.' He looked at Nathan. 'What happened? Was it an accident?'

'We're not ruling anything out at this time,' said Nathan carefully, which I knew meant no, it wasn't an accident. Harry had been murdered... Nathan turned to Camilla. 'We need to take statements from everybody here. I have some more officers on their way to help with that, but for now DS Turner and I will start with the contestants.'

Camilla looked annoyed. 'It's a been a long day for our talent, DCI Withers. I'd prefer it if you started with Russell and our judges, so they can leave.'

Nathan smiled, pleasant but firm. 'I'm afraid it will take some time, and as your contestants live locally they probably have family commitments to get back to...' his eyes rested on me briefly '...dogs waiting for them, that sort of thing. Whereas everyone else is staying at the Travelodge in Okehampton, I believe?'

Camilla reluctantly agreed and backed down, although I could tell she wasn't happy. Barbara began to unpin her wig and start the process of turning back into Russell. Nathan smiled at me, then turned to Elaine. 'If you could talk to DS Turner, I'll start with Ms Parker here...'

He led me off to the corner of the tent, but not before Matt had leaned towards him and muttered, 'I think you owe me a pint, Guv.'

'What was all that about?' I asked, when we were away from the others. He grinned.

'Matt bet me that you'd be the first person to ask a question,' he said.

'And you didn't think I would?' I shook my head. 'It's like you don't even know me...'

He pulled out his notebook and pen, then looked around to make sure no one was listening. 'So come on then, who did it?'

I laughed quietly. 'I'm good but I'm not *that* good. It was definitely murder, then?'

He nodded. 'Head bashed in with something hard. I reckon it was probably a branch or a rock or something like that. One of the crew found him sitting by the river, so there's plenty of natural murder weapons to hand.'

'Not easy to find, then. They probably threw it in the water.'

'Yeah, that's what I reckon.' He turned and gazed around at the rest of the tent's occupants. 'So, was Harry well liked?'

I snorted. 'Nope. He was a bit of a dick, if you ask me.'

'What makes you say that?'

'For starters, he just came across as a bit ... I dunno, *sly*. Like he was giving you the once-over—'

'Yeah, but you and I do that.'

'But that's different. Don't look like that, you know it is! We do it *professionally*. We're not judging people, are we? We're just taking their appearance in. But anyway, apart from that, he wasn't the most conscientious crew member here. He was a bit sloppy, and he took great delight in winding Russell up.'

'Did he now?' Nathan looked at Russell thoughtfully.

'You spotted it too, didn't you? Russell looked almost as if he was expecting bad news, just not *that* particular bad news.'

'It might genuinely have been his high heels,' said Nathan, but I shook my head.

'Nah, I don't think it was that. He was furious with Harry for ripping his dress. Do you know what the time of death is?'

'Not officially, but we've narrowed it down to some time after 1.15 p.m., when filming stopped for lunch. That seems to be the last time anyone saw him alive.'

'And that's when loads of us left the tent,' I said. 'Including Russell, who stormed off like a bat out of hell the minute Camilla said cut.' I watched the drag queen discreetly, as she accepted a box of wet wipes from the make-up lady and started taking her face off, revealing the good-looking but pale Russell underneath. 'He was late getting back for the afternoon's filming.'

'Was he? Interesting…'

'And not only that, he'd had a complete change of clothes as well.'

'Really? That's even more interesting.' Nathan

scribbled it down in his notebook. 'What about everyone else? The other contestants.'

I told Nathan about Ravi and Martin staying at their baking stations, while Elaine and Lynda had found a nice spot for lunch under a tree.

'The other thing that might be relevant,' I said, 'although equally it might not be... But Camilla told Harry off for screwing something up, and she said that he was only there because Indira had got him a job. So he hadn't been part of the crew for very long.'

'Long enough to make an enemy of someone,' said Nathan. 'Or maybe they were already enemies.'

'Indira?' He nodded. 'Maybe... I don't know, she seems nice.'

He laughed. 'A lot of murderers are "nice", as long as you don't upset them.'

I remembered that lunchtime, when the poor hopeless sound guy's flirting had been met with complete indifference by Indira. Maybe she was indifferent because she was interested in someone else?

'Maybe we—' I said. Nathan raised an eyebrow and I stopped. 'All right, babe, *you* need to look into Harry and Indira's relationship. Why did she do him a favour and get him a job? To bump him off, or to get closer to him?' I thought of something. 'Was he married?'

'Yes. Not wearing a ring, though.'

'A lot of men don't.'

'I would,' said Nathan absentmindedly, as he jotted something down in his notebook. He looked up sharply. 'I mean – I wasn't suggesting…'

'No, no, I know!' I smiled, although I wasn't sure whether to be relieved or disappointed.

'Although I'm not saying we shouldn't—' he started, then stopped as Matt Turner appeared next to us.

'Sorry to interrupt, Guv, Jodie,' said Matt. 'I just wondered if we were letting people leave after we've interviewed them? Only I've finished with the first one.'

'Oh yes, of course,' said Nathan. He smiled. 'Thank you for your time, Ms Parker.'

'You're welcome, DCI Withers,' I said. 'Are you staying at mine tonight?'

'I don't know, I think I might be stuck here for a while so it could be late before I can get to you. I'll call you when I'm done.'

'Cool.' I rose from my seat and he followed suit. We stood and looked at each other awkwardly. 'It feels wrong to leave without kissing you goodbye,' I said quietly, and he laughed.

'Yeah, I know. We'll make up for it later…'

I left the tent and walked through the production village that had sprung up outside. More tents, including the canteen we'd been in earlier, a hair and make-up one, and another that was sheltering camera and sound equipment from whatever meteorological vagaries the British weather was capable of throwing at it – spring showers, Arctic blizzards and Sahara-like temperatures were all equally likely at this time of year, although at the moment it was just pleasantly warm sunshine. Thanks, climate change. I passed the portable toilets and a row of small but luxurious shepherd's huts, which I assumed were where the 'important' people spent their time between filming – although not necessarily where they got ready; Russell needed space to morph into Barbara, and her wigs and dresses must take up a lot of room. Pete would want space to chill out when he wasn't on camera, and Esme in particular would definitely need somewhere comfortable to relax; filming could be a long, boring and drawn-out process and, sprightly as she was, at eighty years old she couldn't be expected to spend all day on her feet. Besides, the judges weren't allowed in the tent during the blind technical challenges, and also didn't tend to wander around and talk to the contestants while they baked as much as Barbara did.

A group of crew members sat together in the sunshine, talking amongst themselves, as a small team of uniformed officers moved among them, taking statements. I recognised Davey Trelawney, a veritable man mountain who appeared to have muscles on top of his other muscles. I nodded to him as I passed. His butch exterior belayed a gentle nature; I'd seen him both wrestle two drunken fighters to the floor at the same time outside a pub, and calm down a runaway horse, talking calmly to the frightened beast until its wild eyes had quietened and it had ended up nuzzling his huge hand. Sergeant Trelawney had been one of my late father's recruits, one he had been very proud of. But Eddie Parker's Boys (by now a complete misnomer, as many were approaching retirement age) were a rapidly diminishing band, and although I recognised most of the other coppers I didn't know their names.

I walked along an avenue of trees that followed the river and led towards the house. Boskern and its grounds were open to the public (although not this week, because of filming), and the production vehicles were parked in what was normally used as overflow parking. Because I'd been a bit late that morning, I'd missed out on a space near the tent and had ended up in the car park reserved for visitors to the house. I didn't mind though, because it was a nice walk. A walk which happened to take me past the crime scene, I discovered, as I could see the tent that the forensics team had erected over the body. There were a couple of vans parked nearby as well as the ambulance whose sirens we'd heard earlier, the crew standing around chatting, enjoying an unexpected but well-earned break. Their passenger wasn't quite ready for them, and wouldn't be in a hurry to see a doctor.

As I approached, I recognised one of the forensics guys from the station at Barnstaple. He was dressed from head to toe in a white bio suit, to avoid contaminating the scene, and had ripped off his face mask as he headed back to his van.

'All right?' I said, as I drew level with him. He looked at me suspiciously, then his face cleared as he recognised me.

'Oh, hello. What are you doing here?'

I nodded back towards the production village. 'Competing, if you can believe it. What have we got here? Any clue as to the murder weapon?'

He rolled his eyes and shook his head. 'Oh no you don't. You might be Eddie Parker's daughter but you ain't Force anymore. You know I can't tell you.'

'You can't blame a girl for trying,' I said, craning my neck to get a look at the river bank crime scene. He laughed.

'Go on with yer, before my boss sees you and has you arrested.'

'I thought you were the boss?'

'Don't you try and flatter me, it don't work. You want me to call that boyfriend of yours? Tell him you're making a nuisance of yourself?'

'You think he'd be surprised?' I said, grinning. 'It's all right, I'm going, I'm parked down by the house. I haven't come to nose about, honest...'

He laughed again at that and flapped his hands at me, moving me on. I sighed. Sometimes I really wished I hadn't quit the police.

I thought over the events of the day as I drove home. Harry had clearly not been bothered about making friends amongst the cast and crew, and although everyone had been very shocked, the only person who had been even mildly upset was Indira. But she obviously *had* been his friend, because she'd got him the job. If she'd had any strong feelings for him – if she'd pulled strings for him because she'd had romantic notions about him – then surely she would have been more upset? Unless she'd bumped him off. He was married; maybe she'd hoped luring him away from his wife would increase her chances and, when that hadn't worked, she'd done him in? But I was only really basing that on the fact that the sound guy, who seemed very sweet and was nice looking, had been trying so desperately (but respectfully) to flirt with Indira, and she hadn't responded at all. She might have her eye on someone else (possibly Harry, possibly not). She might be gay. She might just not fancy the sound guy. I might be clutching at straws.

Clutching at straws. Yes, that seemed like the most

likely explanation. I shook my head in exasperation and drove on.

Apart from anything else (I told myself), Indira had been in the tent, being flirted with by the aforementioned cute sound guy, when I'd left for lunch. Had she been there when I'd come back? I couldn't remember. I couldn't say for certain either way. And that had been around the time Harry had been murdered.

Of course, Barbara had left the tent just before Harry. She'd been gone a long time, and had been wearing a completely different outfit when she returned. Barbara had been royally pissed off with Harry most of the day, especially after he'd ripped her dress and made no attempt to hide his amusement over it. And there had been the snide way he'd called Barbara 'he'; which wasn't wrong in itself – Barbara was only a character and, as far as I was aware, Russell identified as male, not female or even non-binary – but it kind of went against the spirit of it. Everyone else involved in the roadshow, including the contestants, referred to Barbara and Russell as if they were two different people, and it had just felt a bit mean and petty, calculated to get Barbara/Russell's back up even more than it already was.

Barbara had completely changed her outfit. Why? The obvious reason, if you were a suspicious, cynical ex-copper like me, was because she'd murdered Harry and had got blood on her outfit, so she had disposed of it in order to hide or destroy the evidence against her. But it was such a clumsy thing to do; it drew attention to her. Barbara thrived on attention, of course, but from the little I knew of Russell, he wasn't stupid. And drawing attention to yourself if you'd just bashed someone over the head really would be stupid.

But... Barbara had been on edge all day, and *really* on edge after lunch. She'd gone through the afternoon's filming on automatic. Russell was a pro, but he was still rattled, and it felt like he'd been peeking out from under Barbara's outrageous costume, waiting for the hammer to fall. And then when it had, it hadn't been the blow he'd been expecting. What was he so nervous about, if he hadn't killed Harry? And was Harry being an annoying git enough of a motive for him to do it anyway?

By the time I got home, having swung by Debbie's to pick up Germaine, I'd thoroughly convinced myself that Indira was innocent, then guilty, then that she had been working in cahoots with Russell, who was actually totally blameless and had neither the motive nor the personality for murder, even though he'd had the opportunity... In short, I had no idea and I really should leave the detective work this time to Nathan.

Yeah, right.

'Thank God you're home, I am literally starving,' said Daisy, who had opened the door as I parked on the drive and had started moaning before I'd even switched off the engine. 'Nana is threatening—'

'Offering,' I gently corrected.

'—to make shepherd's pie, and you *know*—'

I put a finger against her lips to shush her. 'Mummy's home. I'll save you from Nana's lumpy mashed potato.'

I managed to stop Mum making dinner (to be fair, she'd only really been making a half-hearted effort by putting the oven on; I think she'd been hoping I'd get home before she had to actually cook), much to both Daisy and Germaine's relief. I'd learnt to cook with my mum, and she was still really good at it when she could be bothered, but she'd got used to me cooking most days, and she had to be in the mood.

'It's getting late,' I said. 'Shepherd's pie takes too long. Fancy spicy meatballs?' Germaine pricked up her ears at 'meatballs' and Daisy stopped moaning about how she was wasting away, so I took it as a sign of approval.

I got her to peel and grate a couple of big cloves of garlic while I diced a red onion. I heated some olive oil in a pan and gently fried the garlic and onion with some finely chopped mushroom, added a handful of dried oregano and a dash of Worcestershire sauce, then a large dollop of tomato purée. Daisy boiled the kettle and carefully made up some vegetable stock with a stock cube – the ingredient besmirched by every TV chef in the land but a lifesaver for busy home cooks everywhere. I added the stock and turned it down to a low heat, with a lid on the pan.

I had some spicy Italian sausages in the fridge, so I de-skinned them and chopped them into pieces, rolling them into balls. Meanwhile Daisy used the rest of the boiling water to put spaghetti on to cook. I browned the meatballs in the pan, then after tasting the tomato sauce and adding a good pinch of black pepper and a smaller one of sugar, tipped in the meatballs and left them to simmer and cook all the way through.

Spaghetti drained, I tipped it into the pan of meatballs and tossed it in the sauce, adding the final ingredient: a handful of fresh basil leaves, torn from the plant in a pot outside my back door.

'Oh my God, that smells so good!' said Daisy, and I thought of Nathan, stuck at the roadshow with nothing to eat except cake. Which would have suited me just fine, but he was more of a savoury person and he would have hoovered this up.

'What is it they say in Italy?' asked Daisy, as she put three plates of steaming spaghetti and meatballs on to the table.

'Grub up!' said Nana, and Daisy groaned.

'No, Nana. In Italian.'

'Grubbio upio!' she said, in the most outrageous (and terrible) Italian accent I had ever heard, and we all laughed, apart from Germaine who looked at her as if she was constantly being surprised by just how weird her human guardians were. *Yep, I really should just stick to cooking,* I thought, and tucked into my dinner.

Chapter Six

So, to misquote Dickens, Harry was dead: to begin with. But his ghost seemed to hover over the baking tent the next day.

I'd woken that morning, alone (Nathan had texted me around 11 p.m., saying he was only just finishing up at the crime scene, and that he didn't want to disturb Mum or Daisy by coming round so late). I'd fallen asleep swearing that I would not get involved in the investigation this time; I had the competition to think of, and although Nathan was too lovely to say anything he probably didn't really want me getting in the way. Even if in the past he'd made a point of involving me, grilling me for local information and giving up (fairly easily) at my repeated attempts to insinuate myself into his detective work. But that had probably only been because he fancied me, and he'd wanted an excuse for us to spend time together. We didn't need to do that now.

I'd fallen asleep thinking that, but of course the next morning I woke up and immediately thought, *I wonder if Forensics came up with anything?* And I knew the chances of me concentrating on Italian meringues, croquembouches and sponge cakes when there was a murderer on the loose were pretty slim.

After taking Germaine for an early morning walk, making Daisy's packed lunch and kissing her and Mum goodbye, I drove to Boskern. I made sure I parked by the house like the day before, giving me an opportunity to skulk past the crime scene again, but the tent was still up and there were a couple of uniforms guarding it, standing around and trying to look important as more Roadshow people drove past. All except one, who was probably supposed to be logging visitors to the scene and recording numbered evidence bags.

'Sergeant Adams!' I said, loudly, and the rather elderly police officer in the fold-up chair jerked awake. I'd known him since I was a little girl, and he'd seemed old then, although he couldn't really have been. God knew how he hadn't been forcibly retired by now. He must be younger than he appeared. And fitter. And more alert.

'All right, young Jodie?' He fished in his lap for a

crumpled paper bag and held it out to me. 'Sherbet lemon?'

'Bit early for me,' I said. He took one, unwrapped it and popped it into his mouth.

'My Peg says I shouldn't be having these, on account of me debitees, but I needs the sugar to keep me awake.'

'You mean diabetes? Yeah, you should probably lay off them for a bit…' I wondered again how he could still be in the Force, but then most of his duties these days involved sitting behind the reception desk at the station. He was only wheeled out on special occasions like this, when most of the Penstowan officers seemed to be here.

He rubbed his hands together. 'Exciting, innit? Another murder! In the old days it was just blokes getting drunk outside the King's Arms, but now… I'm going out with a bang, ain't I?'

'What do you mean?' Surely his diabetes wasn't that bad? He really should stop with the sherbet lemons…

'Retiring, ain't I? Should really have gone five years ago, but we had staffing shortages and they let me stay, as long as I stuck behind me desk. No one wanted to be a copper down here, they all wanted to be up in the big smoke where it was more exciting.'

I blushed. 'Yeah, like me…'

'Oh I don't mean you. You had your own reasons for leaving. Wouldn't have wanted to work under your dad, would you?'

'I...' I started to protest – my dad had been a brilliant and well-loved chief inspector at Penstowan – but then stopped, because he was right.

'I get it. Your dad got it, too. Gotta spread your wings, you young 'uns.' He sucked on his boiled sweet and smiled at me. 'So what you doing here? You baking?'

I nodded. 'If I can get my mind off the investigation...'

He shook his head. 'I reckon I got more chance of being made chief superintendent in my last week on the job than you have of keeping your nose out of things. Just like your dad. He could never leave stuff alone, neither. Chip off the old block, you are.' He gave me a sudden, sweet and sincere smile. 'And that's a proper compliment, in case you didn't realise.'

I returned his smile, feeling suddenly a bit emotional. 'I realised. Now, no more sherbet lemons! Or jelly babies. Peggy's right.' He snapped off a surprisingly sharp salute and I returned it with a grin, then turned on my heel and headed towards the baking tent. I knew without looking back that Sergeant Adams would already be half asleep by the time I was back under canvas.

The mood amongst the crew loitering outside the tent was subdued, but business-like. *The roadshow must go on*, I thought. I nodded to a couple of production assistants who were standing around chatting in quiet voices, then made my way into the marquee.

On the first day of the roadshow we'd been told to get there for 8 a.m., for a briefing on how filming would go, not to swear on camera please, wear something bright and cheerful if we had it, etc., etc., but on subsequent days we didn't have to be there until ten, although filming didn't always start on the dot. The crew, of course, had been there since eight every morning, setting up. There was no sign of Camilla, Barbara or the two judges, but Indira was standing off to one side, looking tired; she obviously hadn't slept well. I'd got there an hour early to factor in a bit of nosing-about time, so I was surprised to see all of the other contestants already there.

'Here she is,' said Elaine, as I approached the trio of my fellow bakers. They all looked at me expectantly.

'Morning,' I said. 'I thought I was early. Did they change our call time? Where's Camilla?'

'She'll be here in a minute, with the others,' said Ravi. 'She's going to give us a bit of a pep talk.'

'We got here early because we want to know what's going on with the police,' said Martin. And they all looked at me expectantly again.

'What?'

Elaine rolled her eyes. 'Come on, we all saw you with that hunky copper yesterday. You know each other, don't you?'

You could say that, I thought, but I didn't say it. Martin looked impatient.

'And the young one winked at you when they came in,' he said. 'I saw him. They're from your neck of the woods, aren't they?'

'All right, yes, I do know them, but they're hardly going to tell me anything, are they?' I said, ignoring the fact that actually, yes, Nathan already had told me a little bit.

'Why are they questioning everyone? Was it a murder?' asked Elaine. I shook my head.

'I honestly don't know.' I looked at them, reluctant to share Nathan's suspicions, but I could see they weren't going to leave it at that. 'I doubt if they know either yet. It was probably an accident, but whenever an unexplained death occurs they have to investigate it. They have to treat it as an intentional death—'

'You mean a murder,' said Martin. I nodded.

'Yes, okay, they have to treat it as a potential murder case before they can rule it out. But nine times out of ten it'll just be an accident.'

'How do you know all this?' asked Ravi.

'I used to be a police officer.'

Martin looked at me sharply. 'A police officer? I thought you were a chef?'

'I am. But I was in the Met in London before I moved back home. So believe me, I do know what I'm talking about. We just need to carry on as normal, get on with the show, and let the police do their job.' As I spoke, I wondered who exactly I was talking to – my fellow contestants, or me. 'We're not in any danger, I'm sure—'

'Oh God, I hadn't even thought of that!' exclaimed Elaine. 'What if there's some sort of mass murderer around? A serial killer?'

'In Cornwall? At a baking roadshow?' Ravi scoffed, but gently, as we could all see that Elaine was genuinely worried. 'I don't think so, do you?'

'No, I don't think so either,' I said. 'Look, there are TV cameras and crew members all over the place, and police too now. Statistically speaking, the scene of the crime is probably the safest place to be, because it's swarming with Old Bill. It's like that old saying, lightning never strikes twice.'

'Well actually, it *does*...' Ravi looked at me, and then shut up, realising he wasn't helping. 'She's right, Elaine. We're all quite safe here.'

'Plus we have access to a whole lot of knives and heavy pans,' I joked, but no one laughed.

'I'm sure that won't be necessary.' I whirled around at the sound of Nathan's voice. He looked at me with an attempt at a stern expression, but I could see a smile lurking around the corners of his mouth. I could feel the others watching us, particularly Elaine, her head turning from me to Nathan and back again like she was watching a game of tennis. Camilla stood next to him, and behind them Barbara, Pete and Esme. Several crew members filed in after them, carrying equipment, talking quietly amongst themselves as they set up. Camilla smiled at us.

'Thank you for turning up,' she said. 'I wasn't sure if you'd all be here today.'

'The show must go on,' said Ravi, and she nodded.

'That's exactly what we think. You've all put so much time and effort into being here, not to mention the hard work of our judges and the whole crew, it would be a shame to waste it.' She gestured to Nathan. 'I've been talking to DCI Withers and he assures us that it's perfectly safe for us to continue.'

'That's right.' Nathan nodded, his gaze travelling around the bakers and lingering for a moment on me, making me smile. 'We're still looking into how Mr Dodds died, so officers from Penstowan police station will be here for some time yet. We may need to talk to some of you again, and we are still collecting forensic evidence from the scene, so please avoid that area of the grounds.'

'We will cooperate completely,' Camilla reassured him. Nathan's mouth twitched again.

'Yes, I'm sure *most* of you will,' he said. I stifled a laugh; he knew me too well. 'I'll leave you to it. Good luck.' He gave us all a sharp nod and turned on his heel, leaving us gazing after him.

'Now ain't that the tastiest dish you've seen all day...' said Barbara, watching Nathan walk away. 'I'd let him handcuff me any time he wanted to.' And most of the women (and probably some of the men) in the tent agreed with her.

After another hour or so of us bakers standing around, chatting, and getting in the crew's way, it was on with the contest... I forced myself to concentrate as the most glamorous housewife in Essex, our very own Barbara, explained the day's challenge. She seemed slightly less stressed out today, almost as if the worst had already happened and it actually hadn't been that bad; but at the same time, I still had the feeling that she was metaphorically looking over her shoulder the whole time, ready for – what? What could be worse than someone being murdered? Well, *yourself* being murdered, I supposed, but surely she couldn't be that scared or she wouldn't have turned up for filming.

Focus, Jodie! I reprimanded myself, as Barbara took centre stage and the cameras rolled.

'Well done, my baking babes, for making it this far!' she said. 'Today is Technical Challenge day, and although it ain't an elimination round, it will count towards who goes and who stays tomorrow. So it ain't like you can relax or nothing! Esme?'

Esme stepped forward, a beaming smile on her face. She really did look like the world's loveliest, fluffiest grandma, but I suspected that her beatific countenance was masking the fact that she was about to be completely evil and ask us to bake something flipping impossible.

'Morning, bakers. Today I would like you to make Baumkuchen. It's a famous German cake, traditionally cooked on a spit, and should have ten distinct layers of sponge separated by jam.' *Traditionally cooked on a spit?!* I exchanged horrified looks with my fellow bakers. 'Each layer of sponge should be the same thickness. And I would like you to finish your Baumkuchen with the decoration of your choice.'

Barbara smiled at us. 'You have five hours to make your bumcocken...' We all sniggered and she beamed even wider. Naughty Barbara! She was back on smutty form. 'So *eins, zwei, drei* – get yer bake on!'

I turned over the page of instructions in front of me. Next to it, all the ingredients I would need were covered by a large gingham cloth.

As I scanned the long, long list of instructions (*oh so many instructions*) I couldn't help cursing the fact that it was going to be a long-drawn-out bake today, when all I really wanted to do was go and find Nathan and get the latest on Harry's murder. But I couldn't ignore the little voice at the back of my head that kept reminding me that it was a non-elimination round. So if I wanted to do a half-arsed job of my cake and sneak off to investigate, it wouldn't *really* matter as I wouldn't get sent home. Although it would mean I would have to ace it tomorrow, and I do have such a thing as pride. I didn't want to give Barbara the opportunity to make a joke about my bum – my bam – my German spit cake, like she had on the first day. The fact that I had made it past the first elimination round had allowed a little voice in my head to start whispering that maybe I could get to the final. Maybe I could even win this…

I began whipping up the sponge mixture, glancing discreetly round at my fellow bakers. They all seemed to be back in the zone, murder forgotten. Elaine had a little furrow in her brow as she read the instructions, concentrating hard. Ravi had set everything out very neatly once again, methodically adding ingredients and clearing up as he went. Martin – it was difficult to watch Martin, as he was on the bench behind me, but when I managed to get a quick look at him it was completely pointless as he'd done the same thing as yesterday; piled everything up along the edge of his counter top, so no one could see what he was doing. Of course he looked up as I turned slightly in his direction, and his eyes narrowed. As if I was spying on him! I mean, I was, sort of, but I didn't give a damn about his cake; I was more interested in how yesterday's events had affected him. Not a jot, by the looks of it. Pillock.

One person the events clearly *had* affected was Indira. The production assistant stood in the corner of the tent. She was facing the bakers, but I doubted that she was actually watching what was going on; she appeared to be miles away, in a dream. Pete and Esme had left the tent – this was a blind challenge, meaning they wouldn't know who had baked what – but Barbara was nearby. Occasionally she would cast a quick, concerned glance at Indira. I obviously wasn't the only one who could see that she was out of sorts. Understandably so. Indira had got the dead man his job on set. Maybe she was blaming herself for his death?

I thought back on my conversation with Nathan the evening before. We needed to find out more about Indira's relationship with Harry. I assumed Nathan had asked her but sometimes, when it comes to matters of the heart at least, people prefer to talk to a woman about it. But how could I get out of baking and get Indira on her own?

'Ow!' I was jolted back to the present by Elaine exclaiming loudly in pain. I turned to look. She was clutching her hand, a thin stream of red blood trickling down it. I rushed over.

'What's happened?'

'Cut my finger. Ow ow ow! Bloody hell!' She grabbed a tea towel and wrapped it around the bleeding digit before sitting down on the stool behind her counter. Camilla appeared next to us.

'Oh dear,' she said. 'Can we have the first aider, please?'

I looked round for the first aider, and spotted Indira waking up from her daze. She grabbed a first-aid kit from the pile of equipment at the front of the tent and rushed over. As she passed Barbara she looked at her, and the drag queen gave her a sympathetic smile.

'Let me see...' Indira gently took Elaine's hand and held it up. She carefully peeled away the tea towel, which was now stained bright red. 'Keep it elevated for me,' she instructed the invalid. I peered in for a closer look. There was a long but not very deep cut along the top of Elaine's index finger.

'Is it bad?' asked Elaine anxiously. Indira shook her head.

'No, it's fine. It's not deep. It's just one of those parts of the body that seems to bleed a lot.' She took a Steri-strip from the first-aid kit and applied it to the cut. She took out another, wider plaster, and talked Elaine through what she was doing. 'The bleeding is already slowing down, and the Steri-strip will help stop it. We need to keep it really clean, so I'm putting another plaster over the top and then you should be able to wear a plastic glove over it while you're cooking. But just sit there for five minutes and keep it elevated. Do you feel okay?'

'Yeah, I'm fine.' If anything, Elaine seemed more embarrassed about all the fuss. She started to get up. 'I've got to get my first layer of sponge in the oven—'

'Five minutes won't put you behind schedule,' said Camilla, firmly. Elaine nodded reluctantly and sat herself back down on the stool. Indira seemed satisfied that the invalid was fine and began packing the first-aid kit up.

I took a deep breath and swayed. Nobody noticed. I swayed again, more violently this time, and put out a hand to steady myself on the counter. Indira looked up at me, concerned, and reached out to hold onto me.

'Are you okay?' she asked. I shook my head.

'No… I mean, yeah, I'm fine, it's just the sight of blood…' I swayed again, trying to ignore the way Elaine looked up at me, sharply.

'Do you feel faint?' asked Indira, concerned.

'A little bit… It just feels really hot and stuffy in here. I need some air…' I thought I was quite convincing, but Elaine was still watching me, a look of mild disbelief in her eyes. Indira took my arm.

'Come on, let's go and sit outside for a bit,' she said, and for a moment I genuinely felt bad; nothing to do with the blood, more that I was taking advantage of Indira's caring nature. I let her lead me outside, aware of Elaine's gaze following me.

Indira led me over to a couple of chairs that had been placed under a tree. It was actually a bit chilly in the shade, but of course I was supposed to be feeling hot and shaky, so I forced myself not to shiver.

'Just sit and take some deep breaths,' said Indira. She

looked for a moment like she was just going to leave me there, so I reached up and grabbed her hand.

'Will you sit here with me for a bit?' I said. 'Sorry, I just hate feeling faint...'

'Of course,' she said, sitting down next to me. She let out a sigh before she could stop herself, and smiled at me ruefully. 'Glad of a chance for a bit of peace and quiet myself, to be honest.'

'Of course. This horrible business with Harry must be really upsetting for you.' I paused, not wanting to push her too hard. But nothing ventured... 'He was a friend of yours, wasn't he? From before?' She looked at me sharply. 'I overheard Camilla yesterday,' I said quickly. 'After he had that bother with Barbara's dress.'

'Oh, yes... Yes, we knew each other from university.'

'Were you close?'

'No, not really.' She sighed again. 'I *am* upset about his death, but to be honest I'm more sorry for dragging the roadshow into it. The producers don't like trouble. First whiff of a scandal and people are out.'

'Do you think they'll try and get rid of you because of it? They can't blame you, surely?'

'I was the one who put in a word for him. I persuaded them to take him on.'

'All the same...' I sat for a moment, trying to form my next question diplomatically. 'Can I ask you, if you weren't close, why did you get him the job? Why did you put yourself out?'

'Well, you know, he was an old friend...'

'Had you stayed in contact?'

'We were connected on LinkedIn – that's how he contacted me – but I hadn't actually spoken to him since our uni days.'

'So, what, eight years? Ten years?'

'About ten, yeah.'

'Bit cheeky of him to contact you after all that time and ask for a massive favour like that. And extremely generous of you to help him.'

Indira fiddled with the hem of her top, avoiding my eyes. 'Not really...'

'Why did he want this job? Is it what he normally did?'

'No...' She was starting to look flustered. I reached out and took her hand.

'If there's something bothering you about it, you should tell the police,' I said, but I was thinking, *don't tell the police, tell me!*

'It's nothing,' she said, and that little voice in my head went *ah-ha!*

'But it is bothering you.' I gave her a gentle smile. 'Look, why don't you tell me what it is? I know the detective leading the case, I can tell him off the record if you like, and if he thinks it's significant he can come and talk to you.'

'Are you sure you don't mind? I'm keeping you from your baking...'

'No, it's fine, honestly. I don't like to see people upset, and you clearly are.' I wondered if I was laying it on a bit thick, like I was some kind of Samaritan, but she suddenly smiled and nodded.

'OK. Thank you. Yes, I did think it was a bit weird the way he suddenly contacted me, but he had his reasons. He said he was between jobs and he'd seen me post about the roadshow on social media, and he was really keen to give production work a try.'

'Is that what the two of you did at university?'

She shook her head. 'No. I did English and Drama, and he did English and Philosophy.'

'Do you know what he normally did?'

'He was a teacher, but he said he'd had trouble getting a permanent job and had just been doing substitute stuff, and he didn't have any work on for the next couple of months.'

'It's quite a change from teaching, though.'

'I know. I said the most I could get him was a job as a runner, and of course being a roadshow meant he'd be away from home a lot of the time, but he said he didn't mind. He told me he was a really big fan of Barbara's and it was really just the experience he was after.' She looked at me, troubled.

'But you don't believe that now, do you?' I said softly, and she shook her head. 'Was he desperate for money, do you think?' She gave a low snort.

'I hope not. Do you know how much a lowly production assistant gets paid? Not a lot. Being away on the road, the production company do give us a bit extra for food and stuff like that – an evening meal and a few drinks in the pub – but it's not as well paid as being a teacher, even a substitute one.' She stopped and waited for a couple of crew members to walk past, before continuing. 'He claimed to be a big fan of Barbara's, but once he got here he didn't really seem that keen on her. You saw the business yesterday with the mike.' I nodded; if anything, I'd thought Harry had been quite hostile, and certainly rude, to her.

'So why was he so keen to get a job on the roadshow?' I asked. She shook her head.

'I don't know. Maybe it *was* the money. Even the rubbish pay he was getting here was better than nothing. Maybe he'd had enough of teaching and wanted a career change. I don't know.'

'It could be that,' I mused. 'Wanting to work behind the scenes, seeing how the magic happens. What I'm still not sure about, though, is why you put yourself out for someone you didn't really know anymore? It's not like he was ringing you up and pestering you. It's really easy to ignore a message on social media, or even block someone.'

Indira looked irritated for a moment, then gave a resigned shrug. 'Oh what the hell, it was such a long time ago now anyway... We went out for about eighteen months, while we were at university.'

'Eighteen months? That must have been serious.'

'It was. On his side, anyway.'

'Ah...'

'I wanted to dump him, but I'm a terrible coward when it comes to things like that. I hate confrontation.'

'Oh, me too,' I said soothingly, but it was actually a complete lie. I've never had trouble dumping anyone, apart from my ex-husband. I've always had a very good sense of my own worth, except for when it came to Richard Doyle, cheating swine extraordinaire, crap but thankfully mostly absent parent, and a 'Dick' in more ways than one. 'So what did you do? Ignore his calls, that sort of thing?'

'Yes. I suppose I ghosted him before ghosting was even a thing. I wasn't very nice, really. And then one evening he came round to my house and found me with someone else.'

'Ah...'

'Yes. He was very upset. But he did get over it, and by

the time we finished uni we were more or less friends again.'

'More or less. But you still felt guilty.'

'A bit. And when he contacted me he mentioned our past relationship and made me feel guilty all over again, so I helped him.'

'I understand. He was married, wasn't he? Did you ever meet her?'

Indira shook her head. 'No. He mentioned her name – Sarah – but he never really talked about her. I don't know anything about her or their relationship.'

'It must be hard, being away so much,' I said. 'If you've got a relationship, I mean. Someone waiting at home for you.'

She gave me a rueful grin. 'The only thing waiting for me is my houseplants. As long as my neighbour remembers to go in and water them.'

'Everything okay?' I looked up to see Nathan standing in front of me. His expression was a weird mix of concern and *what-is-she-up-to-now?*

'Jodie was feeling a bit faint,' Indira explained. Nathan now looked genuinely worried, and I felt bad again. 'One of the other bakers cut their finger and there was quite a lot of blood.'

The genuine concern disappeared, to be replaced now by a combination of relief and amusement. 'Oh dear,' said Nathan. 'Are you feeling better now?'

'Yes, thank you.' I smiled brightly at him. He rolled his eyes, then turned to Indira.

'I need a quick word with Ms Parker anyway. I won't keep her long.'

'Oh – okay.' Indira stood up, looking at me. 'Are you sure you're all right?'

'I'm fine. Thank you so much for looking after me.' I smiled at her until she turned and left. Nathan sat down on the chair she'd just vacated. 'I remember you telling me about your time in the Met,' he said. 'I remember you telling me that your record for dealing with stabbing victims was ten in one month. You'd think someone who'd seen that many knife wounds would be used to a bit of blood by now.'

'Okay, I lied. I just wanted to get Indira on her own...'

'I'd worked that out. I'm a detective, remember. And you're supposed to be a baker, not Miss Marple.'

'Yeah, right,' I snorted, then looked at his face. 'Oh, you're being serious. Bless you, did you really think I would stay in the tent cooking when there's a dead body a couple of hundred metres away?'

'The body's not there anymore.'

'You know what I mean.'

He shook his head, exasperated (but not really), then glanced around surreptitiously and took my hand. 'This contest could be a really good opportunity for your business. You could win this! Can't you keep your nose out just for once and let us get on with it?'

'Have you met me?'

He laughed. 'Yes, yes I have, and I really should have learnt by now. So what did you find out that I don't already know? Because I did interview Indira last night.'

'Did she tell you she and Harry used to be an item?'

Nathan looked surprised. 'No, she didn't… When?'

'Oh, years ago. But that's why she got him the job. She felt guilty for dumping him.'

'Interesting. Not sure it makes any difference, but interesting. Anything else?'

'Only that he lied about why he wanted the job.' I filled him in on my conversation with Indira.

'Hmm… Again, interesting, but not sure if any of it's relevant. He probably didn't think he'd get any teaching work for the next few months, for whatever reason, and figured this would be better than sitting at home on the dole.' He glanced around again, then moved his chair a bit closer. 'If I wasn't on duty I would kiss you right now, Ms Parker.'

'Damn your professionalism.'

He laughed. 'I know, it's a pain in the backside. I missed you last night…'

'I missed you too. Will you be round tonight?'

'Definitely.' He looked around again, then leaned in

and kissed me hard on the lips. I gave a big, over-the-top mock gasp.

'DCI Withers! I'm shocked by your blatant disregard of the high standards of behaviour your post demands—'

He laughed and shut me up with another kiss. 'Yeah, whatever. I never wanted to make superintendent anyway…'

Chapter Seven

I headed back to the tent. I was definitely behind the other bakers now, and probably behind schedule. As long as I managed to present *something*, it wouldn't be a complete disaster that ended in me being sent home. My bowl of sponge mix sat on the counter where I'd left it, and the oven would certainly be hot enough by now. I reminded myself of the instructions again. Baumkuchen was normally cooked on a spit, but obviously there weren't any spits in the tent, so Esme had come up with a recipe that we could cook in the oven. A thin layer of sponge was baked, then another layer added on top and put back into the oven. Every third layer was of jam, and then the next layer of sponge would be spooned on top and baked in the oven.

'Bugger!' At the work station in front of me, Ravi threw down the instructions in frustration.

'You all right?' I asked him.

He shook his head. 'We have to make the jam,' he said, reaching for a bowl of apricots that was nestled amongst our ingredients. 'I can't bake any more layers until I've made the jam.' At the next bench along, an *aargh* of frustration indicated that Elaine had just made the exact same discovery. I put down my bowl of sponge mix and turned my attention to preparing the apricots instead.

I managed to focus long enough to get a pan of crushed apricots and jam-setting sugar boiling away on the hob, then ladled out four tablespoons of sponge mix into a cake pan. I popped it into the oven, then took my jam off the heat and carried it over to the fridge; it needed to cool down before I could use it. The sponge layer only took six minutes to cook. I added another four tablespoons of cake batter and stuck it back in the oven. I might have been behind everyone else when I returned to the tent, but making the jam first meant that I had soon caught up with Elaine and Ravi at least. Martin, as before, was keeping himself to himself, but the (real or imagined) waves of smugness I could feel wafting over from his bench made me think that he'd spotted the jam issue before he'd started.

As each layer of sponge was so quick to cook, I couldn't really start working on the topping; every time I started doing something else, I had to check on my sponge and add another layer of batter or jam. So instead I just stood and thought about my conversation with Indira.

Why had Harry been so keen to get this job? Did it matter? It seemed obvious to me he'd lied about being Barbara's number one fan and wanting an opportunity to work with her. The money wasn't great, according to Indira. But if he'd been out of work, maybe Nathan was right; maybe he'd preferred to do something, *anything*, rather than be bored at home, on the dole. But … he was a substitute teacher. The very nature of the job meant that you probably never knew when you would be working, but you would surely be prepared for that? And how could he say that he wouldn't have any work for the foreseeable future? I could understand if the summer holidays were just around the corner, but it was March – spring had only just sprung, and the long six-week summer break wasn't for months. Didn't being a substitute or supply teacher mean you would stand in for teachers who were off sick, or where people left abruptly and the school hadn't had a chance to fill the position? So you could feasibly be called in at very short notice for a day or two or to cover long-term sickness.

Why would someone swap a relatively well-paid (if potentially sporadic) job for a minimum-wage position on a TV show that would take them away from their loved ones and the comforts of home for weeks at a time? From what Indira had said, and from what I remembered of the film set I'd catered for back in October, being a runner was considered the lowest of the low. Did he want a career change? It was an entry-level position, the sort of job that *could* lead on to better things, but only if you really gave it your all and put thought and energy into it. You had to have passion and enthusiasm to be a runner, because goodness knew you'd get all the worst jobs, and it would only be your love of film or TV that would keep you going. Harry had forgotten (or deliberately failed) to check the battery levels on Barbara's mike, and he hadn't exactly been careful when attaching it to her dress. He'd looked bored most of the time, or sullen, and had made no effort to endear himself to cast, crew or contestants. He didn't have that passion.

Maybe he'd needed to get away from home? Maybe he owed someone money, and he was desperate to get away until the heat was off him. But if he needed to actually disappear, then that suggested that whoever he owed (a drug dealer, perhaps? or were they gambling debts?) knew where he lived, and his poor wife was still there. It would be like throwing her to the wolves. And the roadshow didn't go on *that* long; he'd have to go home at some point in the not-too-distant future, so the problem would still be there. Maybe…

Maybe I should concentrate on my baking, I thought, as a faint waft of burning sponge assaulted my nostrils.

Sponge finished, I decided to cut out some chocolate shapes and make some sugar work for decoration while it cooled. I thought I would cover the whole thing in a chocolate ganache and then decorate it with flowers or leaves or something. I made a few chocolate leaves, then had a go at making a rose out of sugar paste, but it didn't quite go according to plan.

'Ooh, what you making there, babes?' asked Barbara, tottering over on her heels. 'You going for a roadkill theme, are you? That's a bold choice.'

'It's meant to be a rose,' I said, and she patted my hand.

'Of course it is, love. And there's me thinking it's a squashed badger.' Everyone laughed, including me, because now I looked at it critically there was definitely a hint of something-you-scrape-off-the-road about it. I sighed and threw it in the bin. Barbara gave my arm a sympathetic squeeze.

Camilla called lunch, and most of the crew left the tent. Indira was back in her trance at the front of the tent, but she looked up and smiled as Barbara stopped to speak to her.

I decided I needed a break from (unintentionally) making small, dead woodland creatures to decorate my cake with – I possibly needed to rethink my decorating plans – and headed outside. The other bakers stayed in the tent, chatting amongst themselves as they waited for their own cakes to cool and modelling chocolate to set. I probably should have stayed there as well, but I wanted to find Nathan, to grill him on what he'd found so far, and (I'm not ashamed to admit it) maybe have a bit more of a snog. That man made me feel like a daft teenager, and there was no point pretending otherwise.

I grabbed a sandwich from the catering tent and then casually sauntered down towards the crime scene.

'And where do you think you're going?' I whirled around to find Matt Turner standing behind me, grinning. I held up the sandwich.

'I was taking Nathan some lunch,' I said, and he grinned even wider.

'You've started eating it,' he pointed out, and I laughed.

'OK, it's a fair cop. I'm being nosey.'

'You? With your reputation?' He shook his head. 'The guvnor was in the car park over there, last I saw of him. How's the contest going?'

'Don't ask. If there was a prize for worst cake

decorator in Cornwall, I'd be the winner. Top three, anyway.'

'Don't you believe it. My mum made me a Harry Potter cake for my birthday one year – I was really into the films at the time – and it looked more like Darth Vader sucking a lemon than a boy wizard. Gave me nightmares for weeks after.'

'Oh dear. How old were you?'

'Twenty-seven.' He laughed. 'Nah, nine or ten. You don't want to hear about the Pokémon cake she made for my next birthday.' He shuddered.

I left him reminiscing about (or reliving the horror of) past birthday cakes and went to find Nathan. He was sitting in his car, door open, talking to someone on the phone. He looked up and smiled at me, but carried on his conversation.

'And you're sure she's headed this way?… No, I don't think it's a good idea, but we can't legally stop her, can we?' Was he talking about me, I wondered? 'Yeah, seeing where it happened is the last thing I'd want to do, either, but grief affects people in different ways, I suppose. At least it gives me the opportunity to talk to her while she's here. I'll tell Uniform to keep an eye out for her.'

'What was that all about?' I asked, as he disconnected the call.

'Victim's wife wants to see the scene,' he said. 'She's

down here identifying the body as his next of kin, and she just left the mortuary saying she's on her way here.'

'Where did they live? Did she drive down here on her own?'

Nathan nodded. 'Yeah. They live on the outskirts of Bristol, apparently. The local force went round and told her the news last night. They should really have offered to drive her down here today.'

'Maybe they did. But it's got to be a lot to take in, hasn't it? Perhaps she thought a couple of hours in the car on her own would give her time to process it, prepare herself. Or maybe it still hasn't really sunk in. It hits people differently, doesn't it?' I thought of the day I'd heard about my dad's death. I hadn't cried during or after the phone call. My dad was a hero to me, the strongest man I knew (even though he was in his sixties and coming up for retirement, I still saw him that way). He couldn't really be gone. I'd gone home to my parents' house and had helped my mum, who was of course devastated; the man who had been a massive part of her life for more than half of it was gone. I still hadn't cried. I had arranged the funeral, and had gone along and stood by his grave, and not one tear, not even as they lifted his coffin into the hole. Nothing. I'd gone to the memorial held by the local police. Nothing. And then one day, about two weeks after his death, I'd gone to the station to pick up his belongings. Sergeant Adams had packed everything up for me, so I didn't have to go into his office, but I wanted to have one last look round. The sight of his desk, without him behind it, had almost brought me to my knees. I still couldn't go into the station without thinking about him, even when I was going to meet Nathan.

Nathan was looking at me. I smiled.

'Grief is a funny thing. It sneaks up on you when you least expect it,' I said, and I knew he'd guessed what I'd been thinking about. He got out of the car and pulled me into a hug, not even caring that there were other people around.

'So,' I said, pulling away after a few moments, 'give me the latest.' He opened his mouth to speak but I stopped him with a finger against his lips. 'Don't tell me you're not allowed to. I know you're not, and you know you're going to tell me anyway…'

He took my hand away from his mouth, laughing. 'I've given up trying to keep things from you. And occasionally you're even helpful.'

'Only occasionally?'

'Yeah. Four times out of ten, I reckon.' I poked him in the side with my finger and he jumped out of the way, laughing. 'You want to hear this or not? I'm a busy man, you know. And you have a cake to bake.'

'Don't remind me. So?'

'So we got some of the forensics back. Harry Dodds

was bashed in the head by an irregular-shaped object, which we haven't yet found.'

'A tree branch, or a rock?'

'Could be either. Plenty of both at the scene.'

'Where exactly was he killed? I mean, I've seen the tent over the scene, but—'

'The River Ottery runs through the grounds, although it's not much more than a narrow stream in most places on the property. But there are a couple of wider spots with little wooden bridges across it. Dodds was sitting on one of them, looking at the river, his legs through the wooden railings—'

'Dangling into the water?'

'Yes, but not actually *in* the water – the bridge is too high for that. It looks like the blow to the back of the head is what killed him, although until we've got the autopsy results we don't know that for sure. From the position of the body when it was found, though, it looks like he slumped forward, against the railings. They stopped him toppling into the river.'

'Whatever the murder weapon was, the murderer probably tossed it into the stream, don't you think?' That was certainly what I would do, I thought. It would be almost impossible to find, and if there was any incriminating DNA evidence on it, the water would probably wash it off.

'It's what I would do.'

'What about DNA, or is it too early for that?' I asked.

'Too early. But we did find blonde fibres snagged on one of the victim's fingernails.'

'Fibres? Or hairs?'

'I'm waiting for the lab to get back to me on that.'

'But blonde suggests hair, surely? Why are you calling them fibres?' Nathan looked at me steadily. I suddenly caught on. 'Hang on – are you suggesting they could be from a wig? So they look like hair, but they might not be?'

'And who do we know who was wearing a blonde wig on the day of the murder?'

'And then appeared after the murder without it. And in a whole new outfit.' I looked at him. 'The new outfit thing was suspicious anyway. Add in the blonde hair...'

'I think we should go and have a chat with Ms Strident, don't you?'

'We? You're letting me in on it?'

'You'd only lurk nearby and eavesdrop if I didn't.' He smiled. 'Consider yourself deputised, Ms Parker.'

I checked my watch as we made our way over to Barbara's trailer. I reckoned I still had about ninety minutes left to finish my Baumkuchen. Would they notice if I stayed away a bit longer? They didn't just film us bakers. They would shoot things from different angles, including the judges discussing the challenge amongst themselves, and of course they would film Barbara sashaying her way around the bakes. I could spare a bit longer, I thought, but I reminded myself that if it went badly today I would have to be brilliant tomorrow. I ignored the little voice that pointed out that I was no more likely to be able to focus on the baking rather than the murder tomorrow than I had been today; it wasn't helpful.

Barbara's shepherd's hut was kind of a shed on wheels, but a very luxurious one. Pete and Esme had one each as well. The huts were painted bright colours, had cutesy retro curtains at the windows, and little stainless-steel chimneys poking out from a shingle roof; they must have a wood burner, or little stove, which would keep them toasty and warm. Away from the main baking tent, which was really hot with all the lights set up and ovens turned on, it was still a bit nippy, so I imagined Barbara's hut would be warm and toasty.

Nathan went up the wooden steps and knocked on the door of the hut.

'Mr Lang?'

There was movement inside, then Barbara opened the door. 'I'm sorry, love, he ain't here at the moment.'

Nathan smiled and without missing a beat said, 'That's fine, Ms Strident, it's you I need to talk to.'

Barbara looked at him, then at me, for a moment, then

shrugged. 'You'd better come in, then,' she said, only now she sounded more like Russell. This was going to get confusing.

The hut really was snug and cosy. Most of one end was taken up by a big day bed, with a colourful patchwork quilt flung carelessly over it, as if we'd disturbed Barbara (or Russell) from a lunchtime power nap. There was a wood-burning stove in the corner, no longer aflame but still radiating a gentle warmth. There was a table with a stack of magazines and a very serious-looking non-fiction book on anthropology on it, next to a couple of mugs with the dregs of tea in the bottom.

Barbara gestured to us to sit on the day bed, and plopped herself into a small tub chair that was far too low to the ground for her long legs.

'Ms Strident—' Nathan began. Barbara reached up and unpinned her wig – today's 'do' was a glossy chestnut mane, the sort of thing you normally only see in slow motion on a shampoo advert – before dropping it carelessly onto the table.

'Call me Russell,' she – he – said. It was remarkable how they really did seem like two entirely separate people, just through the hair and the voice. The voice was much more leafy Surrey than Essex.

'Mr Lang – Russell – I just need to ask you a few more questions about the murder of Harry Dodds.'

'Really? And there's me thinking you were here for an

autograph,' said Russell sarcastically, sounding like Barbara all over again. He suddenly drooped. 'Sorry, that was rude of me. I'm just under a lot of stress at the moment. I apologise.' He looked over at me. 'You're not the police, though. You're supposed to be baking.'

'Ms Parker is actually a consultant for the Devon and Cornwall Constabulary,' said Nathan, and I beamed proudly. I was almost a copper again! But without the hassle of shift work! And absolutely no powers of arrest! Dammit, I knew it was too good to be true. Russell raised a heavily plucked eyebrow.

'A consultant? What does that mean?'

'It means I was on the Force for twenty years, and I know the local area, and in this case I was on the spot when the murder happened,' I said. 'And my cake's cooling down…'

Russell shrugged. 'Fair enough. It's no skin off my nose who you are, to be honest. I've done nothing wrong.' So why did he sound like he had?

'I just wanted to ask you about your costume change after lunch yesterday,' Nathan started.

'I already explained about that,' Russell interrupted. 'I told you, Harry ripped my dress when he was putting my mike on. It lasted the morning, but by midday it was coming apart, so I changed it. End of the story.'

'Why did you change your wig, though?' I asked thoughtfully. 'Camilla was fuming, wasn't she, because of continuity. You would have known that would happen. Okay, if your dress was literally falling apart, that change could have gone unnoticed—' Russell snorted in disbelief. 'Okay, with your outfits maybe not completely unnoticed, but they could have just shot close-ups of your face or something. But changing your wig... There's no way viewers won't notice that you had a complete change of look.'

'It doesn't matter, I shot a piece to camera saying Barbara felt like a change halfway through,' said Russell, but Nathan shook his head.

'You know I don't give a damn about "continuity". What I want to know is, why did you change your wig? Especially when you knew it would cause issues.'

'You don't understand, DCI Withers. Every outfit is like a different persona. The one I started with yesterday was Dolly. Big hair, leopard print and rhinestones. Definitely a blonde. The afternoon's outfit was Selina, smooth, sophisticated, a bit of a femme fatale—'

'Where's Dolly now, Mr Lang?' asked Nathan. His voice had that steely politeness that I knew was masking the irritation he felt.

'Over at Wardrobe,' said Russell, carelessly gesturing towards the tent production village outside his hut.

'Right. So if we go over there now, you'll be able to show it to me?' Nathan was still polite, but persistent.

'Really, Detective, she won't go with your

colouring…' Russell attempted to laugh, but he was nervous. I leaned forward.

'Russell, come on. You know Wardrobe is the next place we'll be heading after this, so if you've got any reason to doubt the whereabouts of your wig, or anything else to tell us, do us and yourself a favour and tell us now.'

'You're a better cop than a baker, do you know that?' said Russell defiantly, but he was on the back foot and we all knew it.

'Yes, I do know that. So?'

Russell looked from me to Nathan then back again, and sighed.

'I lost it.'

'What?'

'I lost the wig.' He looked at us, like he was desperate for us to believe him. 'When I left the tent at lunchtime yesterday, I was hot and bothered. I'd had a pig of a morning, and – well, let's just say it's not just work that has been causing me a bit of stress lately.'

'Problems with your personal life?' I asked, remembering the argument we'd witnessed in the pub on Monday evening. Russell looked at me, irritated.

'Do you know why it's called "personal life"?' he asked. 'Because it's personal.' He turned back to Nathan. 'I was hot and bothered, so I ripped Dolly off my head to cool down – she sheds a bit, and it was making my face itchy. I came back here, and...' He stopped abruptly.

'What is it?' asked Nathan. 'What happened when you got back here?'

'Nothing,' Russell said. 'I'm just trying to remember. I could hear someone approaching, but I just didn't have the energy to deal with anybody. I was desperate to get inside but I couldn't find my key, so I dropped Dolly on the steps and searched through my pockets until I found it. And then I came inside for a lie-down.'

'You left the wig outside, on the steps?'

'Yes. And then when I came out later – when I realised I'd have to change out of that dress because the rip had got bigger – the wig wasn't there. At first I thought it had just fallen down between the steps, but it wasn't on the ground. Someone had taken it.'

'Did you tell anyone?' I asked, but he shook his head.

'No. I assumed that someone had seen it and taken it to Wardrobe, to put it back with all my other wigs, but when I went there no one had seen it.' He looked worried. 'I didn't tell Camilla, because the production company paid for a whole new wardrobe for this series, including the wigs. They own them. I didn't want anyone getting into trouble about it until I'd had a chance to look for it properly.'

'It's only a wig,' I said, but he shook his head.

'It's not "only" a wig, it's a handcrafted, made-tomeasure wig, made from one hundred per cent human hair. It's not some cheap nylon tat. Even if Dolly *was* a bit prone to moulting...' He looked at Nathan. 'Why are you so interested in my wig, anyway?'

'Because we think Harry Dodds's killer was a blonde...'

Chapter Eight

Russell stared at Nathan in shock, his mouth open. 'You think I killed him?' He looked genuinely astonished. 'Why on earth would I kill him?'

'You didn't exactly hit it off,' I pointed out. He shook his head in disgust.

'Oh *please*. I'm a drag queen. I spent the early days of my career working the pubs and clubs in Soho. I'm used to dealing with homophobes like Harry Dodds.' His voice became pure Barbara again. 'I eat muppets like that for me breakfast, love, washed down with a Bacardi Breezer.'

'I'm sure you do,' said Nathan calmly. 'But I'd have thought dealing with a drunken heckler in the audience was different to dealing with someone who's right there, in your face, trying to make you look stupid or trip you up.'

'He "forgot" to put batteries in your mike and then he "accidentally" ripped your dress,' I said. 'And then he made a point of calling you "him" when you were dressed up as Barbara, which isn't exactly wrong, but it's not in the right spirit, is it?'

'I can handle morons like him without resorting to violence,' said Russell defiantly. 'And anyway, I'm not the only blonde on the bake off, am I?' He looked at me. 'Just in the tent, there's Camilla, and that weirdo guy at the back—'

'Martin,' I said. 'But why would either of those kill Harry?'

'Camilla was gunning for him after the mike incident,' he said. 'And that Martin – well, all right, I don't know why he'd want to kill Harry, but he's strange, isn't he? All the stuff with the yoga and his travels, yet he talks like he's never got past the Tamar.'

'He's just super-focused,' I said, although I wasn't sure why I was defending him after he'd dissed my cake-decorating efforts on the first day. 'And Camilla could've fired Harry if she was that annoyed with him.'

'Believe me, she was going to, I'd lay money on it.' Russell sat back, his arms crossed. 'Anyway, none of that changes the fact that it wasn't me.' He looked at his watch. 'Now if you'll excuse me, I've got a show to film.'

. . .

We left Russell rearranging his wig in front of the mirror and headed back towards the tent. I really needed to make a reappearance before they disqualified me or something. I turned to Nathan.

'Did Forensics find enough hair to get DNA from?' I asked. 'Can they do that, if it's just a strand? Because if it *did* come from Russell's wig, there won't be any root attached.'

Nathan nodded. 'They should be able to get something from it.' he said, 'We quite often only get strands. Without the root, though, it'll just be mitochondrial DNA.'

'Let's pretend for a moment I don't know what mitochondrial means…'

'Passed down the maternal line. Mitochondrial DNA won't necessarily identify a specific individual, but it does let us narrow it down to that matriarchal line. So as long as we don't have any members of the same family in our pool of suspects, we'll be good.'

'And if the DNA doesn't match anyone here, then you know it's from Barbara's wig,' I said.

'Which would be a right pain in the backside, because although that means I can tie Russell to the crime scene, it doesn't rule out other suspects,' said Nathan. 'Because technically, *anyone* could have been wearing the wig.'

'Maybe the murderer wanted it to look like Russell had done it?' I said, thoughtfully.

'Maybe. But why? Would you say he's well liked on set?'

'Definitely. Much more so than Harry, anyway.'

We drew level with the Wardrobe tent. I stopped.

'Have you had a look at Barbara's outfit from yesterday? The one that was supposedly too ripped for her to carry on wearing?' I asked. Nathan looked at his watch.

'I sent Matt to have a look at it and get it bagged up for Forensics,' he said. 'I haven't seen him since.' We exchanged glances as the sound of laughter reached us from inside the tent.

'He must've been on his way over when I saw him earlier...' I said.

'What the—' Nathan stood in the doorway of the tent, hands on his hips. I peered over his shoulder and burst out laughing.

Matt Turner sat in a chair in front of a mirror, wearing an outrageous ginger wig and flirting even more outrageously with the make-up lady, who was young, attractive and (I noted) blonde. *Like half the flipping crew*, I thought. If we – I mean, they – didn't get any DNA off those hairs, it would leave us with a very wide field of suspects.

Matt turned in his seat and, seeing his superior officer, blushed. He leapt up, grabbing at the wig on his head, but it had been pinned on and wasn't that easy to remove.

'Sorry, Guv, I was just talking to Shanice here about Barbara's outfit—' he said.

Nathan looked at him sternly, but I could tell he was trying not to laugh himself. 'So how did you end up looking like a Spice Girl on steroids?' he asked, and Shanice and I both giggled again. Matt looked mortified.

'Sorry, I just—'

'Oh come on, Nath,' I said, coming to the poor detective sergeant's aid. 'Don't you have the slightest urge to try one on? I do.'

'Everyone does,' said Shanice, looking Nathan up and down appraisingly. 'Especially men, for some reason. It's always the first thing they want to do. The more macho, the more likely they are to go for something glamorous.' She reached out and carefully picked up a blonde bobbed wig from a nearby stand; there was a whole row of them, displaying a variety of hairpieces, except for four, which were empty. One for the wig Barbara was wearing today, two for the wigs Matt and Shanice currently had, and one for the missing-presumed-a-murderer Dolly. 'This one would really suit your colouring,' she said to

Nathan. Matt and I both snorted with suppressed laughter.

'No, no, that one!' I said, bursting. I pointed to a short, dark, curly one. 'Oh my God, you'd look like a proper Scally in that one.'

The look on Nathan's face was a picture. Matt gave up trying to hold in his laughter. 'What's the matter, Guv? I thought Scousers liked curly perms?'

'And little moustaches,' I said. I was in danger of peeing myself, I was laughing so hard. Women of a certain age. It happens.

'All right, calm down,' said Nathan, but that just made us laugh even harder. Nathan raised an eyebrow, watching us like we were a couple of complete morons, waiting for us to stop. But every time one of us did, we'd catch sight of the other and start again. Nathan sighed.

'Just put it on,' I gasped. Nathan shook his head.

'Never going to happen. Can we get on now, please?' He was starting to look genuinely irritated, so I forced myself to stop laughing and averted my eyes from Matt, who was quite red in the face.

'Sorry, babe,' I murmured.

'Sorry, Guv.' Matt cleared his throat, and I could hear laughter threatening his voice again, but he took a deep breath and gestured over to a clothes rail. 'Barbara's outfit from yesterday. I was just about to start bagging it up. It's definitely ripped.'

Nathan wandered over to the rail and, pulling on a pair of latex gloves, turned the dress towards him so he could inspect it. There was indeed a very long rip along one seam, from the armpit all the way down to the bottom of the skirt, where the horizontal stitching along the hem was the only thing keeping it together.

'I see why she had to change it,' said Nathan. 'A bit daring, even for Barbara.' He turned to Shanice. 'Barbara came in earlier in the day, and you managed to patch it up,' he said. 'Is that right?'

'Yes,' said Shanice, 'although it wasn't me, I'm Make-up. Julie's the wardrobe mistress. She's at lunch. I saw it though, and it wasn't anywhere near as bad as this.'

'From what I saw of it, it was just a little hole about here...' I pointed to a spot that would have been just above Barbara's hip when the dress was on. 'It had pulled away a bit of the stitching along the seam, but nothing like this.' Shanice nodded in agreement.

'From what you saw of the repair to the dress, should it have lasted the rest of the day?' asked Nathan. 'If it was just worn normally, like standing up in the tent, sitting down for a break, that sort of thing?'

'I don't know, to be honest, but I would have thought so,' said Shanice. 'Julie's used to making running repairs on things during the shoot, she would have done a good enough job on it that it should have lasted at least until we wrapped for the day.'

'Right...' Nathan leaned in and sniffed at the dress.

'What is it?' I asked, leaning in as well, but I smelt it too, before I'd even got close.

'It reeks of perfume. Barbara must've really overdone it yesterday, because I didn't smell any on her today.' He stood up and looked at Matt. 'Get that bagged up and sent over to Forensics, please.'

'Yes Guv.'

'Oh, and Matt?'

'Yes Guv?'

'Take that stupid wig off.'

I left Nathan and Matt to it and forced myself back to the baking tent. Camilla rushed over to me as I entered.

'Is everything okay?' she asked, but she seemed more relieved than annoyed. 'What with – everything that's happened – we were starting to get concerned.'

'Sorry—' I started, but Barbara appeared behind me and interrupted.

'Oh, she's fine. Just doing her bit to help that dishy detective.' Camilla looked at her, confused. 'She's with the filth, Camilla.'

'I *was* with the filth – I mean, police,' I explained. 'I'm a consultant these days. I just got a bit caught up with the investigation, what with being on the spot when it happened and that. Sorry. How long have we got to finish our cakes?'

'Fifty minutes,' said Camilla. 'As you've been helping the police I'll try to give you a bit more time, but it's not really fair on the other contestants.'

'Fifty minutes is plenty,' I said hastily, although it would be pushing it. I headed back to my bench, ignoring the questioning looks from Ravi and Elaine (Martin probably hadn't even noticed I'd left the tent). I set about making a chocolate ganache. That wouldn't take long; I just had to break up some good-quality chocolate, then heat some cream and pour it over the pieces, stirring until everything melted and combined.

Except none of the rings on my hob were working. I fiddled with the knobs, trying all of them, and let out a cry of frustration. I didn't have time for this! I would have used the work space that Lynda had been using before her exit yesterday, but it had been covered over with a cloth and the bench top next to it had production notes and bits and pieces of camera equipment on it.

Ravi looked round at my *aargh!*. 'Everything all right, Jodie?'

'No! My bloody hob's stopped working. It was fine earlier. Nothing's coming on…' I ran my fingers through my hair, beginning to get stressed. Ravi waved over towards Camilla, but she was talking to a production assistant and didn't see him.

'Where's it plugged in?' asked Ravi. We both looked around. The cables for all the electrical equipment were taped down to avoid a trip hazard, so it was easy to follow the line of duct tape all the way from my counter to the bank of power sockets at the side of the tent, out of camera shot.

There was a plug on the floor, out of its socket. Ravi bent down and plugged it in, and immediately all my cooking rings came on.

'There you go, panic over,' he said, and carried on with his own decorating.

'Thanks, Ravi,' I said, smiling at him, but inside I wasn't smiling. All the cables were still firmly stuck down with tape. It was clear that no one had tripped and accidentally tugged the plug out of the socket. *Someone unplugged me on purpose,* I thought. Add to that my white chocolate going missing the day before, and it definitely seemed suspicious... Or was I being paranoid? The problem with being a copper is that you do sometimes tend to spot a crime or malicious intent where there isn't any.

Whatever, I didn't have time to think about it now. I heated up some cream in a pan and melted my chocolate in it. The ganache was rich, thick and gorgeous, the way I liked my men (before I met Nathan).

I let the ganache cool slightly, then poured it over my cake, working it out to the edges of the sponge and letting it run down the sides, then smoothing it over. The ganache had a beautifully smooth finish and looked pretty good just as it was, but simplicity was not going to win the day, not looking at Elaine and Ravi's masterpieces. Both of them had also gone for a chocolate ganache frosting (it was the traditional way to top it), but that was where any similarities had ended. Ravi had gone for a nature theme, like my original idea, but instead of horrible misshapen roses that looked like they had been struck down by the horticultural equivalent of the bubonic plague, his looked like they'd come straight from the Chelsea Flower Show. Alan Titchmarsh would have been proud of them.

Elaine, meanwhile, had gone off on a completely different tack. We'd had a variety of ingredients with which to decorate our cakes, and she'd taken some hazelnuts and dipped them in hot caramel, leaving the caramel to run as it cooled so they looked like delicious teardrops of sugary nuttiness. The cake was covered with dark chocolate ganache, then edged with swirls of white chocolate frosting topped by the hazelnuts.

I could only imagine what Martin's would look like. I was in trouble.

I cut out more chocolate leaves; the ones I'd done earlier had disappeared, but I couldn't actually remember what I'd done with them. I assumed I'd left them on my bench top, but I didn't have time to wonder about that now. Luckily they were quick to cut out and I soon had tons. Once the ganache on the cake had set – and with five minutes left on the clock – I started to place the leaves in a spiral pattern on top, whirling out from the centre of the Baumkuchen. I figured that although it was quite simple it would still look impressive, by dint of the sheer number of leaves on it.

'One minute left, bakers!' called Barbara. 'So if you've not finished, *schnell, schnell*!'

I placed the last leaf on and stood back to admire my cake. For such a last-minute, rushed job, it actually looked really good. Not as good as Elaine's or Ravi's, and I was betting Martin (the jammy git) would have made something AMAZING, but hey-ho.

'Time's up! Step away from your bakes!' cried Barbara. I looked up and smiled at Elaine as we all stepped back from our counters.

'Oh my God, yours looks brilliant!' I said. She smiled.

'For someone who's been missing half the afternoon, so does yours! Where have you been?'

But I couldn't tell her right then, as we had to carry our Baumkuchen down to the front of the tent and put them on a table for the blind judging. Pete and Esme came in, all smiles, and stood in front of the cakes. And we all got an eyeful of Martin's cake.

Like the rest of us, he'd covered his cake in the ubiquitous chocolate ganache. But when it came to decorating cakes, Martin liked to think big. He'd carved a brown bear, rearing up on its hind legs, out of chocolate. The bear was supported by a chocolate tree stump, and surrounded by carved acorns, beautifully modelled and so realistic. It was so far ahead of the rest of us, it was embarrassing. It was like Usain Bolt taking part in the school sports day three-legged race.

'Holy moly!' muttered Elaine, and I had to agree.

The judges inspected all the cakes. Pete raised his eyes at Martin's. I got the impression that, although it was a blind judging, they knew exactly whose cake it was.

'Wow,' said Pete, and Esme nodded in agreement. 'That looks incredible. Whoever carved that bear is an artist, not just a baker.'

'It's fantastic,' enthused Esme. Barbara, however, did not look quite as impressed.

'Yeah, well, it's cool, I'll give you that,' she said, 'but I was under the impression that the bear was a symbol of the Black Forest, in the south-west of Germany, innit? And as everyone knows...' she winked at Ravi, because of course none of us knew anything about Baumkuchen apart from what was on the list of instructions '... Baumkuchen originated in Salzwedel, in the Saxony-Anhalt region, which ain't in the south-west, is it, babes? It's in the north-east...' I heard an annoyed grunt from behind me; Martin was less than pleased by her comments. He really did not like criticism.

'I think we can let him – them – off for that,' said Pete, smiling. Esme cut them both a slice of the cake and it was, of course, delicious.

Elaine's cake and decoration were also pronounced very good, but Ravi's layers of sponge weren't cooked evenly. I was surprised. His decorations were still better than mine, though. I waited with bated breath as the judges reached my cake.

'Oh, now this is pretty,' said Esme. 'It's like you, Pete – simple, not too flashy—' Everyone laughed except Martin, who I felt stiffen behind me, annoyed that someone else (but specifically me, I thought) was receiving praise. 'This is probably the closest to a traditional Baumkuchen in terms of decoration. I like it.'

Pete nodded. 'Yep, it's very clean, very classy. Also like me. Of course, if you go with something simple, it has to be done perfectly...' I held my breath as he cut into the sponge; maybe I was a lot more invested in this contest than I'd realised. Pete held up the slice of cake. 'Look at that. The layers of sponge are all perfectly cooked, all equal. Nice amount of jam, too.'

The judges both took a big bite, and for a moment didn't speak. Had I poisoned them? Esme smiled at the bakers before taking another bite. She liked it.

'Now that is yummy,' she said. 'I do like that one a

lot.' I let out my breath in relief as the two of them and Barbara went off into a little huddle to decide who the winner was.

'Okay,' said Pete, returning to the table. 'In fourth place, this one.' He pointed to Ravi's. Ravi nodded. 'Looks fantastic, just tastes a bit dry in places. A real shame. In third place, this one.' He pointed to Elaine's. She raised her hand. 'It was really close between this one and the one in second place, and your nuts almost swung it—'

'I went out with a bloke like that once,' said Barbara, and we all sniggered.

'They're delicious, but the layers, again, could be a bit more even. Whose is this one?' asked Pete, pointing to mine. I raised my hand. 'Really lovely. Perfectly cooked, but the decoration let you down a bit.'

'I liked it very much!' protested Esme. 'Very pretty.'

'It is,' agreed Pete. 'But look what you're up against.' He gestured to Martin's cake. 'I just wish we'd gone for an Italian recipe, we could've had Michelangelo's *Statue of David* rendered in chocolate on the top.'

Everyone laughed, again apart from Martin, who just looked smug. 'Nice one, mate,' I said, but he just looked at me like he'd known all along that he was going to come out on top, and my congratulations meant nothing to him. I bit my tongue as Pete pronounced Martin's

Baumkuchen the winner and joined in the round of applause from my fellow bakers.

I looked out for Nathan as we all left the tent and headed home, but he was nowhere to be seen. I was disappointed, but hardly surprised; he *was* supposed to be working, and not hanging around waiting to see how his girlfriend's dodgy German cake had got on. Or to let her in on his latest discoveries in the case. But I would work my magic on him when he came round later and find out anyway.

'How did you know toad in the hole's one of my favourites?' asked Nathan, sitting back in his dining chair and exhaling. Under the table, Germaine lolled about hopefully with her tongue out; it was her favourite, too. 'I'm so full, if you weren't here, Shirley, I'd take my trousers off and give my tummy more room.'

'Don't mind me,' giggled Mum. Daisy and I exchanged eye-rolls, but she spotted me. 'Don't you roll your eyes at me, young lady! I remember when you were little and I showed you how to make this, you kept asking me where the toads were.'

'Why *is* it called toad in the hole?' asked Daisy,

thoughtfully. 'Sausages don't look anything like toads. And Yorkshire pudding doesn't look like a hole, either.'

'Bubble and squeak doesn't have bubbles or make a noise when you bite into it,' I pointed out.

'And pork scratchings sound like something you'd get off a pig with eczema,' said Nathan.

'Eww…' said Daisy, and Germaine gave a little whine as if agreeing with her.

'Spotted dick's my favourite,' said Mum.

'Why does that not surprise me, Nana?'

I jumped up – as much as the plateful of sausage, batter and mashed potatoes I'd just consumed would allow me to jump – and began to clear away the plates.

'Who's going to help me with the dishes?' I said, knowing the answer already. The dog followed me, and I knew she was offering to dispose of the leftovers. Just as a favour to me, obviously. There wasn't much left, but there was a tiny bit of sausage on one of the plates, so I threw it up in the air (not that high, of course – Germaine's a Pomeranian, not a Great Dane) and watched as she sat up, alert, and caught it. Good girl.

'I've got homework,' said Daisy, pushing her chair back and legging it out of the room. Germaine, her sausage craving assuaged, trotted after her, tail wagging.

'That's convenient. Mum?'

'*The Chase* is on, love. You can't expect me to miss Bradley Walsh and his cheeky grin.'

Nathan laughed. 'You go and sit down, Shirley. Me and Jodie can do it.' Mum gave him a warm smile and turned to me.

'This one's a keeper,' she trilled, then fled before we changed our minds. She had a much faster turn of speed than you'd expect from a seventy-one-year-old. I shook my head.

'You spoil my mother,' I said, and Nathan laughed again, taking the dirty plates from my hand and setting them down on the counter, then pulling me towards him.

'I know how to handle little old ladies,' he said, grinning. 'And nosey young ones...'

After we'd finished the washing up, I put the kettle on and we sat at the kitchen table nursing mugs of hot tea.

'Go on, then,' said Nathan. I raised an eyebrow. 'Ask me what else I found today. I'm amazed you've lasted this long without bursting.'

'I was buttering you up with home cooking first,' I said. 'So what *did* you find today? Other than that ginger doesn't suit Matt Turner.'

'The victim's wife came to the scene.'

'Dammit! And I was cooking. I would've liked to have talked to her.'

Nathan laughed. 'Bold of you to assume I'd have let you.'

'You would have.'

'No, I wouldn't in this case. She's a grieving widow.' He looked suddenly serious. 'You know, sometimes investigating stuff feels a bit like a game. Less so with murders, obviously, but even then, when it's someone you don't know and who doesn't appear to have been well liked, it feels kind of competitive – like you're pitting your wits against the criminal.'

'It's like Sherlock Holmes, innit? It feels like a cerebral challenge, not a moral one,' I said, and he nodded.

'It does. It doesn't mean I don't feel for the victim, but you probably know from your own experience, you can't let yourself get emotionally involved in every case, otherwise it would drive you mad.' He sighed. 'And then you talk to the grieving relatives and you remember why you're doing this job.'

'Was she really upset? Sorry, that's a stupid question. Of course she was really upset. But people don't always show it.'

'She did show it. It was hard to get much sense out of her. I have to admit I was quite worried about her driving herself home.'

We sipped at our tea for a moment, and without even thinking about it I reached out to take Nathan's free hand. The thought of losing a loved one under such horrible circumstances – under *any* circumstances – just made me want to gather him and Daisy and Mum all together so I could hold them close and not let them out of my sight. But of course I couldn't do that; I had to let them all live their own lives and trust that the universe would take care of them. But I could, for now, hold on to Nathan.

'So, what did she say? Anything useful?'

'Not really. She said he took the job on because he was fed up with teaching and wanted to try something new. He'd never shown any real interest in TV production, but apparently he was a big fan of Barbara's, and having an "in" – Indira – that's what gave him the idea of working on the roadshow.'

I frowned. 'She really said he was a fan of Barbara's? Because like Russell said, he struck me as a homophobic weasel, not a fan.'

'That's what he told her, and she believed him.' Nathan looked thoughtful. 'Maybe…'

'What? You've either had an epiphany or you need the toilet.'

'A little bit of both, actually. But what about this? Harry's married. He's relatively young to be married, by today's standards – only twenty-eight. Why the hurry to get hitched?'

'She was pregnant?'

'If she *was*, then something happened because they didn't have any kids. No, I was thinking, maybe he got married because he *was* such a fan of drag queens…' Nathan gave me a look, and I suddenly caught on.

'The lady doth protest too much, you mean? The biggest homophobes often turn out to be in denial themselves.' I thought for a moment. 'So, Harry Dodds is a closet homosexual. He gets married at an early age, to try and ignore his doubts about his own sexuality. He's a genuine fan of Barbara's, and he thinks if he meets her, works with her (or with Russell, more to the point – another gay man), it might help him get up the courage to come out. But all it does is make him more confused and more in denial.'

'It's a theory,' said Nathan.

'Yeah…' I started.

'But…' Nathan finished.

'But he would have to be in deep, deep denial to get married, and to act the way he did. So deep in denial he could see de pyramids… And who in this day and age cares that much about being gay or straight or whatever?'

'And why would he end up dead?' asked Nathan.

'Maybe his wife worked it out. She wouldn't be very happy about it, I'd imagine.'

Nathan shook his head. 'She was at work all day.'

'What does she do?'

'She's a nurse. Works in home health care, mostly private clients. She spent most of the day looking after a disabled patient who had been taken ill. The agency she works for backed her up.'

'Dammit! It's always the husband or wife,' I said, and Nathan laughed.

'Really? You do remember how we met, right?'

We'd met when Tony Penhaligon had hired me to cater his wedding, not long after I'd moved back to Penstowan. Only the wedding had never taken place, because his ex-wife Mel had turned up, first to have a go at his wife-to-be, Cheryl, and later as an uninvited, dead guest. Nathan had been convinced of Tony's guilt, and if I hadn't known him I probably would have been, too. But I knew my oldest friend in the world was not and never could be a killer, and I'd set out (much to Nathan's irritation) to prove his innocence.

'Okay, fair point,' I conceded. 'But who else had motive to kill him? He was a bit of a dick, but most people would need more than that to bump someone off.'

'We're still looking into anyone who might have had a grudge against him,' said Nathan.

'If only we knew the real reason for him taking the job...' I murmured. Nathan shook his head.

'We might never know that, and to be honest I'm not sure it would make that much difference if we did,' he said. 'But that's enough shop talk. Have you planned what you're baking tomorrow?'

'White chocolate custard-filled hot cross doughnuts,' I

said, absentmindedly. 'I know it's not Easter yet, but by the time they show our episode it will be.'

'Wow! When did you come up with them? And why haven't I had one?'

'I haven't tried making them before. They only mentioned it should have an Easter theme this afternoon, so I only just came up with the idea,' I said. Nathan looked amazed.

'What? But it's an elimination round tomorrow—'

'I know.' I smiled at him with a confidence I didn't entirely feel. 'It'll be fine. I work better under pressure...'

Chapter Nine

'What do you mean, it's Inset day?' I grabbed a piece of toast as it leapt out of the toaster and interrogated Daisy as I buttered it.

'That means it's teacher training day,' said Daisy, dangling the belt of her dressing gown in front of Germaine, making her bounce around in excitement.

'I know what it means, I mean, what do *you* mean by it's today? Why didn't you tell me before?'

'I forgot.' Daisy smiled brightly at me. 'So I'll have to come to the roadshow with you today.'

'Why can't you go to Jade's?'

'She's going out this afternoon.'

'Nana will be here,' I said. Mum entered as if on cue.

'No I won't, I've got to go back to my house and then I've got an appointment,' she said.

'What appointment?'

'A private one.'

'With the doctor?'

'No.'

Nathan entered the kitchen, which was beginning to resemble a madhouse, what with Daisy and Germaine leaping around and my mother being enigmatic, while I was busy trying to get ready. Nathan had stayed the night. He'd started off only staying at the weekends, so even if he was working the rest of us probably weren't and the morning chaos was slightly calmer. But at some point he'd started staying over during the week too. I saw it as something of a trial run; if we were serious (which I hoped we were), then maybe at some point we would move in together, and we'd all have to get used to living under the same roof. I didn't like to think about that too much, because 1) I could foresee problems ahead if we all lived together in this house – Mum was supposedly still independent, but she had to all intents and purposes moved in with us now, and Daisy was getting bigger, and as much as I loved this house, it was probably too small for four adults and a small but energetic dog. And 2) I really wanted it to happen, and if I thought about it too much, made too many plans for our future, then I might jinx it. And it was still early days, really, even if it sometimes felt like I'd known him for years.

Nathan looked at me over the kitchen table. 'Everything okay?'

'Daisy's not at school today and I'm only just hearing about it,' I said.

'Ah. You could go to Jade's?'

'She's going to the orthodontist this afternoon,' said Daisy, smugly.

'What about Shirley?'

'I have an appointment,' said Mum. Nathan looked at me, eyebrows raised.

'She's being enigmatic,' I said, and Nathan grinned.

'Surely not. Debbie?'

'No, she said she was going to Exeter today…' I slapped my forehead. 'Of course! She mentioned she was taking the kids out for the day and I thought it was weird, but her two go to the same school as Daisy so it's Inset day for them, too.' I plopped myself down on a kitchen chair. 'I'm sorry, sweetheart, I've been so busy with the roadshow and everything that it just didn't occur to me. And term's only just started – you'd think they could've done all their teacher training over half term.'

'They never do,' said Mum.

'It's fine, I'll just come to the roadshow,' said Daisy. I narrowed my eyes.

'You sprang this on me on purpose, didn't you? So I'd have to take you with me.' Daisy put on the most angelic, innocent face I had ever seen. I didn't believe it for a moment.

'Who, me? I won't get bored, there's TV cameras everywhere and drag queens, and now there's been a murder...' Daisy had got a taste for playing detective after we'd been snowed in during a catering gig at Christmas, and a murder had taken place. We'd been trapped in the house, and with the bad weather holding the police up, had taken on the investigation ourselves – me, Daisy, Mum and Debbie.

Nathan groaned, but it was good-natured. 'That's just what I need, the Number One Nosey Parkers' detective agency clambering all over my crime scene.'

In the end I arranged for Daisy (and Germaine) to go to Jade's for the morning, and then for Jade's mum Nancy to drop them off at the roadshow after lunch; the orthodontist was in Launceston, so it was more or less on the way for them. At least that way I'd have the morning to get most of my baking done without worrying about Daisy getting bored or the dog getting into trouble (or vice versa). The afternoon would be more about decorating my doughnuts (which sounded like a euphemism but wasn't) and adding the finishing touches to my Easter display.

Daisy went off to get dressed while Mum booked a taxi; I'd offered to drop her off, but I was going in the completely opposite direction, so I was relieved when she said no. I grabbed my bag and car keys and let out a deep breath.

'And relax...' said Nathan, leaning in for a kiss.

I sighed. 'My mornings are not usually that chaotic. Daisy normally lets me know well in advance if she's got a day off coming up, because of what happened that one time...'

Nathan looked at me. 'What "one time"?'

'The one time when I thought term started again on Tuesday, and it actually didn't start until Wednesday...'

His eyes widened. 'You didn't...?'

'Yep. I packed her off to school, on time for a change. It was only round the corner from our old house, and lots of her friends went the same way, so she used to insist on walking there on her own. Half an hour later I get a call from the school secretary asking me to come and pick her up because it was a teachers-only day.' Nathan laughed. 'It wasn't funny! I felt so guilty.'

'I bet you're not the only mum who's done that,' he said, pulling me in for a hug.

'No, probably not, but still... Anyway, I reckon she kept it quiet this time just so I'd have to take her with me. She wants to have a poke around.'

'I wonder where she gets that from?' said Nathan, grinning at me.

'I honestly have no idea...'

• • •

Nathan went his way (to Penstowan Police station) and I went mine – back to Boskern House, and the baking roadshow. I told myself I was determined to concentrate more today. My hot cross doughnuts were rather complicated to make, and would take some time as they had to prove twice. Plus I had to make white chocolate custard, and my track record with making custard from scratch was a bit sketchy, to say the least; I would either end up with the smoothest, creamiest custard you'd ever tasted, or scrambled eggs. Or in this case, white chocolate-flavoured scrambled eggs. Yum.

But... I got out of the car and there were still a few uniformed coppers hanging around, including Davey Trelawney, who winked at me knowingly; knowing that I wouldn't be able to resist sticking my nose in. NO! I would stand firm. I WOULD concentrate on my doughnuts. I WOULD focus on my custard. I WOULD find a spare moment to slip out of the tent and have a word with Davey and find out if anything had come up overnight... Aargh! The temptation was just too much for someone as nosey as me.

'All right, Jodie?' Davey nodded at me as I approached.

'Yeah, you all right?' He nodded again. 'So... what's new?' He grinned.

'Reckon you probably know more than I do, being close to the guvnor,' he said.

I shrugged. 'Yeah … but you're here, on the spot. I wondered what the word was on the ground, so to speak.'

He looked around, but the only people nearby were crew members, and they were all busy getting ready for the day's shoot.

'They say that Barbara's not what she seems,' he said, in a conspiratorially quiet voice. I leaned in closer.

'Really? In what way?'

'Some say…' He looked around again. 'Some say as she's actually a fella.' I looked at him for a moment, then groaned as he burst out laughing.

'Oh you git,' I said, and he laughed harder.

'Sorry, I just couldn't resist. Under strict instructions, ain't I, not to talk to anyone about the case.'

'Yeah, but I'm not "anyone",' I pointed out, not unreasonably, I thought. He patted me on the arm.

'I know you ain't. I did actually hear one of the crew saying people would be surprised if they found out the truth about Russell Lang.'

'Really?' I looked at him, frankly. 'You're not going to say, "because he likes dressing in women's clothing", are you?'

'No I ain't, scout's honour. I didn't hear the rest of it, though. It could have nothing to do with any of this. He don't seem like a murderer to me.'

'He doesn't to me, either,' I said, because despite the

blonde fibres that I somehow felt sure would come from the missing Dolly wig, I couldn't see him bashing someone in the head. Cutting them down with a sarcastic remark, yes. But actual physical violence? He didn't seem the type.

But then most murderers probably didn't. Most murders are spur of the moment, crime of passion things; outside of that 'moment', many murderers actually *weren't* 'the type'. They were ordinary people who, for whatever reason, temporarily lost it in a flash of madness, and then had to live with the guilt of what they'd done. Even if they covered it up, even if they legally 'got away with it', they were punished by the knowledge they'd taken a life, every single day.

If Russell were a murderer, what could have caused that moment of temporary insanity? And how would Harry – someone who, as far as Nathan had been able to ascertain, had no connection with him – be able to provoke such an extreme reaction?

'I know that look,' said Davey. 'You look like your dad used to, just before he told us we'd be putting overtime in on a case.'

'It's a tricky one, innit?' I said, and he nodded.

'Like I said, we'll be putting some overtime in on this one, I reckon…'

• • •

I gave myself a stern talking-to as I walked to the baking marquee. Today was an elimination day. Although I'd tried to convince myself that I wasn't that bothered about winning (I certainly didn't expect to), I didn't like the idea of losing either, and I at least wanted to make it through to the last day if I could. The whole point of me being here was to get publicity for my catering company, so the longer I was on the show, the more publicity I'd get. *Imagine the publicity I'd get if I won the Cornish leg of the roadshow, then went on and won the national final AND solved the murder at the same time?!* I thought, but that was ridiculous. I couldn't possibly do that...

...could I?

No. *Focus, Jodie!*

I tried, I really did. I made the dough for my doughnuts, adding sultanas and cinnamon for that hot cross bun taste, then left it to prove for an hour. I made the custard (it needed to be cold when I piped it into the doughnut), made scrambled eggs instead, started again, and it came out perfectly. While it was still hot I broke white chocolate into pieces and added it, so it melted into the custard and oh my God, it was lush. A bit sickly, but delicious, and it didn't matter that it was so sweet as there would only be a small amount inside each doughnut.

'Jodie, do you have a moment?' I looked up to see Camilla standing in front of me. *Uh oh*, I thought. Were they going to give me my marching orders because I kept disappearing?

'My dough's proving, so, yeah…' I said, wishing I'd taken the contest more seriously. Although there was a tiny (to be honest, not *that* tiny) voice at the back of my mind telling me that being chucked out would give me more time to join the investigation. Camilla smiled and patted my hand.

'Don't look so alarmed, we just need to film your interview piece. Every time we've wanted to do it, you've been missing in action.'

'Interview piece?'

'You must have seen it in other episodes, where we talk to you about your love for baking and what winning would mean to you. We've done everyone else's, it's just you.'

Phew, I thought, and I realised that perhaps this show meant more to me than I'd thought. Camilla led me outside the tent, to a quiet spot overlooking the river, where another camera and a couple of crew members were waiting. In the distance I could see another tent – the tent over the crime scene, further down the river; it looked like the uniformed officers were starting to take it down. The body was long gone and the forensics team must be satisfied that they'd got all the evidence they were going to get.

'Maybe just move a little over to your right…'

murmured the camera operator. 'We don't want any of that police stuff in the background.'

'Of course,' I said. 'What kind of thing do you want me to say?'

Camilla smiled. 'When we're ready, I'll ask you a couple of questions…'

They tested the sound and checked the lighting was OK, discussing whether or not daylight was enough or if they needed to set up a light. I fidgeted around, needing to get back to my baking but also desperate to go along to the crime scene and have a chat with whoever was still there. Finally they were ready.

'So, Jodie, what does baking mean to you?'

I'm not really a baker. I'm a chef. So maybe the best way to answer that was to think about what cooking in general meant to me. Cooking, to me, meant helping my mum in the kitchen when I was a little girl; spending time with her, hanging out, talking, laughing, and occasionally licking the bowl clean. It meant doing the same with my own daughter, the two of us – or three of us, as these days Mum was just as likely to be part of it – simply enjoying being together. Cooking has always been my happy place. After a stressful day on the Force, I used to love getting home and changing into comfy clothes, putting some music on, and then following a recipe. Emptying my mind of the events of the day, and just focusing on chopping and dicing, frying and roasting.

Some days, the more complicated the recipe, the better. It was my way of meditating; my way of finding my Zen.

Cooking also meant feeding – not just myself, but the people around me. The people I loved. Someone ill? Make them something warm and comforting that reminds them of their childhood – chicken soup, eaten wrapped in a blanket on Nana's sofa, that kind of thing. Upset? Getting over a break-up? Something decadent, calorific, that represents a great big two fingers up at whoever upset them. Who cares about a stupid man when you've got your girlfriends and a big pile of profiteroles and ice-cream? Celebrating? Bake them a cake. It doesn't have to look good (although it does have to taste good). Feeding people shows that you care about them, that you're thinking of them. Food, to me, equals love. Which was probably why I'd put a bit of weight on recently.

I found myself saying all of this to Camilla and getting a bit emotional, and was surprised and gratified to see her dabbing her eyes with a hanky. She cleared her throat.

'That's lovely, Jodie. What would winning mean to you?'

'You know what, I'm really not that bothered about winning. It would be fantastic, but I already feel like a winner, being here with such wonderful fellow bakers,' I said, hoping I didn't come across as being ridiculously sentimental or completely insincere. Because it kind of was true. Murder notwithstanding, I was enjoying my time on the roadshow. Most of the people involved were nice, and it was pushing me to try things I wouldn't have otherwise done.

'That's great, thank you,' said Camilla. 'I think we've got enough?' She looked at the camera operator, who nodded.

I escaped back to the tent. Elaine looked up as I made my way back to my bench.

'How did it go?' she asked.

'Fine, although I think I was just waffling really. When did you do yours? I didn't even notice.'

'Lynda and Ravi did theirs on the first day, me and Martin did ours yesterday,' she said. She looked around, glancing over at Martin, but he was on the other side of the tent putting something in one of the fridges. 'I overheard the crew talking about Martin's, and they were all laughing,' she whispered.

'Really? Why?'

'He was really up himself. He said he hadn't come along to take part, he'd come to win. He said something like "second place is just first loser".' We both snorted.

'What a muppet,' I said. She nodded.

'That's not a healthy attitude, is it? What will he do if he loses?'

I shrugged. 'He'd better hope he doesn't... What did you say in yours? Why did you enter?'

Elaine smiled. 'I wanted to prove to my kids that I'm not just a pretty face. I want them to be proud of me. And I'm so used to just being Mum, I wanted to be Elaine for a bit.' She laughed. 'Daft, innit?'

'No, not at all. When you have kids it can definitely feel like your own life gets put on hold, certainly when they're little. How old are yours?'

Elaine took her phone out of her back pocket and clicked on the photo app. 'Here are my little monkeys. Alfie's six and Lola's four.' I took her phone and looked at the photograph displayed there. Alfie had the cheekiest grin I'd ever seen, and Lola had beautiful auburn hair like her mum's.

'They're gorgeous,' I said, and she smiled proudly.

'They look like little angels, don't they? Sometimes they even act like them. But not very often...'

I checked on my dough; it had doubled in size. I cut it into twenty-four small balls and left them covered on a tray to prove again, for another hour. I was starting to regret choosing a recipe that called for so much proving, because once I'd made the chocolate custard filling all I could do was wait. It was making it almost impossible for me to focus on the baking, rather than the murder. The final stages of my doughnuts – the actual frying, filling and decorating – wouldn't even take that long. It was just all this hanging around for the dough to rise again… I was just debating whether or not I could contrive a way to sneak out and go and poke my oar into the investigation when I felt the phone in my back pocket vibrate.

The victim's wife has disappeared…

Nathan was waiting for me outside the tent. He grinned.

'Got any cake?'

'Come back in a couple of hours. What's happened?' Nathan took my arm and steered me away from a couple of loitering crew members.

'I was missing you, that's all,' he said, innocently, but it wasn't washing with me.

'Come off it, a couple of hours ago you said the last thing you needed was me and Daisy sticking our nose in, and now you're texting me in the middle of the contest?'

'Sorry, I'll let you get on with your baking if you'd prefer—' he said, starting to walk away, but I grabbed at him.

'Don't be ridiculous, I want in.'

He laughed. 'OK, I have to admit I do actually need a bit of local knowledge on this one, but Matt's busy digging into the victim's background.'

I laughed. 'Right … and no one else here's a local?'

'Well, I *could* ask one of the uniforms, but where's the

fun in doing that when I could be getting my sexy baking crime consultant girlfriend in on the action.' He grinned. 'Plus I have to admit to being amazed and a little bit offended that you hadn't already found a way to get out of cooking and come and find me.' He looked around to make sure he wouldn't be overheard. 'Sarah Dodds has apparently done a runner.'

'How do you know that?'

'When she identified the body yesterday she was supposed to sign a statement confirming the victim's identity, but she was so upset it got overlooked. Mortuary staff tried to contact her to let her know, but she didn't answer her home landline or her mobile.'

'If she was as upset as you said she was, she might just not want to talk to anyone,' I said. 'She wouldn't have recognised the number.'

'She was supposed to be going home,' said Nathan. 'I was concerned, so I contacted the local force and asked them to go and check on her, but she's not there. And neither is her car.'

'Oh no! Do you think she might have done something to herself?' I asked. Nathan shook his head.

'No. I did at first, so I asked Matt to see if we could trace the GPS on her mobile phone or car. She was so distressed when she left here, I had genuine fears for her safety. And the GPS came back that she hadn't left the county. Matt checked, but she doesn't seem to have any family or known friends round here that she could've gone to stay with. And then, when I was beginning to think that maybe she had thrown herself into the Ottery or something, she rang me.'

'She rang you? So where is she?'

'She apologised for missing my call, said she'd taken some sleeping pills and had been asleep all morning. And that she was at home.'

'Curiouser and curiouser... Did you tell her you knew she wasn't there?'

'No. I'd quite like to work out where Mrs Dodds *really* is and pay her a surprise visit. The trouble is, you know what mobile reception is like round here. We can't pin her exact whereabouts down. And she hasn't used her bank card since yesterday morning, so we can't trace that either.'

'And you think I can help you?'

'Well, if you were a grieving widow, where around here would you stay?'

'Mrs Dodds! Fancy seeing you here.' Nathan gave the grieving widow a smile as she walked into the pub dining area, where we were enjoying a light lunch while waiting for her to come out of her room. She looked pale and shocked, but quickly recovered herself.

'DCI Withers,' she said. Her eyes rested on me for a

moment, then went back to Nathan, and I got the impression she was trying to decide whether it really was a coincidence – whether he was just there on his lunch break, with his civilian girlfriend – or whether we were waiting for her. In truth, we'd made a list of every pub within a ten-mile radius, and this was the only one that had rooms to rent. When we'd got to the Fox and Hounds, a beautiful, half-timbered old pub with a big stone fireplace and a very tempting food menu, the landlady had excitedly told us (in a completely unnecessary whisper) about the mystery woman who had turned up the day before, asking for a room for the next couple of nights. Nathan hadn't wanted to go and knock on her room door – she wasn't under suspicion, even if she was acting slightly strangely, and she *was* a grieving widow – so the landlady had told us that Sarah Dodds would have to come through the bar to leave the building, and had pointed out a table that would give us an unhindered view of the door into the pub's guest rooms.

She stood awkwardly in front of us. Nathan smiled.

'I thought you'd gone home,' he said. 'That's the impression I was under, anyway.'

Sarah smiled uncertainly. 'I know this looks bad, but it's not what you think.'

'What do you think we think?' I asked, and her smile flickered.

'I don't know,' she admitted. Nathan stood up and pulled another chair over to our table, and gestured for her to sit down.

No one spoke for a moment. If someone has a guilty secret, and they suspect that you know about it, if you keep quiet and just smile at them for a while it really freaks them out. And before they quite realise what they're doing, they're telling you all about it.

'OK, I did say I was going home, and I know I should have done,' she said finally, 'but I just can't leave Harry here.'

I reached out and touched her hand gently. 'I know it's hard, but you have to. It won't take long for the police to release his body—'

'That's not what I mean!' she said, distressed. 'I know they have to – do things to it. I know they'll release him and I'll be able to arrange the funeral and everything soon enough. I just – I needed to see where it happened—'

'We discussed this yesterday,' said Nathan, firmly but not unkindly. 'You came to Boskern and we had our chat, didn't we? But I can't let you onto an active crime scene. And I can't imagine why you'd want to be there.'

Sarah looked down at the table. 'I can't explain it, I just—'

'I think I know,' I said calmly. She glanced up at me, alarmed. 'You feel like you can't just sit back and let the police get on with finding out what happened. You feel like you need to be doing something.'

She looked at me gratefully and nodded. 'Yes! That's it, exactly. It's not that I don't think the police will find who killed Harry, it's more like, I should know something. I'm his wife. I should know if someone wanted him dead.' She choked back a sob. 'Sorry, I'm all over the place at the moment…'

I patted her hand. 'It's understandable. You lost someone dear to you and you want to know why. And you want to know why *now*, while it hurts so much, because if you understand what happened it might make you feel better.' She nodded. 'Only it won't, Mrs Dodds. Nothing will make you feel better except time. That, and being kind to yourself.'

Nathan looked at me, and I could see a touch of admiration and pride in his eyes. I was pretty proud of myself too, remembering those lines from a TV cop show I'd watched a few weeks ago. I fervently hoped Sarah Dodds hadn't watched it as well.

'It's not your fault he died, Sarah,' I said. I could really feel myself getting into the part now. 'We can't know every single person our loved ones interact with, we can't know everyone they upset or pissed off or made fall in love with them. There's no way you could have known this would happen.'

Nathan nodded. 'She's right. You need to go home,

Mrs Dodds, and let the police handle it. Go home, maybe get a friend or family member to come and stay with you for a few days. When you're back in familiar surroundings and you can properly take in what's happened, you might find you can think of people who may have had a reason to hurt Harry, or perhaps had a grudge against him. And if you do, I will be happy to personally come up and see you and hear all about it.' He stood, and I stood too, surreptitiously slipping the uneaten half of my lunchtime baguette into my bag. 'But you need to go home, Mrs Dodds.'

We sat in Nathan's car in the pub car park, watching as Sarah Dodds left the building and got into her own car.

'Nice speech earlier,' said Nathan mildly. 'I can't remember, was it from *Law and Order* or *CSI Miami*?'

I snorted. '*CSI Miami*? How dare you. If you're going to bring *CSI Miami* up, the least you could do is take your Ray-Bans off and stare moodily into the distance.'

'I haven't got any sunglasses with me,' he pointed out. 'This is Cornwall, in March. It's as likely to snow as it is to be sunny.'

'Exactly! And it was from an episode of *Big City Crime Squad*, actually.'

We watched in silence as Sarah reversed out of her parking space and drove off.

'You reckon she's really going home?' I asked. Nathan shrugged.

'I don't know. I'll get the local force to check in on her later, and I'll warn Uniform to keep an eye out here. Bloody amateur detectives, getting under my feet...'

We waited for her to drive out of the exit, then Nathan started the car and we headed back to Boskern. Daisy would be dropped off by Jade and Nancy in an hour, so I really needed to get back and fry my doughnuts (not a euphemism).

'At least we know one thing now,' I said, as Nathan eased the car along the twisty roads.

'What's that?'

'Sarah Dodds doesn't know anyone who would have reason to kill her husband.'

Nathan glanced at me. 'And that's helpful, is it?'

'It could be. It could be that the reason she doesn't know the murderer is that it's not someone from their circle of friends. It could be someone Harry only just met, that she hasn't.'

'Someone from the roadshow, you mean? Hmm...' He looked thoughtful. 'You could be right. How would the killer even know where to find him? The roadshow moves around a lot. We've found a couple of social media accounts for Harry, but he doesn't appear to have posted about it or mentioned it to his friends, not so far as we can see.'

'Camilla asked us not to talk about where we were filming on social media, to avoid fans of the show turning up,' I said. 'I think it was even in the contract we signed, that we could talk about the show but not post any pictures or mention the location, not during filming, anyway.'

'So the only people who would have known where Harry was…'

'…would be other people working on the roadshow.'

'Like Russell. As we already suspect.' Nathan slowed the car as we approached the turning into Boskern House.

'Yeah…'

He groaned. 'Don't tell me. It's not Russell.'

'I just can't see him bashing someone's head in!'

'He's a big bloke, even without his high heels. He's certainly strong enough.' Nathan nodded to a uniformed officer who watched us as we drove past. 'And don't forget the hair. I'm hoping to get some forensics back on that this afternoon.'

'Like Russell said, he's not the only blonde on the roadshow. Several of the crew are blonde, and they probably had much more to do with Harry than Russell did. The talent don't really mix with the crew.' I ran through the rest of the road-showers in my head. 'Martin's hair's proper straggly, that pony-tail of his would probably come out really easy in a struggle – it'd be the first thing I'd grab and tug at in a fight.'

'You don't like him, do you?'

'Not much, no. He's taking this contest far too seriously. No sense of humour.'

'It probably just means a lot to him. Just because you had to be strong-armed into entering…' Nathan switched the engine off and turned to me. 'Have I been forgiven for that yet?'

'Are you kidding? It dropped me right into the middle of another murder investigation! Of course you're forgiven.' I leaned across and kissed him. 'And now if you'll excuse me, I left my doughnuts proving, and they'll be the size of space hoppers by now. If I don't rescue them soon I'll never get them in the deep-fat fryer.'

Chapter Ten

I entered the tent trying to look nonchalant, as if I'd only nipped out to the toilet and not disappeared for close to – I looked at my watch – ninety minutes. Holy moly, I needed to motor on with my doughnuts, and fast.

Elaine, Ravi and even Martin all looked up curiously from their benches, but before any of them could speak Camilla rushed over.

'There you are!' she said. 'I was beginning to think you weren't coming back.'

'Sorry,' I said. 'I've been helping the police again—'

'I know, one of the uniformed officers told me you'd gone off with CID. That's fine. Are you going to have enough time to finish, though?'

'Oh yeah,' I said confidently, but, truth be told, I had

no idea if I would. 'I hope me not being here didn't hold up filming?'

'No, we managed to work around you. We will need to get some more footage of you this afternoon though, otherwise it'll be obvious you were missing for half of it. We can edit it together so no one will notice you weren't here.'

'No problem,' I said, but I was wondering how that would work once Daisy and Germaine turned up later. No point worrying Camilla about it now, though. 'I need to get on, so…'

'Of course! Don't let me stop you. Carl?' She turned and gestured to the cameraman to follow my every move. Which wasn't at all distracting.

My dough had risen rather a lot, but at least it was already divided into balls, so all I had to do was punch them down a little bit and then they were ready for deep frying. I heated up the oil and dropped a tiny piece of dough into it, to see if it was hot enough; the dough sizzled, and I knew it was ready.

I deep-fried the doughnuts until they were golden brown, then left them to cool and drain off the excess oil on some kitchen paper. There wasn't actually that much left to do; I just had to make a small hole in the bottom of each one, and then pipe in the chocolate custard, although that in itself was quite fiddly and would take a bit of time. But maybe I should glaze them first?

'Them balls look tasty.' Barbara had popped up behind me while I was thinking, the cameraman close behind.

'I'm just deciding whether or not to glaze them,' I said.

'I was talking about Martin, babes,' she said, and we all laughed – apart from Martin, of course. 'Oh no, my mistake, it's just the way he's standing. I do love a good doughnut. I like anything deep fried. I'm particularly partial to a battered sausage.'

I snorted. 'Aren't we all?'

'I bet you are, love.' She gave what was possibly the dirtiest laugh I'd ever heard. 'A woman with a healthy but straightforward appetite, I reckon. Sausages all the way.' She picked up one of the shiny stainless-steel saucepans sitting on a rack next to my work top and studied her reflection. 'Now, me? Pansexual, I am. I bloody love a nice bit of kitchen equipment.' Everyone laughed. Barbara winked at the camera, then said to Carl the cameraman, in a very Russell-like voice, 'You got enough?' He nodded. Barbara patted me on the back, a bit harder than was strictly necessary, and said, 'Nice to see you concentrating on the cooking, Jodie, and not being – *distracted* by stuff that has nothing to do with you.' Then she turned on her high heels and strode off, out of the tent, leaving me staring after her.

Elaine scuttled over to me. 'What was that all about? And where you been?'

'It's a long story,' I said, discouragingly, but she just smiled.

'I'm waiting for me buns to cool,' she said. 'I've got time.' She leaned in close. 'It *was* murder, then? Why do you think Barbara did it?'

'I don't,' I said uncomfortably.

'But it was murder?' Ravi had joined us. *Not you and all*, I thought. The two of them exchanged excited looks, Elaine's eyes shining.

'This is proper exciting, innit?' she said. I didn't answer – it wasn't my place to go spreading that sort of information about, not to people I didn't really know I could trust, anyway (if it had been Tony and Debbie, I'd have been spilling my guts about now) – but she took that as a yes and looked around the tent, her eyes narrowed. 'I don't think that Harry had many friends here, do you? It could be anyone.'

'Murderers do normally have a motive,' I said, trying to dissuade them both without sounding sarcastic or too dismissive. 'It's more likely to have been someone who *was* a friend. There must have been *someone* who knew him well enough to dislike him.'

She gave a harrumph. 'I didn't know him, and I didn't like him. He were right nasty to Barbara. Is that why you think she did it?'

'I told you, I don't think she did it. But—' I bit my lip, trying to stop the words coming out, but Ravi pounced on it.

'But the police do? Oooh…'

'I've told them they're wrong.' I went over to the fridge and took out my chocolate custard, then nearly dropped it as I turned round; they'd both followed me across the tent and were standing right behind me, waiting for me to say more. 'Sweet Jesus! Look, I really don't know anything. I'm just helping the police with a bit of background, what with me being on the spot. I need to get on with my doughnuts. Don't you have bakes to finish?'

'Just letting it cool and then it won't take long. Are you filling them with that?' Elaine nodded at the custard.

'I am, and it is LUSH.'

'It looks good. Can I have a taste?' she asked. I nodded, and she grabbed a spoon from a nearby bench and took a tiny bit. I watched her face, proudly waiting for her to tell me just how delicious it was, but instead she gave a little grimace.

'What's the matter?'

'It tastes a bit weird…' she said diplomatically. I dipped my finger in the custard and licked it, involuntarily screwing up my face as I did so.

'Eww! It didn't taste like that before. It's really salty.'

Ravi dipped his finger in as well – I *definitely* wasn't

using it now. 'You weren't going for a salted caramel kind of thing?' he asked, but I shook my head.

'No, I can't stand the stuff. I'm telling you, it didn't taste like that when I put it in the fridge. Someone's tampered with it.'

'Who would do that?' Elaine asked, but I didn't want to answer. Who would benefit if my doughnuts tasted disgusting and I got sent home? My fellow bakers, that's who. But it couldn't be either of these two, could it? It would take some bloody nerve to stand there in front of me and taste the sabotaged custard. Plus they surely wouldn't want me to know it tasted disgusting? They'd want me to use it. So that only left one person.

'I don't know. More to the point, what am I going to do now?' I asked, feeling not just annoyed but also like I could cry. It was fine if I got sent home because I wasn't good enough, or because I'd been distracted by the investigation and not focused on the cooking, but to get sent home because someone else had tipped a load of salt or something into my custard when I wasn't looking… That just wasn't fair.

Elaine glanced at me, and at the bowl of unusable custard in my hands, then smiled. 'I know! White chocolate ganache. Quicker to make than another custard, and just as tasty.' She grabbed some cream from the fridge and carried it over to my work bench, while Ravi found some white chocolate buttons for me.

'Thank you,' I said gratefully, then set to work. I had about twenty minutes left, which would really be pushing it. I made the ganache, then popped it into the freezer for five minutes. I needed it to cool and slightly thicken, but it needed to still be a little bit runny so I could get it into an icing bag.

The phone in my back pocket vibrated again. *Daisy!* I thought. I'd almost forgotten she was coming. It was her.

Just got here, me and Germaine having a walk around the grounds txt me when u r done

And then another one, immediately after:

Saw N he said it was ok

That was a relief – I could concentrate on this properly now. I spooned the cooled ganache into a piping bag, then cut a small slit in the bottom of a doughnut and stuck the piping nozzle into it. I squeezed the bag, sending ganache into the doughnut, then pulled out the nozzle, fully expecting the cream and chocolate mixture to run straight out again. It didn't. *Phew.* I repeated the process on the rest of the doughnuts.

'Five minutes!' cried Barbara.

I melted what was left of the white chocolate in the microwave, then drizzled it across the doughnuts to make them look like hot cross buns. I'd just placed the last one on the cake stand when—

'Time's up!' called Barbara.

I grabbed my phone and sent Daisy a quick text to let

her know I was almost finished, and then we stood and waited for Pete and Esme to enter.

'Martin!' said Ravi, peering around me to the work station at the back. 'Wow, man, that's another masterpiece.'

We all turned to look at the basket of Easter goodies at the end of Martin's bench. He'd not only made small, individual cakes, he'd made tons of mini chocolate eggs to decorate them, and a family of chocolate rabbits. *I'm going home*, I thought.

Barbara and the judges went straight to the back to try Martin's cakes. They did look and smell delicious, I couldn't deny it. They were *Nidi di Uccelli* – birds' nest cookies, although they were more like little tarts than cookies. The pastry shell was rich and crumbly, and the filling of walnuts and brown sugar smelt divine. My tummy rumbled, and I suddenly remembered the remnants of the prawn baguette from the pub in my bag. Oops. Martin's cakes were drizzled with melted chocolate and topped with lots of tiny eggs, which he'd tempered and modelled himself.

Pete took a small bite into one cookie, then smiled and put the whole thing into his mouth. Esme gave a small moan of pleasure.

'Oh my goodness, that's wonderful,' she said. 'This is another Italian recipe, isn't it? You're terribly good at Italian baking. Is there any Italian in your family?'

'No,' said Martin. 'We're Cornish, through and through.'

Pete swallowed his cake and held up his hand to high-five Martin.

They moved on to Elaine's bench. Elaine had made individual Easter simnel cakes; mini rich fruit cakes, topped with a layer of marzipan and decorated with colourful, delicate spring flowers, which she'd created from sugar paste. They looked incredibly life-like. *I really AM going home,* I thought. Esme cut one of the cakes in half, and even from here I could smell the fruit.

'Ooh, that's moist,' said Esme, groaning a little bit again, and Ravi and I caught each other's eye and started giggling. Barbara patted Esme on the back.

'Somebody run Esme a cold shower!' she called out to the crew. 'And bring her one of my emergency HRT patches, she's having a hot flush.' We all laughed, even Esme.

'It is *that* good,' said Esme. Pete nodded.

'Yep, well done.' And he held his hand up again. We all looked at each other in shock: TWO high-fives in one round? Unheard of! I felt a little stab of Cornish pride, even though I suspected I wouldn't be getting one.

Put me out of my misery! I thought. But they didn't. They went to Ravi's counter instead. Ravi had made one big (and very impressive-looking) cake, covered in a smooth creamy frosting and decorated with rose petals and a sprinkling of some kind of spiced nut mix.

'What's this?' asked Pete. 'It certainly looks the part.'

'It's a vanilla sponge, covered with a masala doodh frosting,' said Ravi. 'Masala doodh is a spiced milk drink. My nani used to give it to me before bed when I was little, but only on special occasions, like my birthday or Diwali.'

'That sounds lovely,' said Barbara, sounding genuinely sincere. Maybe she (or Russell) was thinking of her own grandmother.

Pete cut a big slice. There were three layers of cake, sandwiched together with more of the frosting; a little bit uneven, but it still looked great. Esme took a spoonful of the frosting first.

'Oh that's yummy,' she said. 'So unusual, but very yummy.' Pete took some too.

'That is nice,' he said. 'A nice hint of spice.' He prodded at the sponge cake. 'This seems a bit soggy.'

'The sponge is soaked in saffron-infused milk, to keep it moist,' explained Ravi, watching anxiously as Pete and Esme tasted the cake layer.

'Hmm... It's got a very nice flavour, but I think you've overdone it with the milk,' said Pete. 'It's just a bit too soggy.'

Esme nodded. 'I agree. Lovely flavour, but the texture is a bit odd. It feels a bit claggy.'

'Okay,' said Ravi, trying not to look or sound too disappointed, but he obviously was. I knew how hard he'd worked on his cake – how hard we'd all worked, even me. When I'd been there…

'Ooh, now these look fun!' said Esme, approaching my work bench. 'They look like hot cross buns at first glance, but they're not. Your doughnuts are lovely and golden.'

Pete cut one in half, and the white chocolate filling oozed out slowly. Thank goodness it had had time to cool and thicken up. He dipped his finger in the ganache and tasted it.

'You were originally planning to use custard as your filling, weren't you?'

'Yes,' I said, debating whether or not to mention the sabotage and deciding against it. 'It went a bit wrong so I went with a white chocolate ganache instead.'

'I'm glad you did, I think this works far better as a filling,' said Pete, and I sent up a silent prayer of thanks to whoever had spiked my custard with salt. He and Esme both bit into their halves of doughnut, and chewed them without saying anything. *I AM going home*, I thought, and was surprised at how disappointed I felt. The two judges exchanged glances, then turned to smile at me.

'That is so clever,' said Esme. 'It has all the flavours of

a hot cross bun, but the nice springy texture of a doughnut. And that filling is divine.'

Pete stuck out his hand and I thought, *don't tell me I'm getting a high-five?!* But then he grinned and reached for another doughnut.

'I do like that. I think it *is* a clever idea, and it tastes great, but compared to what some of the others have done, technically, it's quite simple. I'd have liked to see you do something that really pushed you.'

The judges went off into a little huddle, and the four of us got into our own little huddle – well, me, Elaine and Ravi did, Martin just kind of loitered awkwardly next to us. I still thought I was probably going home, but maybe I'd done enough?

The judges came over and Barbara stood in front of us.

'Well done, baking babes,' she said. 'The judges were really impressed with everybody's efforts today. But sadly, it's an elimination day, and that means one of you is going home. And the baker that's leaving us today is…' I waited to hear my name…

'Well done, Mum, I'm really proud of you,' said Daisy. Germaine jumped up, putting her front paws against my legs, and panted at me to tell me how proud she was as well. I laughed, patted the dog and kissed my daughter.

'Thank you. I still can't believe it. Ravi is such a good baker, I have no idea how I beat him.'

'Because you're such a good baker too!' Daisy said, as ever my biggest cheerleader and supporter.

'Thank you. So, did you have a nice walk?' Germaine's ears pricked up at the 'w' word.

'We didn't get very far. We ended up eating jelly babies with Sergeant Adams while he told us stories about Grandad.'

I smiled. 'Aww, that's lovely. As long as he didn't tell you any about me.'

Daisy laughed. 'Oh yes, he did. He told me about the time you and Tony drove his car onto the beach and it got stuck in the sand.'

'Oh my God, I'd forgotten all about that!' I said, remembering it as clear as day now. 'Tony had only just got his licence. He'd been watching this TV show about bodyguards or the CIA or something, how they were taught to drive in all sorts of conditions, and he wanted to try it. He was showing off about how easy it was to drive on the beach, as long as you kept up a certain speed and didn't stop, otherwise you'd sink. And then he stopped, I can't remember why, and of course we got stuck. It was hilarious.' I remembered running up to the police station and begging Sergeant Adams to come and help us, but not tell my dad. Of course, he *had* told my dad, who had strong words for my old friend, putting his daughter in harm's way, but I'd never really been in any danger and Dad had just been winding Tony up.

Germaine barked and tugged at the lead in Daisy's hand. 'She's still full of energy,' said Daisy. 'Should we take her for a walk here, or wait till we get home?'

'Let's do it here,' I said. 'Nicer surroundings.' Daisy eyed me suspiciously.

'That's the only reason, is it?' she said, and I gave her an affronted look.

'How dare you cast aspersions!' I said. 'Now if we head that way, towards the crime scene, it'll give Germaine a chance to stretch her legs properly…'

We kept Germaine on the lead until we'd cleared the roadshow village of tents and the car park – people were leaving for the day in their cars, and we would too, soon. But past that, out into the grounds proper, I unclicked the lead and let her run off. There was no one around, and we were some way away from the crime scene, so there was no chance of her blundering into it by mistake.

'What was Nana acting all mysterious about this morning?' asked Daisy.

'No idea. You know what she's like, she does like a bit of drama,' I said, watching Germaine gambolling along the path ahead of us. 'Talking of this morning…' I added, carefully.

'What about it?'

'Do you mind Nathan being there when you're

getting ready for school?' She looked at me, and I wasn't sure how to read her expression. 'You can be totally honest,' I said, hurriedly. 'If it's weird or whatever.'

'No, it's not *weird*, as such...' she said. 'He's always really careful about using the bathroom and everything. He doesn't barge in, in case I'm in there.' She looked at me thoughtfully. 'It *is* a bit weird, actually, but not in a horrible way. It's a bit like having Dad around again, only not Dad. He's more considerate than Dad.'

'So do you think it's only because you're not used to it? He's only just started staying over, and of course it's not normally during the week when we're all vying for the bathroom at the same time...'

She rolled her eyes. 'Honestly, Mum, just ask me. Would I mind if Nathan moved in? That's what you want to know, isn't it?'

I was surprised, but then I shouldn't have been really, because my daughter was smart and witty and very perceptive for a thirteen-year-old.

'Yes, I suppose that is what I want to know, not that we've discussed or are planning it any time soon,' I said. Daisy smiled.

'I really like him. He makes you smile. I don't remember you smiling that much when we were with Dad. I reckon I could get used to him being there all the time.'

I stopped walking and pulled her into a hug. 'Thank

you, darling. What did I do to deserve a daughter like you?'

'God knows,' she said, her voice muffled against my chest. She pulled back a little bit to get some air. 'It would be easier if we had a bigger house, though. Or another bathroom.'

'Yes…' I said. That thought had already crossed my mind. But I loved our little house. It represented a lot to me. It represented freedom, and new beginnings.

We were interrupted by a splash, as ahead of us Germaine scrambled down a bank and into the stream. The water was very shallow at this part of the river, but it had obviously been rather higher at some point because the bank was slippery with mud. 'Germaine!' I called, not wanting her lovely white fur to get filthy or, more to the point, my car upholstery to get soaked on the way home, but it was too late. Germaine had found something in the water and was biting at it, shaking it and having a grand old time. We quickly approached her.

'Oh no, what has she got?' cried Daisy. 'Is it a duck or a rabbit or something?'

'I hope not,' I said, slipping down the bank and reaching out to grab her collar. I picked her up, a squirming, wet, muddy mess wriggling about in my arms, and carried her back to the path. She still had the unfortunate whatever-it-was in her jaws. I clipped on the lead and put her down on the ground, then squatted next to her and attempted to pull it from her mouth. 'Let go, Germaine!'

The dog dropped it on the path. Daisy, one eye closed, not wanting to see a dead bunny, gingerly prodded it with her foot as I let out a gasp of surprise.

'Is it still moving?' she said, and I shook my head.

'It never was.' We'd found Dolly.

Chapter Eleven

Nathan held up the plastic evidence bag and wrinkled his nose in distaste at the sodden hairpiece inside.

'This Dolly's not quite as glamorous as her namesake, is she?' he said. 'And of course you had to be the one to find her…'

'It wasn't me, it was Germaine,' I pointed out. He nodded.

'Ah, yes. Tell me, did you train her to be nosey, or is it like they say – dogs start to get like their owners after a while?'

'It's the other way round, actually. They say owners start to look like their pets.' Nathan opened his mouth, but I jumped in quick. 'And if you're about to say that I look like the dog, I'd think carefully about it, because it will not go well for you.'

Nathan laughed. 'I was just going to say that Germaine's gorgeous, so…'

'Aww…' I said, fluttering my eyelashes at him.

Behind me, Daisy made puking noises. 'Oh *please*. Can we get back to talking about the murder now?'

'Who's this "we"?' said Nathan. 'The last time I looked, you were a schoolgirl, not a detective.'

'Whatever. If I hadn't turned up with the dog…'

'Have you had the forensics back on the hair found on Harry Dodds's body yet?' I asked, before Daisy got into full flow. Honestly, when you have a teenager you have to pick your battles, and this one wasn't worth it. Nathan nodded.

'Yes. And I have no doubt it'll match this wig. Did you know that it takes on average six full heads of hair to make one wig?'

'No, I didn't know that…'

'Which could explain why there was hair from at least four different people found on the victim's body.'

'I don't know if you've considered this, Nath, but could it just be that four different people got near enough to Dodds to leave hair on him? There are at least four blondes here, just among the crew.'

'Only if all four of them use the same shampoo and

conditioner, and hair dye, and all have heat damage from being styled with curling tongs.'

'Good point. At least you can cross-check it against the wig now. So you think Russell, or rather Barbara, killed Harry and then tossed the wig into the river?' I took the bag from Nathan's hand and studied the bedraggled wig inside. 'But why? If he bashed him on the back of the head with something heavy, like a rock or whatever, he's unlikely to have got anything on the wig, is he? No blood spatter or anything. And by throwing it away he's drawn more attention to himself than if he'd just sponged off any nasty stuff (assuming it had somehow got on there), worn it for the rest of the day and then got Shanice in Hair and Make-Up to give it a wash.'

'Russell Lang's tall, even without his high heels, and Dodds was sitting down. Lang would have had to bend down to smack him,' said Nathan, demonstrating. 'The wig could have fallen off, or forwards, just enough to come into contact with him. There wasn't any hair around the wound, but there was quite a bit on the victim's shoulders, which must have happened when Lang leaned down. Maybe it made him think there'd be enough DNA evidence on it to tie him to the murder?'

'But if that was the case – if Lang did sneak up behind him and kill him – how come he had hair caught under his fingernails?' I looked at Nathan, but I wasn't actually seeing him; I was trying to imagine Harry Dodds's body, from the way Nathan had described it. 'Normally you'd think that would be from the victim trying to fight off their attacker, but Harry just fell straight forward, didn't he? So he hadn't turned around. He had his back to the killer, so how could he pull his hair?'

'Why else would the hair come out? And how else would it end up on him?' We looked at each other, trying to work it out.

'Oof, Germaine! Get off!' Daisy laughed as she gently but firmly pushed the dog away. Germaine had been very excited to see Nathan, who she adored (it was mutual), but then terribly disappointed when he hadn't wanted to play with her, and she was getting a little bit feisty. Daisy brushed at her black leggings and sighed. 'We really should have got a darker dog,' she said. 'I've got white hair *everywhere*!'

'She's moulting…' I said, thoughtfully.

Daisy rolled her eyes. 'I literally just said that.'

Nathan was looking at me. He knew I was onto something, although I didn't quite know what it was myself, yet. 'What are you thinking?'

'Don't you remember? Russell said Dolly kept shedding. She was moulting. So the hair would have come out easy enough, without anyone tugging at it.'

'OK… It still puts Lang at the scene.'

'Does it, though? There's the other thing that Shanice

said.' I felt a bolt of excitement run through me. I knew I had the answer. But Nathan still looked mystified.

'What did she say? Apart from that wig suiting my colour…' Daisy giggled and he poked his tongue out at her, but in fun.

'Everyone wants to try on a wig. It's the first thing everyone does, particularly blokes.' I nodded to myself; I could see it now. 'Russell was telling the truth. He storms off in a big old strop, rips Dolly off his head and flings her on the floor, on account of him being a drama queen. Harry comes by and sees the wig on the caravan steps, and nicks it; he wants to get Russell into trouble after he had a go at him. He goes and sits by the river – maybe he planned to chuck it in there, maybe it fell in when he was murdered – and what does he do? He tries it on, probably admires himself in the water. That's how the hairs ended up on him. It's a long wig, it would have reached down to his shoulders. And that could put a whole new spin on this case.'

'What spin?'

'Was he wearing the wig when he was attacked, or had he already thrown it into the water? Or he could have been holding it and dropped it when he was hit, doesn't matter. Because if he was wearing it—'

'The killer might have mistaken him for Barbara!' cried Daisy. I high-fived her. 'Or Russell, or whatever, I'm a bit confused by the whole thing.'

Nathan shook his head. 'Okay, can I just point out that Russell, or Barbara in this case, is about eight foot tall in her heels, and she would have been wearing a tight leopard-print dress, and our victim was considerably shorter and wearing a black bomber jacket and jeans?'

'True, but he was sitting down, so the height thing wouldn't matter. And the clothes would mostly have been hidden by the fact he had his back to the path and his legs dangling out over the water.' I was getting into my stride now; I *knew* I was right. 'Plus Russell has a very similar black jacket – he had it on, the other night in the pub, remember? The murderer might have thought Russell had just slipped his own jacket on over his costume; at this time of year it's still chilly, particularly when you get away from the heat of the ovens and all the lighting. From the back, all you'd see would be this mass of curly blonde hair and a black jacket. Apart from the height they're actually a similar build.'

'And we know someone who had a grudge against Russell,' said Daisy, trying (and failing) not to look smug. Nathan just looked bewildered.

'We do?'

'Like Mum said, the other night in the pub. He was having an argument with another man. Lovers' tiff, Nana called it.' Daisy folded her arms, as if she was delivering a *fait accompli*.

'He's not the only one,' I said. 'The morning of the murder, I saw him having a slanging match with a blonde woman. He seemed quite upset, but she was absolutely furious.' I saw them again in my mind's eye. 'I haven't seen her on set anywhere, so I don't think she's crew. Maybe not *all* of the blonde hair on the victim came from the wig, after all. Maybe she came back to finish the argument, saw someone in that wig and thought it was Russell.'

'Barbara,' interjected Daisy.

'Whatever.' I turned my full attention on Nathan. 'Maybe the murderer got the wrong person.'

'Hmm…' said Nathan. I could tell he wasn't entirely convinced.

'Look at it this way, who's more likely to have enemies? An out-of-work supply teacher from Bristol who nobody on set really knew, or a celebrity drag queen with a big mouth, who we've recently witnessed arguing with three different people?'

'Three?'

'He argued with Harry, didn't he? Not that Harry's exactly a suspect… But it proves Russell-stroke-Barbara doesn't shy away from confrontation, doesn't it?'

'True. But I thought he was well liked by everyone?'

'Obviously not by *everyone*, or he wouldn't have a target on his bouffant hair…'

• • •

Nathan walked to the car with me, Daisy and Germaine. I strapped Germaine's lead to her special doggy seat belt (I would no more leave her unrestrained in the car than I would a child) as Daisy got into the front passenger seat.

'So what are you going to do now?' I asked Nathan. He smiled.

'You inviting me for dinner again? People will talk.'

'Let them. But no, that's not what I meant. I meant, what are you going to do about Russell?'

He frowned. 'What do you think I should be doing?'

'You should warn him, surely, if someone's after him?'

'We don't know that, do we? Look, I get where you're coming from. On paper he seems a more likely target. But you said yourself, Harry had hardly endeared himself to his fellow crew members, or to Russell – I know, you don't think Russell did it, but I'm not so sure. Harry *could* have been wearing the wig and been mistaken for someone else, or Russell could still have had it on while he murdered him.' Nathan reached out and brushed some of my own hair away from my cheek, grinning. 'I can see from the look on your face what you think about *that*. But you don't know Russell. Why are you so convinced it wasn't him?'

'I don't know…' I said, because I didn't. I liked Russell (or maybe Barbara, because most of my dealings had been with her, rather than him), even if he hadn't exactly welcomed me poking my nose into his business. Which was probably to be expected, even if he *was* innocent. I couldn't help feeling that he was actually hiding *something*, but not murder, surely? Every time I tried to imagine him picking up a rock, sneaking up behind Harry and bashing him in the head, it just felt wrong. If Russell (or Barbara) ever felt the need to murder someone (which I couldn't imagine) this definitely wasn't the sort of murder I could picture either of them committing. 'I don't know,' I said again, 'but it feels too rough, too physical for Russell, and not flamboyant enough for Barbara. A sharpened stiletto heel to the jugular, now *that* I can see her doing. A big flourish of the murder weapon, blood everywhere, drama… Knocking some bloke on the head with a rock or a tree branch or something just feels very dull.'

Nathan laughed. 'I *love* big dramatic murder scenes, they're normally so full of evidence it makes my job easy.'

'But apart from that, what if someone *is* out to get him? What if they try again?' I looked around, but the car park was empty apart from a production van belonging to the crew. Russell and the judges were long gone. 'Shouldn't we go to their hotel, warn him—'

'No.' Nathan spoke gently but firmly. 'Look at the murder. The victim was off on his own, the murderer saw him and picked up the nearest heavy object, and did the deed. It was a spur of the moment thing. Russell is now at a two-star hotel on the A39, living the celebrity dream—'

'I've been to that hotel. Everything was very … *beige*.'

'—surrounded by cast and crew. Even if the murderer's among them, they're not going to get another chance like that, are they? Plus it's probably spooked them too much to try again anyway.'

'I hope you're right,' I said, doubtfully.

'I am. You're letting your imagination run riot. We will talk to Russell in the morning, and ask him if he has any enemies—'

'The shouty blonde-haired woman.'

'And ask him who the shouty blonde-haired woman is, yes. If it makes you feel happier, I'll get a patrol car to swing by and sit in the car park a couple of times during the night, make themselves very visible, just in case anyone gets any ideas. But they won't.'

'That'll work, I suppose…'

'You just wanted an excuse to go over there, didn't you?' said Nathan, and I laughed.

'Goddammit, you know me too well. So what *are* you doing tonight?'

'Well, I would love to come to yours again…' Nathan glanced into the front seat, where Daisy was intent on her phone. He sighed. 'But maybe two nights in a row is too much. I don't want to annoy your roomies.'

'You won't,' I said, 'but you're right, we should probably leave it for tonight.' I pulled him towards me. 'Quick, snog me while she's not looking.'

'Oh Mother,' said Daisy, an edge of disgust in her voice. Nathan laughed.

'Sorry, kiddo, I can't help being irresistible to your mum...'

'Aaaand now you're not,' I said. I drew his face close to mine and gave him a quick but passionate kiss. 'Who am I kidding? You're so hot, DCI Withers.' I ignored the *eww* from the passenger seat. 'I'll see you tomorrow, babe.'

Nathan waved as we drove off. Daisy looked at me, and I became aware of the big, cheesy grin on my face. I hastily wiped it off. 'What?'

'You and Nathan are *so* cringe. Sweet, but cringe.'

I called Mum on the way home. She was at her own place for a change, so I offered to swing by and pick her up but she refused. Alarm bells – ones that had been ringing (albeit quietly) all day, since she'd mentioned her mysterious appointment that morning – began to clang loudly.

'I'm almost at yours anyway, me and Daisy'll pop in to say good night,' I said, and hung up before she could refuse.

When we got to Mum's house – I'd almost forgotten what it looked like, what with her actually staying there so rarely – she looked very pleased with herself. I had the feeling she knew that being kept in the dark about where she'd been that day was driving me nuts, and that she was actually enjoying it.

'Don't ask,' she said firmly, holding up her hand. 'You'll know everything, all in good time.'

'You're not ill, are you, Nana?' asked Daisy, and she was obviously so worried that Mum had the good grace to look a bit guilty. She pulled her granddaughter into a hug.

'Of course I'm not! Look at me, I'm fit as a flea!' Mum released Daisy and did a little twirl, then salsa-danced her way into the kitchen to put the kettle on. 'You staying for a cup of tea? Ooh that rhymes. Look at me, as fit as a flea, making the tea—' Her poetic powers abruptly ran out. 'Dee dee da da dee…'

'You're a poet and we didn't know it,' I said. Daisy groaned.

'Please God, tell me it's not catching.'

'Why, what are you *hatching*?' cackled Mum.

'Kill me now.'

We stayed for almost an hour, with Mum still refusing to be drawn when I questioned her about her mysterious appointment. But at least she was cheerful, and she certainly didn't seem to be unwell; that, of course, had been the first thing that had popped into my mind as well as Daisy's, and it had been lurking there all day even as I baked and poked my nose into things. We left her jigging about to *Strictly Ice Dancing* on the small TV in the kitchen, sliding along the polished floor and waving her arms about like a septuagenarian ballerina on magic mushrooms.

'Nana's definitely not ill,' said Daisy, as we settled Germaine back into the car.

'Not physically, anyway,' I said, and we both sniggered.

We got fish and chips on the way home, and sat at the kitchen table eating it straight out of the paper to save on washing up because, quite frankly, nobody's got time for that. Then Daisy went up to her room to watch stuff on YouTube and talk to her mates online, while I sat on the sofa, Germaine snuggled up next to me, and attempted to sketch my showstopper cake for the next day. There wasn't much on the TV so I turned it off and sat in silence, listening to the gentle rain that had just started outside. The house was quiet, quieter than it had ever been, I thought. I could count the number of times I'd sat here on my own on the fingers of one hand. Mum was usually there, chattering away or turning up the volume on the telly, because she was starting to go a little bit deaf but wouldn't admit it. And Daisy was getting older, beginning to need her own space. She was still a bit young to go out with her friends at night, but in the summer, when the evenings were light for longer, they would play outside in the street or be in and out of each other's houses, and I would see less of her.

Germaine sighed heavily beside me. I reached out to ruffle her white fur. 'This is what it would be like, if it was just you and me,' I said. She looked up at me, tongue hanging out, and I was just thinking what a faithful hound she was when she jumped off the sofa and waddled out to the kitchen. I followed her out and opened the back door for her, standing in the shelter of the overhanging eaves as she did her business, watching the stars through the damp night air. I breathed deeply. I loved the soft patter of rain on the roof and the smell of wet grass, even if there was an undeniable waft of sheep from the field behind the house. The meadow, smelly inhabitants notwithstanding, meant the garden had an uninterrupted vista of the sea in the distance and the vast hugeness of the night sky above. In this weather, in the dark, it was a melancholy scene, but I didn't feel sad; it was quite nice to stand there, alone, contemplating the universe. Our house was normally too full of life to do much contemplating.

Of course, if Nathan moved in, it would be even more full of life and I would never get a moment's peace. Over the stone wall at the back of the garden, a sheep suddenly bleated so loudly it made me jump and

Germaine, who had been sniffing about just the other side of it, yelp and trot over to me as quickly as her little legs would carry her. I laughed and picked her up.

'Don't worry, little one, I'll save you,' I said, and carried my wet, furry burden into the warmth of the kitchen.

Chapter Twelve

I might have been in a melancholy mood the night before, but the next morning was almost surreal in its calmness; just me and Daisy, getting ready for the day. Even Germaine had an air of Zen-like peacefulness about her, until she saw next door's cat, Buzz, in the garden and threw herself at the back door, wanting to get outside and warn him off. When Daisy let her out she yapped at our feline neighbour at the top of her little lungs, but she wasn't quite the guard dog she saw herself as and the cat, who had been busy washing himself on top of a wheelie bin, gave her a disdainful and somewhat bemused look before turning back to his ablutions.

I dropped Daisy at school and then Germaine and I headed to the roadshow. I knew Camilla probably wouldn't be best pleased about me bringing the dog, but arranging child and/or dog care for a whole week wasn't an easy thing, and they would just have to lump it. Germaine would quite happily sleep or just laze about for a lot of the day, and I thought I could probably talk Shanice and the other ladies in Hair and Make-Up to look after her. As long as they kept her away from the wigs…

I parked at Boskern and walked up to the production area. The crime scene was still cordoned off with police tape, but there were no officers on the scene now and the forensics tent had been taken away. There was only so much evidence you could get from that kind of scene. The ground directly around the body wasn't muddy, being on the wooden bridge, so there were no footprints or impressions of shoe soles. In TV crime shows they were always discovering murderers based on the unusual pattern on the soles of their one-off or limited-edition trainers, but in all my years on the Force I couldn't recall that ever happening in a murder investigation – most murderers seemed to wear the same bloody Adidas, Nike or whatever trainers as everyone else did. Terribly inconsiderate of them. The police still hadn't found the murder weapon, and Nathan doubted that they ever would. It was probably a rock or a branch, which had then been tossed into the river, so even if they did find it any traces of blood or DNA evidence would have been washed off it. They might even have come across it and not realised.

I still had almost an hour before I needed to be at the baking tent, so I decided to walk the long way round the roadshow village and let Germaine run off a little bit of energy. She had a great time, sniffing at suspicious tree roots and barking at squirrels who had had the temerity to scamper up into the branches of a big old oak rather than stay where she could get at them (not that she ever actually caught anything). I smiled to myself and decided that from now on I should only ever take catering jobs that allowed me to take her along. To be fair, I already took her on seventy-five per cent of my jobs, because my usual dog-sitters (Mum and Debbie) were also quite often my kitchen helpers.

We began to head up the path towards the shepherds' huts where Russell/Barbara, Pete and Esme relaxed when they weren't on set. A wisp of smoke came from the chimney of Russell's hut; he must still be getting himself ready for the day. Of course a lot of his preparation went on in the Hair and Make-Up tent. The copious amounts of make-up, the massive hair, already coiffed and preened into the kind of bouffant you could see from space, and the flamboyant wardrobe, whose designer had heard the phrase 'less is more' once and then completely forgotten about it, all needed space.

Germaine barked, and I shushed her, bending down to clip her lead back on.

'Shh, Germaine, you need to show a bit of decorum and not make a nuisance of yourself,' I said, because she liked me to talk to her properly and not in the kind of ridiculous baby-talk some dog owners use. I sometimes wondered if she would turn round and answer me in similar fashion, but only when I was a bit tipsy or over-tired.

Germaine, however, didn't shush, and she bolted towards Russell's hut before I had a chance to stop her. The extendable lead spooled out behind her as her little legs pumped away like furry white pistons; she certainly had a turn of speed on her when she wanted. What had she seen? Another squirrel? I followed her as quickly as I could, but she got to the hut before me.

It wasn't a squirrel. It was a man, standing on a small metal barrel – I recognised it as one containing cooking oil – under the window of the hut. He was clinging onto the window ledge, ear pressed against the wood, listening to whatever was going on inside. Or at least he had been, because now he was looking down at the mad (but cute) dog yapping at him below.

'You there! What are you doing?' I called. He looked up at me, then leapt off the barrel and fled before I could collect my senses and run after him. I did have enough sense, though, to lock Germaine's lead and stop her chasing after him.

I was reeling her back in to me when the door of the hut flew open and Russell stood at the top of the steps, clad in a colourful boho silk dressing gown, open to show his bare chest and black boxer shorts. He looked around furiously

'What the bloody hell's going on?' he cried. I heard a muffled voice from behind him, but he ignored it. He spotted me. 'Is that your dog making all that racket? What the blazes is it even doing here?'

'She, not it, and she was only barking because you had a lurker,' I said, turning on my heel. I really had gone off Russell, even when he was being himself and not Barbara.

'What do you mean, a lurker?' He tottered down the stairs – he was in bare feet – and I could see now that what I'd mistaken for anger now looked a lot more like fear.

'They've gone now,' I said, studying his face. Yes, definitely nervous about something. 'The dog spotted someone lurking outside your hut, listening at the window. She barked and scared him off.'

'Right...' He looked concerned. 'Who was it? What did they look like?'

'Some bloke, mid to late thirties, short light-brown

hair, faded jeans, grey hoody, dark-green trainers.' I smiled. 'I didn't get a very good look at him.'

'Right...'

'So do you know who that was?' I asked. 'Or why they might be listening to you?'

He instinctively half-turned towards the hut, then stopped himself. 'No idea. I was just in there going over the script for the opening sequence.'

'On your own?'

'Yes,' he said, but I didn't believe him. He dropped to his haunches and reached out to make a fuss of the dog, and I decided I liked him again after all. 'Thank you, er...?'

'Germaine,' I said. He raised his eyebrows. 'Her full name's Germaine Grrr. Her previous owner was a radical feminist.'

He laughed. 'No wonder she's so good at scaring off unsavoury men. Although I reckon you'd be pretty good at that yourself.' He winked at me, looking exactly like Barbara even without the wig and the fabulous wardrobe. 'Thank you, Germaine.' He straightened up. 'Well, there's no harm done. I need to get over to Hair and Make-Up.'

'OK,' I said, and I waited to see if he would head over to the tent, but he didn't, just stood there awkwardly. There was *definitely* someone in the hut with him, I thought, but I didn't understand why he would be so reluctant to admit it. I didn't want to make it any harder for him, though, so I let him off the hook.

'Right, well, I'd better go and get this one settled,' I said, gesturing to Germaine. I gave Russell one of my serious but reassuring looks, the one they'd taught me to do at police college. 'If they turn up again, or you're at all concerned about it, let me know, OK? Maybe we can get the crew to keep an eye out.'

'OK, thanks…' He gave me an uncertain smile, but still didn't move. I turned and walked away.

'Hello.' Nathan answered the phone in a non-committal, certainly non-romantically-involved tone of voice.

'Ooh get you, Mr Professional!' I said. 'How are you this morning, babe?'

'Good.'

'Ahh… I get it. Are you with someone important? Someone with a lot of pips on their shoulder?'

'Uh-huh.'

'Right. I'd better not say anything to make you crack your stony professional demeanour, then.' I smiled to myself. 'Would you like to know what I'm wearing? You know that black lacy set—'

'Um, you're on speakerphone,' said Nathan, awkwardly, and I nearly dropped the phone.

'What? Oh shi—'

Nathan laughed. 'Not really. But it serves you right.' He paused. 'Are you really wearing that—'

'No, it chafes. Are you really with someone important?'

'Not now, I was finishing up, literally just walking out of the room. Had to update the super on the case.'

'The super?'

'Superintendent Michael Hansen of the Devon and Cornwall constabulary. Yeah. Which is why I couldn't have you talking about your underwear…'

'But you're at the station, aren't you? What's he doing there?' Penstowan was a relatively small station, and most of the time Nathan, as detective chief inspector, was the highest-ranking officer there. The superintendent was normally based at Force headquarters, in Exeter.

'I'm not entirely sure. The bigwigs at Middlemoor are doing a survey on staffing levels at the smaller stations, and as part of that he's visiting some of them. And this case is pretty high profile, what with the TV company being involved, so he asked for an update while he was here.' Nathan sighed. 'I wish I'd had a bit more to tell him.'

'It's only been a few days, he can't expect you to have solved it that quickly,' I soothed. 'Anyway, that's why I'm calling you. Not just to tease you with my undies.'

'Well, I'm digging into Harry Dodds's background

now, and Russell Lang's too, for that matter, and so far I haven't come up with anything. So I can't give you any juicy details.'

'Never mind,' I said, feeling smug. 'It's a good job I've got some juicy details to tell you instead.'

'What? I hope you haven't been pestering anyone...'

'Me? With my reputation? Don't answer that. No, actually, Germaine and I may have saved Russell Lang from – something, I'm not sure what.' I filled Nathan in on what had occurred outside Russell's hut.

'Really? That's interesting...' Nathan sounded thoughtful, and I could almost see the expression on his face as he digested the information. 'This eavesdropper or would-be burglar or whatever he was, he didn't look like the guy Lang was arguing with in the pub the other night?'

I thought back to Monday night, waiting for Mum to finish in the pub toilets. 'No... I don't think so. To be honest, I didn't pay the bloke he was arguing with much attention. I was too busy working out if it really was Russell, without his Barbara get-up. But the bloke just now had light-brown hair, and I'm not sure but I *think* the one in the pub had much lighter hair, maybe even grey. And I'm pretty sure it was close-cropped, not like this other bloke's.'

'So not a jilted lover, then. Why was your mum so

sure they were having a lovers' tiff, in the pub? I didn't really see them.'

'I don't know if they were, but they did seem close, kind of touchy-feely. The bloke he was arguing with reached out and laid a hand on Russell's arm. Male friends don't really do that, do they?'

'Don't we?' Nathan sounded amused.

'Not like that, no. You and Matt are pretty close, but I can't see you doing that. You blokes do all the matey backslapping stuff, maybe a man hug. This was – *emotional* touching.'

Nathan laughed. 'That's probably incredibly sexist of you, but you're right. We don't tend to get that touchy-feely with each other. Not like women.'

'And that's why women are so emotionally well-adjusted.'

Nathan snorted. 'Yeah…'

'Did you ever want to see me in the black lacy set again?'

'Yes! Yes. Sorry. Do go on.'

'Anyway… There was definitely someone in the hut with Russell, so maybe it *was* a jilted lover. Maybe Russell was having a secret assignation with the bloke from the pub – he was certainly dressed for one – and the bloke outside was his ex, or his current for that matter, and he suspected that Russell was cheating on him, so—'

'So he was there trying to catch him in the act,' said Nathan. 'Did you get a look at who was in the hut with him?'

'No, I couldn't see, and I got the impression they wouldn't come out while I was nearby. I'll have to keep an eye out, see if I spot the man from the pub around the tents.' I looked at my watch. 'Talking of which... I need to go. We're supposed to start filming soon. Although I think we'll have a delay while Russell becomes Barbara, because he was nowhere near ready when I saw him.'

'I'll pop along when I've finished here,' said Nathan. 'I think we need to have another chat with Mr Lang about his visitor.'

'The one inside the hut or the one lurking outside?'

'Both.'

Nathan wished me luck with my baking – it was the final challenge of the roadshow, the showstopper, with just me, Elaine and Martin, and I thought I already knew who was going to win – and then we exchanged a few soppy words that would have made Daisy roll her eyes hard enough to see into her own brain, before getting on with our tasks. I headed to Hair and Make-Up, where Russell had just arrived. He ignored me as he took today's outfit – a tasteful cherry-red PVC number – from the rack and went behind a curtain with the wardrobe mistress to get dressed. As I'd hoped, Shanice gushed all over Germaine and agreed to look after her. Germaine eyed her suspiciously, then sniffed her outstretched hand – which just happened to be holding out a custard cream biscuit – and decided that maybe she *was* a nice person after all.

'Just one, Germaine!' I warned her, but I was really warning Shanice not to give in to those gorgeous eyes that just begged to be given biscuits, the tasty human kind, not the boring doggy ones. Shanice nodded, not taking her eyes off my fur baby, and I knew that an entire packet of custard creams was more than likely going to form a large part of Germaine's near future.

And so the day's baking began. Russell, now fully Barbara'd up and showing no signs of concern about his (her) earlier eavesdropper, sashayed into the tent, where Elaine and I were chatting and Martin was staring into space, rubbing his crystal pendant and doing what looked suspiciously like tai chi or yoga or something. Seriously. The guy was clearly there to win, and he wasn't above using some New Age meditation mumbo jumbo to get himself in the zone. I wondered if he wasn't above sabotaging the competition, either; I'd forgiven whoever had put salt in my chocolate custard, because the ganache I'd been forced to use instead had turned out to be a better choice of filling, but I hadn't forgotten about it, and I vowed to keep a closer eye on my baking today. Which would mean staying in the tent, away from the investigation.

I could already foresee problems with that, the main one being my incredible nosiness, but hey ho.

'Bakers, well done!' cried Barbara, Pete and Esme standing beside her, smiling. 'You've only blooming gone and made it through to the final round! Whoever wins this challenge will go on to represent Cornwall in the grand finale, against the best bakers from every other county across Britain. Judges, please tell us what the final challenge is. And make it a toughie.'

'Bakers,' said Esme, solemnly. 'Today's challenge is to create a showstopper cake that represents the best of Cornwall. That can be something that you love about it, something that the county is famous for, anything you like.'

'You can make any type of cake you like, but it should be at least two tiers high, and decorated using a number of different techniques,' Pete went on. 'It needs to look amazing, but don't forget, it must taste good too.'

'Blooming 'eck, they don't ask for much, do they? Bakers, you have five hours to create your showstopper,' said Barbara. 'So get ready, get steady … get baking!'

'Good luck,' said Elaine, and I smiled back at her.

'You too.' I turned to look at Martin, to wish him luck too.

'I don't need luck,' he said, pre-empting me. He stretched up and clasped his hands together above his head, breathing deeply. A slight wobble made me think he was standing on one leg, but the counter was (thankfully) in the way. I turned back to Elaine, the two of us sharing an unspoken *What a muppet*, then got on with my showstopper.

I was making a rich fruit cake, flavoured with a hint of saffron as a nod to the traditional Cornish saffron buns. I melted some butter in a large saucepan, then added brown sugar and some mixed dried fruit (sultanas, raisins, glacé cherries – the usual suspects). I poured in some water and brought it to the boil, then let it simmer for ten minutes, adding in a pinch of saffron and the zest and juice of an orange, to keep it moist and give it a bit of zing.

I let the mixture cool before beating in eggs and flour, then poured it into two deep cake tins, one bigger than the other. I was going for two tiers of fruit cake, rather like a traditional wedding cake, but the decoration would be anything but traditional (or weddingy). Both tins went into the oven for about an hour and a half. *I could sneak off for a bit…* I thought to myself, but no. Barbara was in the tent, and she – or rather her male alter ego Russell – was the only lead left to pursue. Not only did we – I mean, the police – need to know exactly who that was, loitering outside his window earlier, but we also needed to know who he'd been arguing with in the pub that night, and on the morning of the murder, and why; were either of the altercations and disagreements bad enough for them to want him dead? Because it still seemed to me that Russell was a more likely target here than Harry, regardless of how unpleasant the production assistant had been. No one had really known Harry on the roadshow. The only person who had known him for longer than the few days it had so far run was Indira. Admittedly they did have a history, but it was just that – history. There was no sign that she'd been wanting to rekindle things with him, or vice versa, so that wasn't a motive. What other reason could she have had for killing him? None, certainly not so far as Nathan had found out during his deep dive into Harry's background, anyway. Plus she'd still been in the tent when I'd left that lunchtime. She might have had time to go and find Harry, bludgeon him to death with a rock and then head back to the tent, but it was far more likely that she'd only have left to get a sandwich instead…

Focus, Jodie! I had a lot of fiddly bits of decoration to make, so it would be a wise move to get started while the cakes were in the oven. I was going to cover both cakes in fondant icing, with a layer of marzipan underneath, but in order to do that I would need to brush the cakes (once cooled) with jam. And being the baking roadshow, it was frowned upon if you didn't make something as simple as the jam yourself. Luckily, I'd already done that once this week for the Baumkuchen, so it was just a matter of making the same simple apricot jam, boiling the fruit and sugar in a pan and then letting it cool. I would need to warm it slightly again before I brushed it over the cake, but it was handy to have it ready to use.

The next step was to make some modelling chocolate. There were going to be various figures decorating the cake, and they all had to be edible. I could make them out of more fondant, but I was trying to impress the judges after scraping by the day before, and Pete himself had said to use a few different techniques. The modelling chocolate needed to be left for a while to cool down and harden slightly before I used it, so again, now was a good time to do it.

I melted the white chocolate and added corn syrup to it, mixing it together well. I poured it out onto a marble cutting board, to help it cool down quicker, and kneaded it until it was smooth and glossy. I wrapped it in clingfilm and put it into an airtight container.

The cakes had been in the oven for just over an hour by now, and there wasn't much more I could do. Camilla saw that I was at a loose end and gestured for Barbara to come over and interview me, which she did, reluctantly, followed by Carl the cameraman.

'Standing around, doing nothing?' she asked. 'We can't have you getting bored, you might wander off and get yourself into trouble.' She winked at me, but I knew exactly what she was getting at. I just wished I knew why she was so keen for me to keep my nose out. 'Tell us what your showstopper's all about.'

'Well, Barbara, I lived in London for twenty years, and the thing I missed most about Cornwall was the sea,' I said. It was true. Sitting alone in my old flat in Streatham (before I'd met Daisy's useless dad Richard aka 'that cheating swine'), I'd think about the waves off the North Cornwall coast, the way they sparkled in the sunlight, and the deep turquoise of the ocean around Elephant Rock, a rocky promontory near Penstowan. I'd remember days swimming in the achingly cold water then drying myself off in the sun on the golden sand, with Tony and my friends Lily and Nina and Callum, and I'd occasionally weep with nostalgia and the fear that I'd made the wrong decision, moving to London. It wasn't the wrong decision, of course, because Daisy had come out of it; but it had been absolutely the right decision to move back again.

'I missed the sea, Barbara, and everything to do with it. The fishing boats, the harbour, even the fish themselves. I missed the old superstitions of the local fishermen, the tales of mermaids and whales washing up. So that's what my cake is celebrating.' I showed her the drawing I'd come up with the night before. 'The bottom level will be covered in a blue fondant icing, to represent the sea, and there'll be a few fishing boats and mermaids and shells around the edge. The top tier is going to look like a stargazy pie, with a fondant "pastry" crust, and lots of little fish heads and tails poking out of the top.'

'That sounds incredible,' said Barbara. 'That will take a lot of hard work and focus to achieve that.' And she looked at me meaningfully, a look that was much more Russell Lang than Barbara Strident, Essex housewife, style icon and karaoke queen. I knew what the look meant, but not why; it was an almost pleading *please don't dig into this any further, stick to baking.* Oh Barbara, if only you realised that looking at me like that was just going to make me worse…

Cooking time for my cakes was up. I stuck a skewer into the middle of them – it came out clean, so I knew they were done – and then left the cakes in their tins on a cooling rack. I looked over at Elaine, wondering how she was getting on; but Barbara was talking to her now. Behind me, Martin had (as usual) piled everything up along the edge of his counter. I still hadn't worked out whether he was doing it on purpose or if he was just really messy, but whatever the reason, the result was the same – no one could see what he was doing until he revealed the finished cake at the end of each round.

I stood there uselessly for five minutes, then turned the fruit cakes out of their tins and onto the rack to cool. They were quite dense, packed with fruit, and would take quite a while to cool completely. I was just beginning to get restless and wonder what I to do now, when my phone vibrated…

Chapter Thirteen

'You mean to tell me that you've actually spent the last two and a half hours baking?' Nathan looked at me incredulously.

'I know, I was about to go mad,' I said. 'Thank God you texted me. What are we doing?'

'I spoke to Camilla,' said Nathan. I already knew that, of course, because she'd come over to my work bench and told me that he was waiting for me outside the tent, just before calling lunch break. She was really being very accommodating with my investigating. 'She's happy to let you have a longer break if you need to. So you and I are going to talk to Brussell.' He grinned. 'I never know which name to use, so that's what our drag queen and her alter ego will be known as from now on. Between us, anyway.'

'Brussell? I like it.'

On cue, crew members began to leave the tent, turning their steps towards catering. Barbara also appeared, looking around warily until she saw us. She didn't exactly look delighted as she approached us.

'Camilla said you wanted to interview me again,' she said, with heavy emphasis on the *again*.

'Yes, we do need to talk to you,' said Nathan pleasantly. 'Let's go somewhere quieter, shall we?'

We headed back to Russell's hut. I noticed that Barbara – or Russell, now that he'd unpinned his wig and was holding it in his hand – looked around furtively when we got there, as if he was expecting (or hoping not) to see someone. His early morning lurker, maybe? I caught Nathan's eye, and he gave me a slight nod; he'd spotted it too.

Russell slipped his feet out of the towering stilettos he was wearing and stopped at the foot of the stairs into his hut.

'I'll talk to you, but I'm not sure what else I can tell you about anything. And Jodie should be concentrating on her showstopper.'

'I assure you, Mr Lang, Ms Parker's presence is particularly necessary as she has pertinent knowledge about the case, including an event that happened earlier today.' I loved it when Nathan got all serious and no-nonsense with people. And Russell clearly wasn't happy that I'd told him about the man outside his hut. 'And as I think I mentioned before, she's an official consultant. Plus this isn't an interview, we just need to ask you a few questions, that's all. Hence we're going to do it here, in the comfort of your green room, rather than down at the station.' Nathan smiled at him, but the mention of the station was obviously meant to imply a threat. It worked. Russell sighed, then led the way up the stairs, unlocking the door and letting us follow him in.

The throws on the day bed were in a tangled mess, as if someone (or two someones, I thought) had rolled around on it before hastily getting up and trying to make it look neat. Hmm... Russell flopped down on the bed and stared up at us, a slightly sulky expression on his face. Nathan just smiled back and sat down on a canvas director's chair opposite, taking out his notebook while I plopped myself into a bean bag. I hoped I wouldn't need to get up again in a hurry.

Russell was no doubt expecting us to lead with what had happened that morning, but I knew the way Nathan worked, and I knew he would bowl him a googly to throw him off balance.

'Mr Lang, who were you at the pub with on Monday night?' I had to stop myself fist-pumping, because that was *exactly* how I would have started. Russell looked confused.

'What? What are you talking about?'

'Monday night. Dinner time. You were seen arguing with a man. Could you tell me who that was, and what the argument was about?'

'I don't know who you mean—'

Nathan looked at me. I nodded.

'You must know him, Mr Lang? You definitely seemed to be old friends. Mid to late thirties, very short hair, close-cropped even. Fair, maybe grey – light-coloured, anyway. You were sitting in a booth away from the bar, not too far from the toilets—'

'All right, all right!' Russell snapped, irritated. 'Yes, I remember now. Lawrence Smiley. My ex-partner.'

'What was the argument about, do you remember that?'

'No.' Nathan raised an eyebrow, but Russell just smiled thinly. 'I do, but that is none of your business.'

'OK.' Nathan made a note in his pad. 'Jodie?'

'On the morning of the murder, we also have a witness who saw you arguing with a blonde-haired woman,' I began. Russell interrupted me.

'What witness?' He was getting angry, but again I thought I detected a hint of something else; not quite fear, maybe, but definitely concern. 'This is ridiculous.'

'Mr Lang, is there anybody who would wish to do you harm?' asked Nathan. The abrupt change of tack turned Russell's anger to surprise.

'What? No. If this is about this morning…'

'We found blonde hairs on the victim's body, Mr Lang. Blonde hairs which match your missing wig.'

'Which is no longer missing, as we also found that,' I interjected.

'Now, as I see it, there are only two ways those hairs could have got onto the victim's body,' said Nathan. 'Either the killer was wearing it to disguise themselves—' I glanced at Russell's face, and he wasn't buying 'the killer', he knew Nathan was accusing him '—or the victim was wearing it when he was murdered.' Strictly speaking, those *weren't* the only ways the hairs could have got there – Harry Dodds could have been wearing it and then taken it off – but it was a shocking enough image to get Russell's full attention. I looked at him again, and I could see that he'd immediately come to the same conclusion I had.

'You mean the murderer thought Harry was me?' He gasped, and I knew then that I'd been right – about him not being the murderer, anyway. The alarm on his face was genuine enough. 'Are you saying that I was the intended victim?'

'That's what we'd like to know, Mr Lang,' said Nathan calmly.

'The incident this morning,' I said. 'The man outside—'

'I didn't see him, so I couldn't tell you who it was.' Russell was quick to interrupt me. I ignored him.

'It looked to me like he was waiting under your window, trying to listen to what was happening inside the hut,' I said. 'Why would someone do that?'

Russell shrugged, but it was unconvincing. 'I don't know. Maybe it was someone from the press, you know what those vultures are like. This is a very popular show, and they're always trying to dig up some gossip.'

'I thought maybe it was someone connected to the person in here with you,' I said. He shook his head.

'There wasn't—'

'I heard someone else. Who was it?'

'I was alone,' said Russell. He leaned forward and looked Nathan straight in the eye, obviously an attempt to convince him how honest he was, but Nathan wasn't falling for it.

'From what Ms Parker observed, and what she told me,' said Nathan, 'I have a theory about what might have taken place this morning. If I may?'

Russell sat back again. 'Could I stop you?'

'Ha! Not really. Thank you. It seems to me that maybe there was some kind of assignation taking place in here this morning, and the person outside, who you had intended to hide it from, had found out, or had suspicions, anyway. I'm thinking that they were a jilted lover, maybe? Something like that.'

Russell wet his lips nervously. Definitely a jilted lover, then. 'Who knows?'

'So I'm assuming from that, that as they lurked outside, you and your visitor inside were – well, we're all adults here, I think we can guess what you were doing, particularly when we take into account your state of undress when Ms Parker spoke to you.'

Russell glared at me, but his cheeks were red and he could hardly deny it.

'Who was in here with you, Russell?' I asked.

'Why is any of this your business?'

'Because if we know who was in *here*, then maybe we can work out who was out *there*.' Nathan gestured through the window. 'And then maybe we can work out who had it in for you enough to want you dead.'

Russell stared at both of us, and I could tell that he was trying furiously to come up with a way to avoid answering the question. I sighed.

'Come on, Russell,' I said. 'You're not stupid. You were in here having it away with someone, yes? And the person outside was some jilted lover who suspected the affair. How are we doing with that?'

'Oh for God's sake – yes, all right? I was having sex and some nutter was outside listening, OK?' Russell was slightly out of breath and red in the face after that outburst.

'Who were you in here with? The man from the pub – Mr...' Nathan checked his notes. 'Mr Smiley?' Russell looked genuinely confused.

'What? No. Of course not.'

'Why of course not? He was your partner.'

'*Ex*-partner. And not that kind of partner. He was my showbiz partner. We had an act together, years ago, when we first started.' He laughed. 'You really are barking up the wrong tree. We're good friends – or rather, we *were* good friends. But not like that.' He laughed again. Nathan and I exchanged glances.

'Why is that so funny?' I asked. Russell smiled thinly.

'Because I'm not gay.' He laughed again, although with little mirth, at our faces. 'I know, I'm a drag queen so I must be gay. Only, I'm not. Never have been.'

'But everyone thinks you are…' I said. He looked defensive.

'I've got a matador outfit I wear to fancy-dress parties. It doesn't make me a closet Spaniard, does it? I have never, *ever*, claimed to be gay. But when we first started Lawrence got us loads of gigs in gay clubs, and everyone just assumed, so it was easier to play along.'

I groaned. So maybe *that* was what he'd not wanted me to dig up?

'That Russell Lang isn't what he seems,' I said. Nathan looked sharply at me. 'Davey Trelawney said he'd heard the crew talking. That's what they said. Russell Lang isn't what he seems. You're really straight?'

'Yes. Look, Barbara is just a character I came up with when I was at drama school. That's where I met

Lawrence. He was really into the whole drag thing, and he had this great routine, but he was too nervous to do it on his own. So I came up with my own character so we could do a double act. It was only meant to be for his first couple of gigs, until he became confident enough to go it alone, but it was so much fun, and we got a following – the audiences loved us.' He smiled with genuine warmth as he remembered it. 'Barbara Strident and Rusty Binfield. We did this musical act, songs of the sixties, only with the words changed. We were pretty saucy.' He laughed. 'Our version of "Son of a Preacher Man" would have made a sailor blush.'

'So what happened?' I asked. He sighed.

'What always happens. We had "creative differences". Lawrence is a great singer, but I was in it more for the comedy. He wanted the act to concentrate on the music, but I'd really had enough. I sounded like a strangled cat next to him. We argued about it, and in the end we went our separate ways.'

'What happened to Rusty Binfield?' I asked.

'Had you heard of her before thirty seconds ago?'

'No.'

'There's your answer. And of course Barbara went on to become a household name. TV – that's what all comedians really want. No one wants to spend their entire life touring, playing dingy pubs and clubs, driving yourself between each one and sleeping in the van. TV is the prize. I'm not just on the roadshow, I've been on *I'm a Celeb*, *Strictly*, all the big ones. And when I go on tour now it's nice hotels and proper venues for a month. Lawrence never got any of that.'

'Is that what the argument in the pub was about?' asked Nathan.

'Sort of…' Russell stretched out on the day bed. 'I feel for him, I do. He's worked just as hard as I have, but I got lucky and he didn't. Barbara struck a chord with people that Rusty didn't. It's not my fault he's struggling.'

'But Mr Smiley doesn't see it that way?' said Nathan, and Russell nodded.

'If he'd just asked me for some money I'd have done what I could,' he said. 'But he started saying that Barbara had been partly his idea, and that I was using material that he'd come up with.'

'And are you?' I asked.

'No, it's all nonsense,' he said vehemently. 'He wanted a writing credit on my shows, as well as backdated royalties on my old TV specials and a regular gig writing my new stuff. Again, if he'd just asked for a job I'd have tried to find him something, but when I said no he started threatening to sue me, said he'd drag it all through the press. And he said that he'd make sure everyone knew I was straight.' Russell looked up and saw our bemused expressions. 'A lot of my fans are gay, DCI Withers,' he said. 'I've never said I was gay, but at the same time I never came out and said I wasn't. I didn't want my fans to think I was using their sexuality to make money.'

'So how did the argument end?' asked Nathan.

'It didn't, really. I got angry with him, he got angry with me, then he got up and stormed off before I had a chance to do it myself. I haven't heard from him since.'

'We'll need Mr Smiley's contact details,' said Nathan. 'I think we need to check where he was on the day of the murder.'

'You don't think – no, not Lawrence, he wouldn't...' Russell shook his head in disbelief. 'No. We might not have kept in touch as much as we should have, but I still think of him as one of my closest friends. He's not a murderer.'

'So who else hates you?' I asked. 'We still haven't got to the bottom of your argument with the blonde woman, or what happened this morning—'

We were interrupted by the sound of footsteps, pounding up the wooden steps, and then the door flinging open. Indira stood in the doorway.

'Is everything all right?' she asked, breathlessly. Nathan and I exchanged glances; we'd both noticed the look of alarm that had passed over Russell's face.

'Yes, the police just had a few questions,' he said carefully. 'Tell Camilla I'll be back soon.'

'It's not Camilla – I'm not here for that,' she said. I

looked at Nathan again and he gave a small nod. I gestured to the day bed.

'Indira, why don't you join us for a moment, get your breath back?' I said. She hesitated, then sat next to Russell, making him budge along. He didn't seem best pleased.

'So, Mr Lang, who *were* you in here with this morning?' Nathan smiled pleasantly at him and Indira, who half-turned to the un-wigged drag queen beside her and opened her mouth, before shutting it quickly.

'I think you know,' said Russell, resigned. 'But if we can keep it between ourselves? I don't want it getting out.'

Indira turned fully to glare at him. 'What, am I a dirty little secret or something? Are you ashamed of me?'

'No! No, of course I'm not, darling,' said Russell placatingly. 'But you know what I said when we started this. If I'm going to come out as straight, then we have to handle it properly.'

'Ironic, innit?' I mused. 'In the old days, gay film stars used to pretend to be straight so they wouldn't get fired by their studio. Most of them even got married to throw people off the scent. And here's you—' Russell and Indira were both glaring at me now, while Nathan looked amused, so I shut up. 'Sorry. As you were.'

'So you and Miss…' Nathan started to flick back

through his notes again, but Indira stopped him impatiently.

'Bakshi. Indira Bakshi. Yes, we were in here, having – an intimate moment – this morning, until we heard barking outside. And then Russell leapt up and went out and found Jodie and her dog.'

'So this man the dog scared off,' said Nathan. 'Do you know who he is? Or why he might be waiting outside?'

'No idea, on either count,' she said.

'Not some kind of jilted lover, maybe?' I asked gently. She snorted.

'Jilted lover? Oh come on. One jilted lover on set's enough, don't you think?' she said. Russell looked alarmed.

'What do you mean?'

'I did have a jilted lover on set, but he definitely wasn't listening outside the window this morning,' she said. Russell still looked confused. 'Harry. Harry was my jilted lover, from years back. I dumped him when we were at university, so when he asked me for a job I got him one because I'm an idiot and I let him make me feel guilty.' She shook her head, annoyed with herself. 'I shouldn't have felt bad, because he'd moved on and he was just using our past relationship to manipulate me.' She looked at me, then at Nathan. 'I don't have any other "jilted lovers". I haven't had that many lovers, full stop, and certainly none recently, other than Russell. And that only started this week.' Her hand snaked across the covers of the day bed and took his hand. 'And it only started properly this morning.' Russell squeezed her hand and kept hold of it.

'*You* seemed to think that it *was* a jilted lover, or something like that,' Nathan said to Russell.

'I never said that.'

'You never said it wasn't, though. I thought it definitely hit a nerve, didn't you, Jodie?' I nodded. 'Who did you think it was?' Nathan leaned forward. 'Who was the blonde woman you were arguing with on the day of the murder? This mystery man wouldn't have something to do with her, would it?'

Indira snatched her hand away from Russell's. 'Blonde woman? Oh God, you don't mean Laura, do you?'

'Who's Laura?' I asked, noticing Russell flinch at the name.

'Laura Blake. She was one of the food tech assistants on the last season,' said Indira. 'She was on the roadshow for, what, four seasons? Five? More than me. Not this season, though.' She looked at Russell, her mouth set in a thin line. 'I thought I saw her the morning of the murder, hanging around the set, but I didn't talk to her and I didn't see her again.'

'Do you know what was she doing here, Mr Lang?'

Nathan asked. 'Apart from arguing with you. Was that why she was here, to have something out with you?'

'Or have something off with you,' I murmured. Russell shook his head.

'It wasn't like that...' he said. Indira scoffed. He took her hand again. 'It wasn't, I swear.'

'What *was* it like?' I asked.

'They were having an affair,' Indira said. But Russell shook his head again.

'No, it wasn't like that! Look, okay, we did have a relationship. She worked on the show, like Indira said, and for the first couple of seasons it was just flirting. I had to be careful not to be too obvious. I didn't want people to know I was straight. She wasn't the first person on the crew I'd – you know – with, but they were just a bit of fun, on both sides, and we were very discreet. Anyway, the season before last, Laura and I got together, and ... I liked her. I mean, I *really* liked her. I'd even started thinking about coming out as straight so we could be together properly.'

'What happened?'

'She didn't want that. She liked the sneaking around, she said it made it more exciting. And when we finished filming, she didn't want to carry on. What happens on the roadshow stays on the roadshow, that's what she said.'

'How did you feel about that?' asked Nathan.

He shrugged. 'I didn't like it, but what could I do? I couldn't force her to feel the same. Anyway, last season she was on the roadshow again, and we started seeing each other like before...' Indira looked upset, and he reached out for her again, only this time she didn't pull away. 'It was just sex. You and I were friends, weren't we? I realised that you were starting to mean more to me, but I didn't know how you'd react when I told you I wanted more, and I was scared that if we did start something it would be like Laura all over again, so...'

'So you carried on sleeping with this Laura. What happened at the end of the season?'

'Same as before. End of the show, end of us. We all went our separate ways and I didn't think any more of it.'

'But she decided not to come back for this season?' said Nathan.

'No, she wanted to, but they wouldn't renew her contract. She thought that I'd had something to do with it. She thought I'd wanted her out of the way so that I could make a move on Indira—'

'Which you did,' I pointed out. Russell looked at me angrily.

'You're making it sound like I'm a complete rat. Well, I'm not. I've played around a bit with women who *wanted* to play around a bit. That's not what it was for me with Laura, and it's definitely not what it is with Indira.

234

For both of us, I hope.' Indira looked pleased, but also like she was reserving the right to still be furious with him, depending on the outcome of this conversation.

'So did you get her out of the way? Pull some strings with the production company? You are the star of the show, after all. You must have some sway.' Nathan looked up from his pad. 'I take it that's what you were arguing about?'

'You said, it's not like that,' I said, remembering the argument. 'You seem to say that a lot.'

'Because it wasn't like that. She accused me of getting her blacklisted. She threatened to go to the press and tell them I'm straight – yes, Jodie, I know that sounds like a ridiculous threat, but when you consider who my fans are it would be a disaster if it wasn't handled right. The main thing was that she threatened to tell Indira that all the time I'd been getting to know her last season, I'd been sleeping with Laura behind her back.'

Indira shook her head in disbelief. 'You really thought I didn't know that already? Laura knew we were growing close last season, and she made a point of dropping massive hints about why you were late for filming, or why her hair was messed up, until it was really obvious what was going on. She was a total cow. I could never understand what you saw in her.'

'To be honest, nor can I now,' said Russell, looking glum. 'But anyway, it wasn't me who stopped her coming back to work on the show. I asked Camilla, and she said Laura had been getting sloppy towards the end of last season, showing up late – which wasn't always my fault – and just not doing her job properly. Camilla said that if they'd been able to fire her during the shoot they would have done, but it would have left them short of crew.'

'So … getting back to who might have had a motive to murder you…' said Nathan, and we all looked at each other.

'You think that cow wanted to kill Russell?' Indira looked confused. 'But how did Harry end up dead, then?'

'He had my wig,' said Russell. 'No, I don't think she wanted to kill me. Because she came back at lunchtime and we – we made up…' He looked at Indira and the guilt written across his face was obvious. Poor Indira.

'Lunchtime?' I said. 'That's why you changed your outfit, isn't it? Your dress got ripped.'

'Yes. Laura had this thing about me staying in character while we…' Russell gulped. 'She wouldn't even let me take the dress off.' Indira let out a sound that was half hysterical laugh, half sob. 'I'm so sorry, darling. It was the only way I could get her to agree to shut up. One last fling, she said. I didn't realise what she meant until afterwards.'

'What did she mean?'

'She told me afterwards that she was getting married. She said her husband-to-be was a real man who wouldn't be caught dead in a dress, so this was her final time being with another "woman".'

'*Somebody* has issues,' I said. Nathan smothered a grin.

'And then she told me that he had a filthy temper, and that if he ever found out about us he'd kill both of us.' Russell had fear as well as guilt and embarrassment in his eyes now, and I couldn't help but feel sorry for him. He'd got himself in a right pickle, that was for sure.

'That's why you looked surprised, but not *that* surprised, when we heard about the murder,' I said. 'You looked like you were expecting something bad to happen, but when it was Harry you almost looked relieved, because it wasn't what you were expecting. When you heard someone had died, you thought Laura was the one who'd been killed, by her fiancé.'

He nodded. 'I'm ashamed to admit that I *was* relieved when they said it was Harry, although I feel sorry for his wife. But this morning – that must have been Laura's fiancé outside. He must've thought I was in here with her. You don't think he could've killed Harry, thinking it was me, do you?'

'Well, along with your ex-showbiz partner Mr Smiley, he certainly seems to have had motive.' Nathan closed his notebook and stood up. 'Thank you for your help, Mr Lang. I'll let you get back to work.'

We left Russell and Indira talking in low but heated voices. At the bottom of the steps Nathan turned to me with a grin.

'You know I love you, but if you ever want me to dress up like a woman, it's over.'

'Not even Nigella Lawson?'

'I know she's your cooking heroine, but that's just weird, babe.'

Chapter Fourteen

There wasn't much more we could do until Nathan had tracked down Laura Blake and her (possibly homicidal) fiancé, or Lawrence Smiley the (also possibly homicidal) ex-Rusty Binfield, so I went back to the cooking tent. I had – I checked my watch – about an hour and a half left to decorate my fruit cakes, which would be cool by now. If whoever had been sabotaging my bakes had left them alone, that was. In my eagerness to join Nathan and help him grill Russell I'd not thought to take any precautions, like ask Elaine to keep an eye on my stuff; but then again, could she be the one sabotaging me? I was automatically ruling her out because I liked her, and ruling Martin in because I thought he was a knobhead, but really it could be either of them. Or neither. There were lots of people buzzing in and out of the tent at various times, particularly over lunch, where lights got tweaked or the food displays in the background were refreshed (which must have been one of the jobs Laura, our food technician with a drag queen fetish, used to do). It could be anyone.

Or it could be no one. Maybe I had just misplaced my white chocolate that time? But then I'd tasted my chocolate custard before putting it in the fridge and it had been delicious, very different to how it had tasted later on. It definitely hadn't been me, mistaking the salt for sugar and adding that instead. And the hob had definitely stopped working – I wasn't imagining that. Someone really was out to get me…

But my fruit cakes were still on the bench, and they smelt good. I bent down low over them and sniffed, just to make sure no one had pricked holes in them and poured anchovy oil or something over them, but nope – still fruity, with a hint of saffron. Phew.

The next step was to make the fondant icing. I sifted some icing sugar into a bowl, then dissolved gelatine in a saucepan of hot water. I added glucose syrup and glycerine, then made a well in the centre of the sugar and poured the liquid in, stirring until everything was combined. I tipped it out onto the workbench and kneaded it, until the icing was smooth.

I divided the mixture into two, then added blue food colouring to one half. I placed the larger of the two fruit cakes onto a cake stand, brushed it with warmed apricot jam, then rolled out the blue icing, laying it over the cake and smoothing it out. I've never been great at doing fancy decorating – I always end up tearing the icing and having to patch it up – but it didn't look half bad. And the blue was the perfect shade for the sea.

The rest of the icing was going to be my 'pie'. I used some yellow food colouring, adding a touch of red and blue to make it look like golden brown pastry, and covered the smaller fruit cake. That then went on top of the other one. Whatever happened from here on, at least I had a two-tier cake. All I needed to do now was all the fiddly bits. Easy...

I made a kind of rope of the icing 'pastry' and ran it around the edge of the top cake, so it looked like a pinched-together pie crust. Then I started to make my 'silver darlings' – a trio of glittering mackerel, gazing up at the sky to give the traditional Cornish pie its stargazy name. I was making the heads and the tails of the fish from modelling chocolate, which I would then cover with edible silver paint and a little bit of blue and green glitter. With the leftover modelling chocolate I'd make as many seashells, mermaids, anchors and so on as I could. I remembered the mermaid cake I'd made Daisy for her eighth birthday. She'd been well impressed with it, and I'd been very proud, but this was a whole other level and

I wasn't sure if I could pull it off. *She who dares*, I thought, and ploughed on.

My phone vibrated with a text message. Daisy. It was as if she knew I'd been thinking of her and her birthday cake.

Good luck Mum hope it's going well!!! You can do it!!! xxx

I smiled and got back to my decorating.

An hour later I was still making flipping chocolate seashells. I had to paint the bloody things yet and I wasn't convinced I'd have time. Outside the tent, the blue skies that had greeted me and Germaine that morning had been steadily clouding over, and now the heavens opened. Rain thundered down, so hard we could barely hear Barbara when she called, 'Bakers! Half an hour left, babes!' It was a good job she had a fine set of lungs on her.

As I hurried to finish my seashells (I'd done a little mermaid to sit on top of the pie, and it had been so fiddly she was sadly destined to be a lone siren) there was another text message, this time from Tony.

I'm here to do the judging! You better promise to be nice to me from now on if you want to win... Followed by a winking face emoji. I was just about to reply when—

'Five more minutes!' cried Barbara. *Holy mackerel*, I thought. I splashed a bit of edible paint on the last seashell and stuck it into place with the others, on the bottom tier of the cake, hiding the join between it and the top tier, which had looked a bit messy.

'Bakers, step away from your showstoppers!' Barbara sang out, and with groans of relief and exhaustion the final three bakers dropped their spatulas and stood back to admire their handiwork.

I was actually pretty pleased with mine. As I always tell everyone, I'm a chef, not a baker. My cakes always taste good, but they don't always look the part. This one did. I could hardly believe the person who had made those fish was little old me. If you didn't look too closely at the mermaid (who was a bit squinty-eyed) it looked like a cake made by a professional pastry chef.

Elaine's cake was gorgeous. She'd done a food-themed cake, kind of like mine, but her bottom tier was covered in red and white icing, so it looked like a gingham table cloth or picnic blanket. Instead of a second full tier, she had several smaller cakes dotted across the top, representing a Cornish feast. Two tiny scones, with real jam and clotted cream on top; a pasty, with icing that really did look like pastry, much more than mine did; and a flagon of scrumpy cider. There was even a separate glass of 'cider' that came with it, made with apple jam. It was so pretty, it was the sort of cake you wouldn't want to cut into. I turned around to see Martin's masterpiece...

Bloody hell, it WAS a masterpiece and all. He'd made

a cliff top, with raging sea below it, and on the cliff a winding house for an old Cornish tin mine. It wasn't as pretty as Elaine's, or as whimsical as mine, but it was a feat of engineering – because the winding house flipping worked. There was a wheel at the side of it, constructed from Meccano or something, and as it turned a little cage rose up from a hole in the deepest part of the cake. It was, I reluctantly had to admit, incredible.

Camilla called cut and stepped forward, making sure the camera had stopped recording.

'Well done, bakers,' she said. 'You've all done magnificently…' Her eyes travelled between the cakes and I thought they rested on mine for a second, but I could have been wrong. 'Your cakes all look fantastic. Now, as I told you on day one, we've changed things around a bit this season, which is just as well with the weather being so bad! We'd normally have the judging today, but this season we're making it a bit more special, as this year is going to be Esme's last roadshow. We'll have the judging tomorrow, which means that you can invite your family and friends along to the unveiling of the cakes, and we can turn it into a proper celebration of all your hard work.'

I suddenly thought of Tony, outside somewhere in the rain, expecting to do the judging now as they had on past shows. He obviously hadn't got the memo, and I hadn't thought to mention it to him when I'd seen him the other day; I'd assumed he knew.

'That's a lovely idea!' said Martin, and I was surprised to hear him say something so cheerful and positive for a change. I would have expected him to want the judging done and out of the way, his win in the bag.

'Yes,' said Camilla. 'I think it will end the show on more of a party note.'

'What's going to happen to our cakes overnight?' asked Elaine, and I was glad she did, because I should have thought of that myself. If someone was going to sabotage me again, what better opportunity?

'They will be locked in the production van,' said Camilla. 'It's nice and cool in there, and they'll be quite safe.' *Unless the saboteur has got keys to it*, I thought.

'I think we should take photos of them before we move them,' I said. 'I know the camera crew have taken some footage of them already, but they're quite delicate and I'm a little concerned that bits might fall off when we move them. It would be good to have something easy to refer to so we can make repairs to them in the morning if we need to.'

'I don't think anything will fall off, the van's right outside,' said Camilla, but Martin (to my immense surprise) agreed with me.

'No, I think that's a good idea. My winding house

mechanism is really complex. If anything gets dislodged, if I've got a photo I'll know where it's meant to go.'

'Yeah, good idea,' agreed Elaine. Camilla smiled, although I got the impression she thought we were making a bit of a fuss, and agreed that we could take photos.

'We should probably get someone neutral, like one of the crew, to take the pictures,' I said. 'So they can check that when all the cakes are ready for judging, they look exactly as they do now. Sorry for sounding suspicious, but if one of these reprobates decides to bung an extra tier on their showstopper I'd like to be able to prove it.'

Elaine laughed. 'Dammit, Jodie, that's what I was planning to do! Foiled again.'

'You don't need to add another tier, your cake is already *amazing*,' I said, and she smiled.

'OK, that's settled then,' said Camilla briskly. 'Take your photos, and then let's get these wonderful cakes locked safely away.'

Pictures taken, Camilla shut the door of the van and clicked the button on the key fob to lock it.

'Right, that's all the cakes safe and sound,' she said. We three bakers and the assorted crew members who had helped us carry our bakes to the van, which had been backed up right into the doorway of the tent to avoid the rain, nodded. *Safe for now,* I thought, wondering if my photographic evidence plan, along with the large number of witnesses who had seen my cake safely ensconced inside the van, meant that any ideas of sabotage the unknown perpetrator might have been fermenting were sure to have been abandoned. It would be pretty difficult to knacker anyone's cake before the final judging now.

As everyone wandered away for the evening I took out my phone and dialled Tony, hoping that someone had taken pity on him and told him his services weren't needed until tomorrow morning.

'Jodie! What's going on?' Tony sounded much less miserable at the other end of the phone than I'd expected him to. I'd been imagining him sheltering under a tree, hoping for cake.

'Judging's not until tomorrow, did no one tell you?'

'Yeah, some bloke just told me they're doing it different this time round. My own fault for not reading the email properly. Where are you? I'm sitting in the hair and make-up tent with Germaine and the lovely Shanice.' I heard giggling in the background and grinned to myself. Since Tony's marriage to Cheryl had failed to take place he'd had a few false starts in the romance stakes, but it hadn't stopped him being a massive (but endearing and respectful) flirt with the ladies. 'I'm quite happy to wait here and help Shanice dogsit...'

'I bet you are, you tart. Just remember, it's a roadshow. She'll be moving on to pastures new on Sunday.' I gratefully accepted a roadshow umbrella from one of the crew and headed out of the tent. 'I'm coming over now.'

Tony had made himself at home. He was sitting in one of the make-up chairs, drinking tea and telling funny stories, while both Germaine and Shanice listened to him, enraptured. I didn't blame them. Tony at forty was better looking than the Tony at fourteen who'd been my very first boyfriend, and he had a big heart and was always good company. It did my own heart good to see him putting himself out there again, although chatting up a woman who was only going to be in our neighbourhood for another twenty-four hours probably wasn't the best way for him to find new love. And I knew that for all his flirtiness, a proper loving relationship was what he really wanted, and deserved.

'There she is! My oldest friend in the whole world!' said Tony, looking up as Germaine shot to her feet and trotted over to welcome me in. She'd missed me. Shanice's eyes narrowed slightly.

'You're friends?' she said, suspiciously, and I thought, *uh-oh*. I hoped he'd disclosed to the producer that we knew each other, and that therefore his judging was not necessarily going to be impartial. Tony, bless him, got the wrong end of the stick.

'Oh yeah, just friends,' he said. 'Nothing more. It'd be like kissing my sister…'

I felt myself blush. He wasn't wrong. Our one-off romantic interlude – an impromptu pash under a hotel gazebo, just before I'd got together with Nathan – had felt weirdly incestuous and had led to a lot of mouthwash when I'd got home. I did love him, just not like that.

'I don't think she means like that, Tone,' I said. 'I think she's wondering how you got to be a judge when we're so close. Not *that* close,' I hastened to add, before he did.

'Oh… Well, they did ask Maurice to do it –' Maurice was the Mayor of Penstowan, and to be fair I was friends with him, too, since I'd catered his husband's birthday a couple of months back '– but it clashed with something else.' Tony shrugged. 'I'm second choice, once again… But the other local judges come from somewhere else, and they won't know Jodie.'

'And when they signed you up to be a judge, there was no guarantee that I'd be in the final,' I said. Tony nodded.

'That's right, I'm as surprised as you are.'

'Oi! Who said I'm surprised about it? I just said there was no guarantee…'

Shanice laughed. 'I can tell you two have known each other for ever,' she said, and just like that I felt

Tony's hopes of getting her number crumble. He knew it too.

Tony drained the last of his tea and stood up.

'Thank you for your kind hospitality,' he said to Shanice. 'I will see you tomorrow for the judging.'

I clicked Germaine's lead on to her collar and we left the tent. The rain had slowed to a light drizzle now, which I was very thankful for as I remembered that we'd parked some way away that morning in order to give Germaine a walk. She could do with one now, I thought.

'Where are you parked?' I asked Tony.

'Right down there, by the house,' he said. 'By the time I got here, the car park up here was chocka.'

'I'm down that way too,' I said. 'I need to give Germaine a bit of a run, do you want to walk with me?'

'That would be nice,' he said. I put my umbrella up and attempted to shelter both of us, but I was too short. 'Allow me.' Tony took the umbrella from me, then linked my arm through his, holding the brolly above our heads, then we headed down a path towards the river.

'How are you? I haven't seen that much of you lately,' I said.

'No, you've been busy with Nathan.'

'Oh…'

He stopped and turned to me. 'Sorry, that was a proper arsehole thing to say. I'm really pleased you and him got together, he's good for you. I'm just a bit jealous.'

'Tony...'

'Not like that, I'm not saying I wish we were together. I meant it back there, it really did feel wrong, didn't it?' We hadn't properly spoken about what had happened, other than assuring each other that it didn't matter and we were still friends, but our relationship had inevitably changed since I'd started seeing Nathan.

'So, so, *soooo* wrong.'

'All right, you don't have to be quite so emphatic about it...'

I laughed. 'I know, I'm messing with you.'

We walked on, neither of us talking for a moment, then he sighed and dropped a bombshell.

'I miss Cheryl.'

'What? After everything she did?'

'I know, I know. But she was under a lot of pressure at the time. Anyway, we've talked—'

'When?'

'I don't know, probably while you and Nathan were playing happy families.' Tony was starting to get irritated.

'Oh right, but you're not jealous?' I snorted, then hated myself for it, because I really didn't want him to be.

'And you're not jealous because I still love Cheryl?' snapped Tony.

'*Do* you love her?'

'Yes. No. I don't bloody know.'

'Because what she did, yeah, maybe she deserves forgiveness, although I don't think I could, but how could you forget it? How could you ever trust her again?'

I never found out how Tony could even think about trusting his ex-fiancée, because he suddenly disappeared from sight, slipping down a muddy bank towards the river which at this point, thankfully, was just a stream – although after the sudden heavy downpour this afternoon, it was fuller than it had been all week.

'Ow! Bugger it.'

I gingerly stood at the edge of the bank and looked down. Tony was still upright, somehow, but his trouser legs were stiff with mud. The look on his face was one of complete surprise and bewilderment. Now that I'd got over the shock of him just suddenly plummeting from view, and I knew that he was OK, I could feel laughter bubbling up inside me.

Tony looked up. 'If you laugh at me, I swear…' I swallowed it down.

'No, no, of course not… Are you all right? You're not hurt?'

'No, I'm fine. My heart is going ten to the dozen! I got a proper bloody fright then.' He took a deep breath and tried to climb up the bank, but it was too slippery.

'Take my hand,' I said, leaning down.

'No, I'll just pull you down here as well.'

'If that happens we can send Germaine for help,' I said. I looked around for her. She was sniffing at a bush some distance away, and hadn't even noticed that her daft human friends had got themselves into a spot of bother. I sighed. 'Or maybe not. Hang on.'

'I'm ain't going anywhere, am I?'

I tied Germaine's lead to a tree, then tottered back to the edge of the bank. I bent down and grabbed hold of a thick tree root, hooking my hand underneath it tightly, then reached out with my other hand. 'See that root there? Get your foot on it, then boost yourself up and grab my hand.'

'I don't know...'

'Or you can wade along the stream until you find somewhere easier to climb out,' I said. 'But it does get deeper further along.'

'All right.' Tony took a deep breath and put his foot on the root, then reached out with one hand to grasp a branch that was sticking out.

'OK? I'm ready when you are,' I said.

'OK. Three, two, one—' He looked down at his other foot. 'Hang on, what's that?' Tony let go of the branch and squatted down. I looked down and watched him fiddling with something.

'What is it?'

'A necklace,' he said. 'I nearly trod on it.'

'Stick it in your pocket and try again,' I said. The rain

was starting to get heavy again, and the umbrella had disappeared down the bank with Tony. He tucked the necklace away, then pulled himself up using the tree branch. I stuck my hand out, clinging on tight to the root with my other hand, and helped him scramble up the bank and back onto the path.

'Bloody hell,' he gasped. He was covered almost from head to toe in mud by now.

'And that's what you get for starting an argument with me,' I said.

We made our way to my car; mine was closer, and I always kept towels in it to clean Germaine up with after walks (she had little legs and a tummy that was uncomfortably close to the ground). I switched on the engine and turned the heater on, to warm us up; we were pretty soggy. We both jumped as the stereo came on, blasting 'Don't Stop Believing' at high volume. I hurriedly turned it down, but not before Tony had caught a glimpse of the radio's display.

'"Jodie's motivational playlist"?' he said, grinning. 'What's next? "Eye of the Tiger"?'

'Oh shut up,' I muttered, cursing the Bluetooth in my car for connecting automatically with my phone. I'd been playing upbeat songs like that (but not 'Eye of the Tiger') on my way to the roadshow that morning, to psych myself up for the showstopper, and it had just picked up where I'd left off. I reached over to the back seat and flung a rather doggy towel at him. Germaine barked. 'See, *she* likes it. My dog's got better taste in music than you do.' Tony grinned but didn't comment any further. He towelled himself dry while I studied the necklace he had found.

It was a silver chain with a medallion on it, kind of like a Saint Christopher, but not. I'm not a religious person, never have been, and I come from a long line of heathens, but even I recognised Saint Christopher, the patron saint of travellers. When I was eighteen, killing time between doing my A levels at high school and starting police college, I'd planned to go travelling around Europe by train for two months, and my extremely elderly aunt up in Herefordshire (who I realised, with a pang of guilt, that I hadn't seen for at least three years) had bought me a chain with a tiny Saint Christopher medallion on it. It had indeed kept me safe, as far as Dover, anyway, when the friend I was travelling with (Hayley something or other) had had an attack of nerves and changed her mind about going. I hadn't been brave enough to go on my own, not through countries where I didn't speak the lingo, so after a massive argument that our brief friendship never recovered from we'd both turned back. I still regretted not going to this day.

'Do you know who this is meant to be?' I asked, holding it up. Tony gave up trying to dry his trousers and looked up.

'Saint Christopher.'

'No, it isn't. He's always shown carrying someone on his back, isn't he? Over a river or something.'

'That'd be apt,' he muttered soggily.

'This is a female saint,' I said, studying it under the car's interior light.

'That narrows it down,' said Tony sardonically. I ignored him.

'She's holding a cross.'

'Don't they all?'

'…and a bunch of flowers, I think… I don't know, it's a bit worn. I think it's quite old.' I turned to Tony. He was wringing out the hem of his trousers, which were soaked. 'Mate, not inside the car!'

'Sorry.'

'Where exactly was this? Was it buried in the mud, or caught in a tree root or what?'

'No, it was just lying there, on top of the mud. I saw it twinkling next to my foot when I looked down.'

'It wasn't caked in mud, was it?' Tony shook his head. 'Hmm… So it was either dropped recently, like, today, or it was in the river, and where the water level's been up and down with the rain, it got washed up on the bank. Would that work?'

Tony nodded. 'Yeah, that could be it. Or maybe it was stuck somewhere and the rain washed it loose.'

'Yeah... Stay here a moment.' I jumped out of the car before Tony could say anything and rushed over to the entrance of the car park, where there was a small wooden bridge, like the one Harry had been murdered on, over the river. Just to my right, upstream, was the crime scene; to my left, downstream, the river bank where Tony had come to minor grief and found the necklace. The Ottery was flowing the right way...

I jumped back in the car and started it, startling Tony.

'I'll give you a lift to your car,' I said, 'although to be fair you can't get much wetter than you already are. I'll see you tomorrow for the judging.'

'Are you going to tell me what you're thinking?' asked Tony, and I laughed.

'I'm not even sure myself yet...'

Chapter Fifteen

It was only 4 p.m. by now, although with the dark, rain-heavy clouds subduing the sun it felt later. I drove to Penstowan, stopping to text Nathan and find out where he was.

I drove round the one-way system and up to the top of Fore Street, turning into a small dead-end street that overlooked the beach. A couple of houses up stood Nathan's rental cottage; a tiny but very cute stone terraced house, no more than a two-up, two-down. Nathan opened the door as I manoeuvred my car into a parking space opposite. Germaine leapt out of the car and raced over to him.

'Yes, all right, I'm happy to see you too,' he laughed, bending down to make a fuss of her.

'What about me?' I said, pretending to pout. He pulled me towards him for a kiss.

'I'm happy to see you too, but you're less high maintenance than Germaine.' He stood back to let me into the cottage first. 'I was just about to put the kettle on.'

'And that's one of the reasons why I love you,' I said. I walked down the narrow hallway and into the small back kitchen.

'So how was your last challenge?' Nathan filled the kettle and switched it on as I got a couple of mugs from a cupboard. 'Did you get it all finished in time?'

'Yes, unbelievably. It actually looks really, really good. Not like one of my cakes at all. You're coming tomorrow, aren't you? It sounds like they want us to bring as many people as we can, turn the final judging into a party.'

'Of course I am,' said Nathan. He poured some cold water into a bowl for Germaine, and she lapped at it thirstily.

'So what have you been up to? Any more leads?' I asked.

'Nope. I checked out Russell's two potential enemies, but they didn't quite pan out.' He led the way into the front room and we sat down on the sofa to drink our tea. 'Lawrence Smiley was at an appointment at the dole office in Swindon on the day of Harry Dodds's murder. I've left Matt to confirm it with the

DSS, but I can't see someone giving such an easily checked alibi unless it's true. The appointment was at eleven thirty, which means there's no way he could've been down here mistaking Harry for Russell and bashing his head in.'

'So he really did need money, then. Bugger. But to be honest I always preferred Laura Blake's fiancé for it. He seems to have a stronger motive.'

'Yeah, I do too. Did too, I should say.'

'What, he's a blow-out as well?'

Nathan nodded. 'Yup. John Barrow. He and Laura live in Plymouth, so near enough to pop down and eavesdrop on Russell without too much trouble. But Mr Barrow works in business finance, and when Dodds was killed he was schmoozing clients – the directors of some big firm of architects in Torquay. I just spoke to their receptionist. She says she signed him into the building at eleven fifty-five, they went out for lunch ten minutes later and her bosses came back at two o'clock, a little bit tipsy.'

'What about Barrow? Did he come back with them?'

'Not to the office, no. She didn't see him come back but she's pretty certain that his car was in the visitors' bay all the time they were out, and not long after they returned she noticed the car had gone. Anyway, if he was in Torquay at twelve he wouldn't have had enough time to get down here and kill anyone over the lunch break.'

'Dammit! Did he admit to coming down and eavesdropping this morning?'

'Yes. Eventually…' Nathan grinned. 'He was very embarrassed about the whole thing. Said his fiancée likes to play games. She'd teased him about having an affair with an ex-colleague, and he'd put two and two together from hints she'd dropped and decided to come down and confront Russell. But then you scared him off.'

'This Laura sounds like a right piece of work.'

'Oh yes, she's a real keeper. They're meant to be getting married this summer. I give it six months. If it even goes ahead.'

I laughed. 'You sound like my mum. So there's no more leads around Russell. And no one appears to have had a grudge against Harry?'

'Nope. Matt spoke to the teaching agency he worked for. He was well enough liked by his colleagues, although he didn't socialise with them. They said they didn't know much about him, but he was always professional. The lady Matt spoke to said that he hadn't quit, he'd just told them he wouldn't be available for work for the next three months. He didn't tell them why, she assumed he was going away on a long holiday or something.'

'Maybe he was dipping his toe in the water about a career change after all,' I mused. 'He was keeping his options open, so he could go back to supply teaching if he needed to.'

'Yes. Anyway, you look soggy. Did you get caught in that downpour?' Nathan put his tea down on the floor and reached out to take mine from me. 'I think this is the point where I'm supposed to say, "We should really get you out of those wet clothes…".' He pulled me into his arms and moved in for a kiss, but I suddenly remembered Tony's riverbank find. I pulled away.

'Hold that thought! I found something at Boskern.' I fumbled in my pocket and pulled out the necklace. 'Tony found it on the riverbank.'

He frowned. 'What was Tony doing, poking about at my crime scene?'

'He wasn't, he came along for the judging. He didn't realise it's happening tomorrow. We walked along the path by the river to get to the car park – we weren't anywhere near the crime scene. It was muddy, he slipped, and he found this. It looked like it had been washed up on the bank. Recently as well, because it was relatively clean.' I handed him the necklace. 'It's a religious medallion, isn't it? I don't know who the saint's meant to be, though.'

Nathan took it, but I could tell he still wasn't particularly happy about Tony's involvement. He knew that we were close friends, had been for years, and he knew (I hoped) that we would only ever be friends, but I still got the impression that he occasionally felt a bit jealous.

'She's obviously a patron saint of something,' said Nathan, turning the medal over in his hands and bringing me back to the subject. 'I don't know what, though.'

'I know nothing at all about saints or anything like that,' I said. 'I'm not exactly a regular churchgoer. Weddings, christenings and funerals, that's it.'

Nathan laughed. 'I don't. Look.' He leaned over and picked up his keys, which he'd left on the coffee table in front of us. 'I've got one of my own.' There was a medallion on his key ring, a different saint to the one we'd found. 'Saint Michael, patron saint of police officers.'

'Saint Michael? I thought he was patron saint of good-quality underwear and Percy the Pig sweets?'

'And Colin the Caterpillar cakes. He's either a multitasker or there's two Saint Michaels.' He jingled his keys. 'My mum bought me this when I graduated from police college.'

'Oh God, don't tell me you're a left-footer,' I said.

'"Left-footer"?'

'Roman Catholic. That's what my grandad used to call them. I told you, long line of heathens in my family. Not much time for religion. Apparently my nana *was* religious, but after she had three miscarriages in a row she changed her mind. My mum was a bit of a miracle baby, but don't tell her that or she'll be even more insufferable.' I studied the female saint on the necklace. 'So what's this one a patron saint of?'

'Could be anything. We have a lot of saints. And I mean *a lot*. Lots of professions have their own. Some have more than one. Fishermen have Saint Peter and Saint Andrew.'

'I thought Saint Andrew was Scotland?'

'Like I said, some saints are multitaskers. I don't know half of them. I *am* a Catholic, but a very lapsed one. So don't go using me, thinking I'll get you into Heaven...'

'Bold of you to assume I want to go there. They say the Devil has all the best tunes... So who would be able to tell us who this is? Do you know the local vicar or something?'

'Priest. No, I don't, but we can easily find one. More to the point, do we really think this is linked to the murder? I suppose Harry Dodds could have been wearing it. When he fell forward it got caught on ... something ... and ended up in the river. And the rain helped it wash up downriver, on the bank where you – where *Tony* found it. This is not the patron saint of teachers, though. That's Saint John. Maybe someone just lost it while they were out for a walk.'

'Or maybe the murderer was wearing it.'

'Maybe...' Nathan sat back, his brow furrowed. 'I think we need to find out who this saint is, don't you?'

'Yep.' I stretched out. My clothes were still a bit damp, but the cottage was warm and I was starting to feel very cosy. 'I love this cottage.'

Nathan looked surprised. 'Do you? I didn't think you would.'

'What's not to love? It's gorgeous. Tiny, but very romantic. I can just imagine us, stretched out on the rug in front of the fire...'

'With your mum in the kitchen and Daisy upstairs playing on her phone,' said Nathan. I sighed.

'Yeah, I know. My house is far more practical. No cavorting in front of the fire, though.'

Nathan grinned. 'I do enjoy a good cavort, I can't deny it. But our days of doing that here are numbered. Look at this.' He stood up and crossed to a sideboard against the wall, picking up a letter and handing it to me. 'From my landlady.'

Nathan rented the cottage from a lovely, but very elderly, lady called Maureen Tyack. She'd lived in Penstowan all her life, and was Cornish born and bred; I doubted she'd ever even got as far upcountry as Exeter. The letter was handwritten, the words shaky, but I could still just about read it.

'Wait, is she evicting you?' I asked, scanning the page.

'Not yet,' said Nathan. 'Her son has taken over all her financial affairs now, and he seems keen to get into the holiday rental market. I don't blame him, they could almost get the same money for a week's rental in high season as I pay for a month. Maureen was more interested in having a long-term tenant who'd look after the place than making loads of money. I think she's trying to hold out, but Sergeant Adams knows her son and he reckons he'll keep pestering her until she gives in and lets him chuck me out.'

'But you've got a lease?'

'I signed a year's rental agreement when I moved in, but I've been here longer than that now, and it's moved to a month by month lease. They could kick me out with only a month's warning if they wanted to.' He sat down and looked at me. 'So I suppose I should start looking for somewhere else to live.'

The question was unspoken, but I knew what he was thinking.

'Don't be daft, you can move in with me,' I said, and then wished I hadn't, because what if that hadn't been what he was thinking? What if I was moving too fast and it scared him off?

'Are you sure? I mean, I think we're heading that way, aren't we?' he said, taking my hand. 'But I wouldn't want you to think I'm only moving in because I'd be homeless otherwise.'

'That hadn't even crossed my mind,' I said, only now of course it *was* crossing my mind. He frowned.

'Bugger, now you're thinking that's why I want to move in,' he said.

'No, no...'

He laughed. 'I know you, Jodie.' And suddenly it was OK. He *did* know me, even though we hadn't been together that long. 'I know we haven't been together that long,' he said, and I thought, *oh my God, we are SO in tune with each other!* 'But when you know, you know.'

I gazed into his eyes. 'I know.' We both jumped as a small, furry and determined head found its way onto our laps. Germaine gazed up at us both and gave a little *ruff!* 'Germaine knows, too...'

'Thank you for agreeing to meet us, Father,' said Nathan. Father Thomas smiled.

'My pleasure,' he said. 'Always happy to help the police.'

Nathan and I had Googled the nearest Catholic church to Penstowan, and had arranged to meet the local priest there. He was young – in his thirties, maybe – and very tall; he looked more like a basketball player than a man of God, apart from the dog collar, of course. We stood outside the Church of Saint Peter, on the outskirts of Bude. Instead of the stained-glass windows and vaulted ceilings that I had been imagining, the church was a modest brick building from the 1970s, 1980s perhaps; it bore about as much resemblance to Westminster Cathedral as the Taj Mahal Indian restaurant on Fore Street did to the actual palace in Agra. But then if God exists, He's meant to be everywhere, and He should be able to find his followers even if they *were* sitting in a building that looked more like a doctors' surgery than a place of worship.

Father Thomas unlocked the door of the church and stood aside to let us in. 'I hate having to lock the door,' he said, 'but unfortunately these days there are people desperate enough to try and steal from the church. Not that we have anything much of value here.'

I entered and looked around. It felt somehow friendly inside, less intimidating than a traditional church usually would to me. I always felt out of place in churches, as if at some point someone would turn around and point at me, and loudly denounce me as a sinner or something. Not here, though. One end of the room – the business end, I thought – had a wall painted a deep red, the brass crucifix glinting against the dark paint. A small wooden altar stood in front of it, and to one side, looking slightly out of place, was a stone font. A thick carpet of the same dark red made it feel warm, despite the damp weather outside.

Nathan genuflected quickly in front of the cross,

almost an automatic reaction despite being 'lapsed', then turned back to Father Thomas. I just stood and smiled like an idiot, not sure whether I should follow suit as a sign of respect, or if that would be even more disrespectful as I wasn't a believer.

'Father, I wondered if you would be able to identify this?' asked Nathan, nodding to me. I took out the necklace, now safely wrapped in a see-through plastic evidence bag, and held it out to the priest. He went to take it and then hesitated.

'Can I touch it? What about fingerprints?' Thomas gave a small laugh. 'I'm sorry, I may have watched a few too many *CSI*-type programmes in my spare time. It's all insight into the darkest recesses of the human mind. Not that we have too many serial killers in Bude.' He stopped. 'Oh dear, I'm assuming we haven't, anyway. I do hope that's not what you're investigating.'

'Don't worry, Father,' I said. 'We only have one body on our hands. So far. And as for fingerprints, we'll keep it in the plastic bag so as not to contaminate it.' In truth, we weren't very hopeful about getting any useful fingerprints or DNA evidence off it anyway. Forensics can sometimes still get usable prints off of metal or glass that has been submerged in the water, as we suspected the necklace had been, but Tony had picked it up with muddy fingers and then automatically wiped it against his jumper in order to see it more clearly before I could stop him, subsequently (probably) also wiping off his and anyone else's fingerprints.

Father Thomas took the bag from me and held it up, studying the medal inside closely. 'Well, she's a patron saint of something, but then I'm guessing you already knew that, which is why you brought her to me. I don't know who she is off the top of my head, but I think she's been well loved. The picture is little worn.'

'Somebody rubbed her for luck?' I asked, but Thomas shook his head.

'Possibly, although it's more likely they clasped her in their hands while praying,' he said.

'So this belongs to someone who is actually religious?' I said. 'I mean, I've got a Saint Christopher kicking about somewhere from my younger days, and this is the first time I've set foot in a church since—' Since my dad's funeral. My parents might not have been religious, but Mum had been insistent that he had been buried 'proper'. I swallowed hard. 'For quite a while, anyway. No offence.'

'None taken.' Father Thomas smiled. 'There is a database of saints that I could look at... Can I take a photograph of her, then I can have a search on my computer when I get home?'

'Of course,' said Nathan. 'Thank you, that would be really helpful.'

'No problem,' said Thomas. 'I do have Mass over at

Our Lady of Victories in Callington this evening, but I should be able to have a look after that. You're welcome to join us.'

'Oh, er, thanks but…' I said, awkwardly. Nathan and the priest exchanged looks and laughed.

'He's winding you up, Jodie,' said Nathan, and I blushed.

'Sorry,' said Father Thomas. 'But even we priests like to have a laugh now and again.'

Chapter Sixteen

W e drove back to Penstowan and headed to my house, Nathan following behind me in his own car. I pulled up on the driveway, then got out and waited for him as he parked out on the road. Germaine sniffed at a lavender bush which, despite my complete lack of gardening skills and months of neglect, was flourishing in the front garden.

'Are we really going to do this?' I asked him.

'No time like the present,' he said. He pulled me towards him, my head resting on his shoulder. 'We have to make sure your mum and Daisy are OK with me moving in before I give notice on the cottage.'

'Daisy is,' I said. He raised an eyebrow. 'We've talked about it. She likes you. Just don't be like her dad—'

'You know I would never try to replace him.'

'No, I mean don't be a dick and you'll be fine.'

He laughed. 'I'll bear that in mind.'

The front door opened to reveal Daisy, in a pinny.

'Oh good, I thought I heard you out here,' she said. 'Nana was threatening –'

'Offering,' I corrected.

'– to make shepherd's pie again, so I made chilli before she could get near the saucepans.' Germaine jumped at Daisy then, nose twitching, trotted off into the house, following the smell of dinner. Daisy laughed and followed suit.

'Let's wait until after dinner to say anything,' I said, and Nathan nodded.

But we didn't get a chance to announce our news, because as soon as the last mouthful of my daughter's delicious chilli was gone, Mum made an announcement of her own.

'Now I know you've been wondering where I went the other day,' she said solemnly, and my heart sank. Daisy and I exchanged glances. I knew that she'd reassured us that she wasn't ill, but this didn't sound good.

'Oh no, Nana, you're ill, aren't you?' said Daisy, and she looked so scared that I reached across the table and grabbed her hand. But Mum just snorted impatiently.

'No I'm not blooming ill! Honestly, the way you lot go on about me you'd think I had one foot in the grave or something. I'm not some little old lady.' We all avoided each other's eyes and she snorted again. 'I'm seventy-one, not a hundred and one. Fit as the proverbial.' I opened my mouth to speak, but she jumped in quick to stop me. 'Apart from the angina, and me high blood pressure, and me cholesterol, but I'm on pills for all of those. Never took a day off work sick in me life.'

It was my turn to snort then. 'Rubbish. What about that time you kept me off school so we could go Christmas shopping in Exeter? You were working at the Co-op then. The next time I went in there they asked if your tummy bug had gone.'

'That's different, I weren't sick, I just wanted a day off with me daughter. Anyway, you want to know where I went or what?'

'Er... I'm not sure I should be in this conversation...' Nathan stood up awkwardly, but Mum motioned him to sit down.

'No, no, this involves you, love,' she said, smiling at him. Nathan sat down again. 'You're family now. Right. OK, it wasn't the doctor I was seeing, it was the estate agent. I'm putting my house up for sale.'

I let my breath out. 'Is that it? Thank God for that. I've been telling you for ages that it's a waste just having it sitting there, empty.'

'I haven't finished. Once it's sold I'll be moving into one of them retirement flats down by the new Tesco's.'

'What?' I stared at her in astonishment. 'You said moving to a retirement home was like throwing in the towel, admitting you're not long for this world and getting a step closer to the undertaker. Why on earth are you moving?'

'It's not a retirement home, it's a retirement flat. This house is starting to get a bit crowded, innit?' she said.

'Oh Shirley…' started Nathan, but she reached out and patted his hand.

'It's all right, love, I can see how it's going with the two of you. Won't be long before you're here permanently, will it? You won't want your mother-in-law —' I growled at her. 'I know you're not about to get married, but you know what I mean. Moving in together is a big enough step without me being here as well.'

'No, Mum, it's fine, Nathan doesn't mind,' I said, but how did I know? We hadn't really talked about her being there, I'd just assumed she always would be and that he understood that.

'Shirley, please don't move out on my account,' said Nathan. 'It never occurred to me that you wouldn't be living here too. I knew when I fell in love with Jodie—' Daisy made a half-hearted puking noise, but I thought she was too upset at the thought of Mum leaving to mean it. 'I always knew she came as a package. The four Parker females.'

'Four?'

'Germaine,' said Nathan. 'Can't leave her out of it. So don't do anything because of me.'

'Please, Mum,' I said. I was surprised at how upset the thought of her moving out made me, and I could see that Daisy felt the same too. I hadn't expected her to all but move in when we'd come to Penstowan, and she could be annoying, and embarrassing, and frustrating, and made the worst lumpy mashed potatoes in the world, but I'd got used to having her around. And I couldn't imagine her not being here. I felt myself getting choked up. None of us know how long we really have with our loved ones. Dad had left us far too early, and although Mum was relatively healthy for her age, I didn't know how much longer we'd have her for. I swallowed back the ridiculous sentimental tears that were threatening. 'Please don't make any hasty decisions. Wait until the house is sold before you even think about buying somewhere else. If you decide you really want to move into one of those flats, then fine, but don't rush into it. Stay here for now and at least see what it's like with all of us here.'

'Is Nathan moving in, then?' asked Daisy.

I nodded. 'Soon.'

'But only if that's OK with you,' said Nathan, quickly. 'I don't want to upset anyone.'

'As long as I don't have to watch you two snogging all the time,' she said, with a roll of her eyes and a *what-are-you-two-like?* expression on her face. I laughed.

'We'll do our best to control ourselves,' I said.

I sat on the wall at the back of the garden, looking out over the sheep field and on towards the edge of the cliffs. Dusk had fallen, and it was starting to get dark out over the ocean.

Nathan joined me with two mugs of tea, and sat down next to me.

'Where are the sheep?' he said, glancing around.

'I think the farmer moves them to another meadow now and again to give the grass a chance to grow back,' I said.

Nathan put on a country yokel accent. 'Ahh, them's the old country ways…' I poked him in the ribs. 'What? That's how you lot talk, isn't it?'

'I don't.'

'No, you sound more Cockney than anything else. All those years in London. I'm surprised you even remember what a sheep is.'

I poked him again. 'You can talk, city boy. You sound

a bit posh when you're on duty, but when you relax you sound like a Scouser again.'

'Strictly speaking I'm from Crosby, not Liverpool, so I don't count as a Scouser.'

'Yeah yeah, Crosby, Liverpool, tomayto tomarto.'

'Yeah, it's like Cornwall and Devon, isn't it? Basically the same county…' He laughed at my furious expression and leaned in to kiss me before I could tell him off. 'Am I still allowed to move in?'

'Yeah,' I said, but then I felt sad, thinking about my mum. He hugged me.

'I was thinking, you know, you've got a lot of room down the side of the house here…'

'So?'

'So we could build a granny annex for your mum.'

I laughed. 'Oh she *loves* being called a granny…'

'Think about it, though. We could build an extension. I put some money aside for a deposit on a house, when I thought Andrea was going to join me down here.' Andrea was Nathan's ex, back in Liverpool. They'd planned to both move down here to raise a family, but she had (thankfully) got cold feet and stayed behind. 'And your mum will have the money from the house, if she wanted to chip in. I noticed the other day, one of your neighbours has done something like that. They've built out over their garage and made a big two-storey extension…'

I followed Nathan's gaze and tried to imagine an extension. It would take up a lot of the garden, but to be honest, with my brown rather than green fingers, the lawn and plants I would lose would probably be relieved to be out of my unintentionally murderous way.

'Or we could buy a bigger house,' said Nathan. 'But I know what this one means to you.'

'We could...' I said thoughtfully. But we were prevented from discussing it further by Nathan's phone ringing.

'It's Father Thomas,' he said, glancing at the screen. He answered, putting it on speaker so I could hear.

'Good evening, Father,' said Nathan politely, and I was reminded that underneath the hunky and occasionally gruff copper's exterior there was an angelic Catholic schoolboy. I made a mental note to ask if he'd been an altar boy, and giggled to myself; I couldn't imagine him in one of those smocks, swinging the incense burner.

'Good evening, DCI Withers. I have some news for you regarding the medallion you showed me.'

'Were you able to find out who the saint was?' asked Nathan.

'I certainly was. Saint Catherine of Siena. She lived in the mid-1300s. Often depicted, as I think she is on this medallion, although it's hard to see because it's clearly quite old and has been worn down a bit – often depicted carrying a rose, a crucifix, a book and a skull. The first three are easy to spot on the medallion, but the skull is harder to see, as it's in the folds of her dress. Anyway, that's how I managed to identify her. She was a lay member of the Dominican Order, and an author who had a great influence on Italian literature.'

'So what is she a patron saint of? Writers or something?' I asked.

'That's Miss Parker, I take it? No, she's the patron saint of several things, actually, but not writers. People use her as protection against fire. She's the patron saint of Europe, of places in the USA and the Philippines, of people ridiculed for their piety—'

'She's a multitasker,' I said, looking at Nathan. He nodded.

'She's definitely a busy woman,' said Father Thomas. 'She's also patron saint of sexual temptation – resisting it, I assume, rather than giving in to it!'

'What about professions?' I asked. 'Nath – DCI Withers has a medal of Saint Michael because he's a police officer. Anything like that?'

'Oh yes. She's protection against bodily ills, for women who have had miscarriages, and nurses.'

'So a nurse might carry one, in the same way that I do?' asked Nathan.

'Yes. I would say, from the quite extensive list of things she's a patron saint of, the most likely person to carry one of these regularly, and pray with it regularly, would be a nurse.'

Nathan disconnected the call and looked at me.

'You know who's a nurse?' he asked.

'Er…well, Debbie used to be one, but I don't think she murdered Harry Dodds…'

'I can't believe you've forgotten her. The victim's wife. Sarah Dodds.'

I stared at him, open-mouthed. 'Oh my God … of course she is! And what did I tell you? It's always the spouse.'

'Except when it's not.' Nathan sighed. 'She has an alibi, remember? She was with a client all day at his home. Matt checked with her agency and they confirmed it.'

'Yeah… But how do they know that she really was there?'

'After we caught her at the pub, after she was supposed to have gone home, I did a little more digging.'

'Oh yeah?'

'Yeah. And it just backs up her story even more. We checked the GPS on her phone, and it was in the Bristol area all day.'

'So she left her phone there, it doesn't mean…'

'And we have proof that her car was parked outside all day. I got the local guys to check it out, see if the neighbours could confirm seeing her, but they did better than that. Her client has one of those video doorbells, so he can see who it is and let them in without having to come to the door. Apparently some days he can move about OK, but other days, like the day of the murder, he can't even get out of bed. Anyway, it records callers to the house and keeps the video for a month, and when they looked back at that day, Sarah Dodds's car was parked right outside the house, in view of the doorbell's camera, from nine in the morning until around five fifteen in the afternoon.'

'So she can't have done it...' I groaned. 'That's a shame, because we've exhausted the possibility that Harry was mistaken for Russell—'

'Yes, I think we have. None of the people who were apparently gunning for him were gunning for him enough to kill him.'

'So we're back at square one. Harry *was* the intended victim after all. But no one on the roadshow really knew him, apart from Indira, but I can't see her motive for killing him. Plus she was in the baking tent for most of the murder window. And it ties in nicely with Sarah Dodds hanging around after she'd told you she was going home.'

'And lying about it when I rang her,' Nathan agreed.

'She could have been waiting, hoping for a chance to come back and find her necklace.'

'If it even *is* her necklace,' I said. 'Maybe it isn't. Or maybe she'd given it to Harry. What was the other thing Father Thomas said it protected against? Sexual temptation? Maybe she didn't trust him, being away from home for months. Maybe their marriage was in trouble and she thought he'd play away.'

'Maybe that was why he joined the roadshow,' said Nathan. 'To have some time away from her. Maybe they were on a break.'

We looked at each other thoughtfully.

'That's a lot of maybes,' said Nathan.

'And maybe they're all wrong,' I said.

Chapter Seventeen

I woke up the next morning an hour before the alarm went off. I lay there in the semi-darkness. It was six o'clock, so it was still pretty dark outside, but I always left a night light plugged in on the landing in case Mum or Daisy (or me) ever needed to get up in the night, and it sent a soft glow under the gap at the bottom of my bedroom door. I rolled over to look at Nathan, but he was fast asleep and I could only just make out the shape of him under all the bedclothes. He was one of those people who are always cold in bed, whereas I was always hot and just as likely to be found lying on top of my duvet as under it. He gave a sudden heavy snore, but I found it sweet, which meant I was absolutely done for; completely smitten, my mum would have said.

I heard snuffling outside my door. Germaine was up and bursting to go outside, and Daisy, whose bed she would probably have spent the night on, had either slept through the commotion or (more likely) just didn't want to get up. *Mum'll do it…* I gently slid out of the bed, not wanting to wake Nathan, and padded downstairs with the dog at my heels.

I stood in the open kitchen doorway as she went and had a sniff outside. It was Judgement Day – in the baking roadshow sense, rather than the biblical one. I wasn't sure if I was nervous about it; I was excited, definitely, but I'd never thought I'd get this far, let alone win, and the other two bakers were much better than I was. Plus I hadn't exactly focused on the contest, had I? I'd spent as much time investigating as I had baking. I didn't really deserve to win. Still wanted to, though…

I left Germaine interrogating a highly suspicious weed and put the kettle on as I thought about the day ahead.

Everyone was coming to the roadshow today, and I mean *everyone*. Mum, Daisy and Nathan, of course; but also Tony, as one of the judges, and his parents, Brenda and Malcolm. Debbie, her husband Callum and their two kids were coming too, and since she'd posted about it on Facebook the night before I'd had a string of 'good luck' texts, and people telling me they were coming along to cheer me on. It felt like I was probably going to lose in front of the entire town, but I actually didn't mind; it was nice to have their support.

Nathan appeared in T-shirt and boxers as the kettle boiled, and we sat at the kitchen table chatting as we drank our tea. We didn't talk about the case, even though I was dying to. I'd noticed with Nathan that, when he got stuck on an investigation, he would get to a point where he stopped talking about it; not because he didn't want to, but because he knew that he would just keep going round in circles if he did. Sometimes deliberately NOT thinking or talking about it would allow his mind just enough peace and quiet to work it out, or at least give him some new ideas. I kind of did the same thing when I was faced with a knotty problem. I'd go off and do something that required almost no mental effort but a fair bit of physical labour, like digging a hole in the garden or cleaning the car (which didn't happen very often). I reckoned that, if I just let him be, he'd be due a flash of inspiration round about lunchtime.

Slowly the rest of the house woke up and had breakfast and got dressed. Mum and Daisy chattered excitedly about the roadshow, telling me that I was sure to win. And now my nerves kicked in. I still knew deep down that the other two bakers were better than I was, and more deserving – they'd put more into it than me –

but my family's (completely misplaced) confidence in me was allowing me to hope...

We drove over to Boskern, and got there in time to see the early morning clouds roll away and the sun come out. There was still a slight chill in the air, but it looked like it was going to be a beautiful day. Members of the crew were putting chairs out onto a grassy area near the baking tent. It was a bit muddy underfoot, so we were left to hang around in the car park until we were needed, Camilla not wanting us to churn up the grass and make it look messy before filming.

Elaine arrived, along with her own supporters. Her two children were adorable, all freckles, wide eyes and curly auburn hair like their mum. Her husband gazed at her proudly as she chatted with the rapidly growing crowd of people who had come to watch. Martin arrived, resplendent in a long-sleeved tunic-type shirt and a striped waistcoat, both of which looked like they were made out of some kind of hessian or hemp or something. The crystal he typically wore around his neck had been swapped for a *Khamsa* – a lucky hand symbol. I thought again of the medallion we'd found, and wondered if Nathan had had his epiphany or moment of inspiration yet. Sarah Dodds had seemed like the obvious suspect, once we'd discovered exactly who Saint Catherine was, but she had a very firm alibi. Were any other members of the crew ex-nurses, perhaps? Or what else had she been patron saint of? She was supposed to protect against miscarriages; were any of the crew pregnant, maybe? I surreptitiously glanced around to see if I could spot any likely-looking tummy bulges, but it struck me that since I'd left the Force and had cut back on exercise, I'd put weight on and would probably pass for at least four months' pregnant, maybe five in a tight-fitting T-shirt. And I could hardly go up to someone and ask whether they were expecting a baby or just a bit chubby; I could end up with a mouthful of abuse or even a black eye, and I wouldn't blame them. Maybe Camilla would know if anyone on her crew was pregnant? I made a mental note to mention it to Nathan. Where was he?

I turned and there he was on the other side of the car park, talking to Tony, who had just arrived with his parents. As ever, I felt a weird mix of emotions watching them together. I was really glad they were friends, but I felt absurdly guilty that Nathan had no idea that Tony and I had kissed. At the same time I had no intention of ever telling him about it. And despite the fact that Tony and I had both agreed that we really didn't want to be anything more than friends, I still felt guilty about him, too; I worried about him being lonely, and when he'd mentioned that he'd talked to his ex, Cheryl – that had *really* worried me. I hadn't liked her when they were together, and she'd turned out to be bad news. But he'd loved her. Sometimes you couldn't just turn it off, even if the object of your affections wasn't worthy of them.

Tony waved and I joined them.

'I was just updating Tony on the medal you found,' said Nathan.

'Patron Saint of Nurses, eh?' mused Tony. 'Could've done with one of them after I fell down the riverbank! Got bruises all up me leg.'

'Oh no! Did you get yourself checked out at the doc's?' I asked. He shook his head.

'Don't fuss, woman! I'm fine.' But he shifted the weight off his leg with a little grimace.

'Really?' I gave him an unconvinced look, and he grinned.

'Does she do that to you?' he asked Nathan.

'What, see through me when I try and lie to her?' Nathan shook his head. 'I wouldn't know, because I've never lied to her...'

I snorted. 'Yeah, right. Not even when we first met... Seriously, Tone, there must be a first aider round here or something. They could look at you.'

'First aider?' said Nathan sharply. I facepalmed.

'Of course! Indira! She looked after me when I, er, felt faint.'

'*Pretended* to feel faint.'

'Whatever. She might not be a nurse, but she's definitely had medical training because she also dealt with Elaine's cut finger. Maybe the medallion belongs to her?'

'Yeah...' Nathan looked thoughtful. 'Which means she could've just dropped it one day walking between the tent and the car park.'

'Except she's always one of the first ones here, so she normally gets a space right up here and not down in the car park.' I looked at Nathan. 'And of course who was Harry's only friend on the crew?'

'Isn't she the one who you said, and I quote, was "too nice" to be a murderer?' Nathan looked amused.

'Yeah, and you told me most murderers are nice until you upset them and they bludgeon you to death with a rock.' I looked around. 'Where is she? I can't see her.'

'I'll ask around,' said Nathan. 'But it looks like things are happening...'

They were indeed. Russell – or rather Barbara – appeared from the hair and make-up tent, staggering across the rough ground in a skin-tight zebra-print outfit complete with matching hat. She spotted Mum and waved to her.

'All right, babes?' she said, seeming genuinely pleased to see her. Mum preened; everyone was watching her talking to the star of the show.

'I'm all right, my love. You don't seem too steady on them shoes, though.' Mum pointed to Barbara's towering stilettos. Barbara groaned.

'Oh, tell me about it!' she said, grabbing Mum's arm and leaning towards her in a confidential way. 'I think I'm getting bunions, just like you said. Some days I could play football in these heels, other days, like today, I can barely walk.' Something sparked in my brain, but I couldn't put my finger on it. She looked over and saw me and Nathan watching her. 'Here for the judges' announcement or to harass innocent drag queens?'

Mum snorted. 'If you're innocent I'll eat that hat of yours.' Barbara looked offended for a second, then burst out laughing. She nudged Mum.

'Being naughty's always been more fun than being good, innit? You're a woman after me own heart, Shirl.' She turned to Nathan, holding her hands out, wrists upwards. 'It's true. I'm guilty of being the most fabulous creature on the roadshow. You better cuff me, babe.'

'I don't have my handcuffs with me, so I'll have to trust you to behave.' Nathan leaned towards her and carried on in an undertone. 'We tracked down your lunchtime companion from the day of the murder and she confirmed your alibi.'

'Straight from the horse's mouth,' said Barbara, and my brain tingled again, but again, I couldn't put my finger on it.

'Hello, everyone!' We all turned to see Camilla and the show's judges standing in front of the baking tent. 'Thank you so much for coming today, and thank you to all the friends and family who have come along to support you!' Her eyes swept the crowd, lingering for a moment on Martin, who was standing to one side, apparently on his own. I felt a sudden wave of sympathy for him; surely he had family, or friends, or *someone* who cared enough to come along and watch? Maybe that explained why he had been so focused on winning; maybe he didn't have much else going on in his life. That was just sad.

'Families and supporters, if you could all make your way to the seats now that would be great.' Camilla indicated the rows of chairs. In front of them was a table, with bottles of champagne and glasses, and some bouquets of flowers, as well as the winner's trophy: a small glass rolling pin with the words 'Regional Winner' etched on it. There was also another, longer table with a buffet of sandwiches, scones and so on laid out on it. They really were pushing the boat out this season, it seemed; they didn't normally make much of a fuss over the regional final. But Camilla had said this was to be Esme's last roadshow, so they were making sure she went out on a high. 'Please help yourself to some food, enjoy yourselves and we'll get to the big announcement shortly. Contestants, if you'd like to come and collect your cakes and unveil them to the crowd, then the judges will say a few words.'

Nathan, Mum and Daisy gathered round me to wish

me luck. Germaine stood up on her hind legs, front paws against my knees, and gazed up at me in a way that meant *'knock 'em dead, Mum'* (don't ask me how I knew that, I just did). I kissed my daughter, patted my dog, and then left them to find a seat or, in Germaine's case, someone gullible enough to fall for her puppy dog eyes and get her a sausage roll from the buffet.

Elaine and Martin followed Camilla. I turned to go after them, but stopped as I passed Barbara.

'Where's Indira?' I asked. 'I wanted to make sure I thanked her properly for looking after me the other day when I felt unwell. I don't want to leave later without saying goodbye.'

'You've missed her.' Barbara looked solemn. 'She's gone.'

'Gone? Gone where?' I said, surprised. 'You and her – you haven't—' Barbara shrugged, but I could tell she was upset. 'Look, I'm sure you'll work things out...'

'Jodie, we need you!' called Camilla behind me. *Dammit!*

'I hope so,' said Barbara. 'But I think I screwed things up.' I patted her on the arm, wanting to say more but not really able to think of anything. Because Russell *had* screwed up. I hoped it wouldn't be the end of them.

The others were waiting outside the production van. I suddenly wondered if my saboteur had managed to get into the vehicle and get their mitts on my cake, but the van door was still locked, and there was no sign of anyone forcing it open then closing it again. So if my cake had mysteriously developed a wonk overnight, or if my chocolate fish suddenly tasted of real mackerel, then it shouldn't be hard to work out who had had access to the keys.

I held my breath as Camilla herself unlocked the doors and flung them open ... and then let it out in relief. My cake was still standing, and it actually looked better than I remembered it. It just had to taste good now.

We all gingerly removed our cakes from the back of the van and tottered across the grass to the judging table. Martin's cake in particular was literally a towering achievement of sponge-based engineering, and as such it wasn't an easy thing to manoeuvre. I'd been worried enough about dropping my own showstopper, but my heart was in my mouth as I watched him carry his masterpiece over the rough ground.

But we all made it to the judges' table safely, and carefully placed our bakes in front of the judges. As well as Pete and Esme, and Tony, of course, there were two other local guest judges; Nick Jackson, a restaurateur who owned a chain of fish restaurants in St Ives, Padstow and Falmouth, and Victoria Benfield, a writer from Cambourne who had penned a series of steamy historical novels set around Land's End – kind of like *Bridgerton* meets *Poldark*. I smiled at them both, then turned to Tony and muttered, 'Bloody hell, Tony, how did you get a place on this judging panel?'

He laughed. 'I know! I feel well out of place. They wanted Maurice really, didn't they? He'd have come along in his mayoral chain and all that. But he finally got a date for his hernia op and it clashed, so here I am.'

'Thank God for Maurice's hernia and the good old NHS,' I said, and we both laughed. But Martin, next to me, did not find it quite as funny.

'Hang on, you know each other?' he said, looking round for Camilla. *Uh-oh*, I thought.

'Yeah,' said Tony. He gestured to Camilla, who had noticed something was going on and approached us. 'I told the boss lady I did, and she said it didn't matter.'

'Well, that don't seem fair,' said Martin belligerently. Camilla glared at him and then cleared her throat.

'Mr Penhaligon told me he knew Jodie when he agreed to be our replacement judge and I said it didn't matter. For starters, he's just one judge out of five.' She turned to Tony. 'Not to sound ungrateful for your involvement, but if necessary the professional judges' votes are taken into account more than the local guest ones, in order to mitigate just this sort of situation. Lynda was from St Ives. If she'd made it through to the end, then Nick Jackson might have voted for her even if he didn't know her, just because he has business interests in St Ives himself.'

'So you don't really expect the guest judges to be impartial?' I asked, and she gave a small shrug.

'We hope they will be, but... Even if they fully intend to be, if there are two bakers who they think are equally good and they can't choose between them, who do you think they end up voting for? The one they have the most in common with. It's human nature.'

'Hmm...' said Martin, but he didn't sound convinced. Camilla glared at him again.

'The guest judges were agreed upon well in advance, and when the previous judge dropped out and suggested Mr Penhaligon to replace him, we didn't have time to find someone else,' she said. 'If Jodie hadn't got through to the final it wouldn't have been a problem.'

I looked at her sharply. My senses were tingling AGAIN but this time it was all about the roadshow sabotage, not Harry Dodds's murder. Maybe I wasn't *supposed* to be in the final? I'd suspected Martin, primarily because I'd thought he was a bit of a dick and he'd upset me on day one with his reaction to my cake decorating, but maybe it wasn't him. Maybe it wasn't one of my rivals at all. Maybe it had been Camilla? She would have had access to every part of the tent, and could wander in and out as she pleased without drawing attention to herself. But why? Because Tony being a judge gave me an unfair advantage of winning? But she'd just completely refuted that.

Tony was looking at me quizzically. I shook myself. Did it matter anyway, as I was in the final round now? I smiled broadly at Camilla.

'Before we start, can I just ask where Indira is? I found something of hers and I wanted to make sure she got it back.'

Was it me, or did Camilla look relieved that I'd changed the subject?

'She's not here today, she needed to go home this weekend,' she said. Out of the corner of my eye I saw Tony shoot me a meaningful look.

'Oh dear, was it a family emergency or something? I hope everything's OK,' I said. Camilla smiled and shook her head.

'No, nothing like that, just a family wedding. She's been looking forward to it for ages. What did you find?'

I made a show of patting my jeans pockets and coming up empty. 'I must've left it in the car. It's a silver necklace, a medallion of Saint Catherine on a chain. I thought it was hers, do you remember seeing her wear it?'

'A saint? You mean like a Catholic thing?' She shook her head, amused. 'I wouldn't have thought it was Indira's. Her family are Sikh.'

'Are you sure? I mean, I guessed her family was from India, obviously, but she's British Asian, isn't she, so I didn't know...'

'Positive. She was telling me about this wedding, how it'll go on for days. I can ask around later and see if it belongs to anyone else, if you like?'

'No, no, it's fine. We should probably get on with the judging, shouldn't we?' I said, and she nodded, necklace forgotten. She clapped her hands.

'Let's get this show on the road!'

Chapter Eighteen

I turned round and looked at the assembled crowd. More people had turned up now but, I was relieved to see, not the entire town as I'd feared. Debbie and Callum were there, their kids playing with Germaine and sneakily feeding her bits of sandwich when they thought no one was looking. A whole other bunch of people had turned up, and as I watched, one of them – a young guy in his twenties – gave Martin a thumbs up. Also part of the group was a woman of around my mum's age, maybe a little younger; she was quite overweight, unlike Martin, who was thin and wiry, but the family resemblance was clear, even if the blonde hair was probably out of a bottle. His mum, surely. I was pleased that he did have someone there cheering him on after all.

I turned and saw Nathan watching me. He gave me a brilliant smile and held up crossed fingers. I grinned and turned back to the judges, but not before spotting Mum giving the woman who I was assuming was Martin's mum a thorough once-over. What was she like? And they called *me* nosey!

'Welcome to the roadshow, mesdames et messieurs, boys and girls, babes and bros!' cried Barbara. 'This is the moment we've all been waiting for! The final judging, to decide which of our magnificent bakers goes on to represent Cornwall in the grand nationwide final!'

The crowd cheered and clapped. There was even a little bit of whooping, which may well have come from Debbie. I exchanged grins with Elaine, who was jigging about from foot to foot with excitement. Either that or she needed to visit the Portaloos.

Pete stepped forward. 'The challenge was to create a showstopper that represented something you love about Cornwall. They all look amazing, but remember they have to taste good too. So let's start with this one here...'

The judges all turned their attention to Elaine's cake. It looked great. Pete cut it into small pieces, and all five judges took a few bites. Barbara edged her way in between Tony and the author, Victoria.

'You don't think I spent the whole week eating salad to *not* get any cake, do you?' she said, elbowing Victoria out of the way. Everyone laughed, even Victoria, despite the fact Barbara's elbows looked pretty sharp in the zebra print and the tip of her massive hat was threatening to poke her in the eye.

The verdict was pretty much unanimous. 'Absolutely scrumptious,' Esme declared. They moved on to Martin's cake, which was in the middle of the table. Everyone admired the engineering that had gone into it, and there were gasps of delight when he reached out and turned the wheel of the winding house, bringing the tiny Meccano cage up out of a hole in the cake.

'Seems a shame to cut into it,' said Nick the restaurateur, and everyone murmured in agreement. But they still did. Again, it was pronounced delicious. Then they moved on to my cake.

'I love this one,' said Tony, and I cringed slightly, because obviously he knew it was mine, and even if he *did* genuinely love it, Martin would be convinced he was trying to sway the judging because of our relationship. Martin did seem to stiffen to attention at the sound of Tony's voice, and I wondered if he was waiting for Tony to say anything else incriminating.

But the other judges loved the decoration too, although Pete did point out that the mermaid had a bit of a squint and probably should've gone to Specsavers. He cut the cake into small pieces, also pulling off one of the chocolate fish and slicing that up too.

'That tastes as good as it looks,' said Tony, and I

almost groaned. But Martin actually *did* groan. The crowd looked at him, and Camilla rushed over to shut him up, signalling the camera crew to stop filming and moving him away from the crowd. Elaine and I exchanged looks and followed them.

'He's her friend, of course he's going to say nice things about it!' protested Martin. Camilla put her hand on his arm, but he shook it off. 'It's cheating!'

'You're worried about cheating, when it was *my* chocolate custard that got tampered with?' I said, and Martin looked shocked.

'What? You think – I didn't know—' he stuttered. The crowd of supporters, who had maintained a bit of distance from the judging table as per the crew's instructions, pressed forward, sensing a scandal or at the very least a bit of an argument, but they were too far away to hear. Barbara, sensing the possibility of some brown stuff (not chocolate) hitting the fan, inserted herself between them and us like the pro she was, and started entertaining them with anecdotes about the filming process. I turned to Nathan, who had joined me with a bemused expression on his face.

'You said, when I got in, that you were surprised they let me enter. You said I must have an unfair advantage over the other contestants.'

He nodded. 'Yeah. The rules said you couldn't be a

professional baker, but they didn't say you couldn't enter if you'd trained as a chef.'

'But someone who's been to catering college *must* have an advantage over a housewife, an anaesthetist and a retired teacher, right?' I turned to Camilla. 'So that's why I got a spot. Martin doesn't work as a baker, but he *does* work as a chef. Technically, it's not against the rules, but it doesn't really seem fair, does it? Not if everyone else in the competition was untrained. So you made sure that he *wasn't* the only trained chef in the tent.' Martin looked aghast but Camilla just stared at me, coldly. 'You know what, I bet I was meant to go out in an earlier round, to make it look even more like having a catering background wasn't an advantage. You weren't happy about me making it to the final, were you? But after Ravi cocked up the last round so badly, you couldn't persuade Pete and Esme to let him through without it looking suspicious. They would have wanted to know why you were so keen to get rid of me and keep Ravi.' I facepalmed as something else occurred to me, something that was really obvious now I thought of it. 'That's why you were so happy for me to keep disappearing to help the police with the investigation. You thought there was no way I'd get through if I was in and out of the tent all the time.'

'What you didn't allow for is the fact that my

daughter is an amazing cook,' said Mum, who as ever had managed to insinuate herself into the action, and I felt a flush of pride. She'd never told me I was an amazing cook before.

'And then when I still kept getting through, things started disappearing from my workbench, and stuff got tampered with. My hob got turned off halfway through a challenge.'

'So – so someone cheated, to get you out?' said Martin, and he genuinely looked horrified at the thought. 'I don't understand—'

'It was Camilla,' I said. 'I'm sorry, Martin, at first I thought it was you, putting salt in my custard and hiding ingredients from me. But I realised you were so intent on winning that you hardly even moved from the counter. You were too immersed in what you were doing to think about anyone else.'

'But why would Camilla be so desperate for Martin to win?' asked Elaine, confused. I shook my head.

'I don't know. Yet.'

'I *knew* I recognised you!' said Mum suddenly, looking Camilla up and down. 'You're Deirdre Hurley's youngest, aren't you? You're the spit of her.'

'What?' I was surprised, but I shouldn't have been, because between them Mum and Tony knew everybody in Cornwall. It certainly felt that way, anyway.

'I told you about her, the one that moved upcountry. To Chelsea.'

'Yeah, but – Camilla?'

'She's got her mother's nose,' said Mum. 'I thought I knew her from somewhere when I first saw her, but I couldn't put my finger on it. But that must be why I remembered that night in Chelsea with DeeDee, when I hadn't thought about her for donkey's years.' Mum shook her head. 'Her family weren't best pleased when she went into modelling, I can tell you, not until she started making enough money to send some back to them. She even bought her sister Sheila a café in Bodmin. She always dreamt of having a little tea shop by the moors.' She sniffed. 'Funny thing to dream of, if you ask me. I always dreamt about being whisked off to Egypt by Omar Sharif and having him ravish me on the banks of the river Nile, but it takes all sorts, I suppose.'

'Oh my GOD, Nana!' muttered Daisy. Mum ignored her and turned to the overweight blonde woman, who was standing on the edge of the crowd, watching everything with her jaw slowly dropping lower and lower.

'How are you these days, Sheila?'

'Not so bad, Shirl. You're looking well.' Sheila looked at Camilla, who facepalmed and beckoned her over; she obviously didn't want everyone else knowing what was going on. Sheila scampered over. 'You have to know, my Martin didn't know about any of this.'

'What?' said Martin. He looked utterly mortified by the turn things were taking, and I couldn't help but feel sorry for him. Families, huh? What are they like? 'Know about what? Mum?'

Camilla took his arm. Seeing them standing next to each other now, looking closely at them, you couldn't miss the family resemblance. Camilla was well groomed and pretty, whereas Martin was a bit of a scruff-bag, but if he had a decent haircut and a shave he probably could have passed as her brother, not just her cousin.

'I'm sorry, Martin, but you know what it's been like between my mother and yours. Even after she bought her the shop, they never really got on.' Camilla looked around at us all, like she was desperate to make us understand. 'My mother said that Aunt Sheila had never forgiven her for leaving her in this shi— this place. She said my aunt was jealous, but deep down I knew she felt guilty. So when she heard I was working on the roadshow and that we'd be coming to Cornwall, she asked me to help her make it up to Sheila.'

'By fixing it so that her son won, and getting her café some great publicity at the same time.' I looked at Sheila sternly. 'And you were OK with this, were you? Letting him win by cheating, not on his own merit? Because if you had any confidence in him, you'd have realised that he probably could have won this under his own steam anyway. He's a fabulous baker.'

Camilla sighed. 'So what happens now? Are you going to tell everyone? I'll lose my job.'

'You probably should have thought of that before,' said Nathan. 'And Martin will be disqualified, of course.'

Elaine, who had been standing quietly all through this exchange, looked up.

'Um, is that a good idea?' she asked. We all turned to look at her in surprise, because I think we'd all almost forgotten she was there. She blushed. 'The thing is, I love this show. The whole country does. If this comes out it'll be a huge scandal, and the roadshow might not survive it. That means all the work we've done is pointless, and if the show gets cancelled, all those other bakers who are looking forward to their spot on the telly won't get the chance to be in it. And it's not a nice way for Esme to go out, is it? Maybe Camilla should be allowed to finish this season and then move on to pastures new? Pastures where there's no family pressure to cheat. And Martin – well, Martin is an amazing baker, but quite frankly so are me and Jodie, so maybe the judges should just be left to make their decision in peace, on talent.'

'It would mean all of you needing to keep quiet about this,' Nathan said. Ever the policeman, I could tell he was reluctant to let Camilla and Martin off the hook. But I had to admit that Elaine had a point. The scandal would mean the end of the roadshow, and none of us wanted that.

'That's fine by me,' I said. 'Martin? Will you accept that?' He was so relieved he almost squealed with joy.

'Yes! Yes, definitely. Thank you.'

So the judges made their final deliberations. I knew Tony would be putting in a good word for me, for all his talk about being impartial, but I also knew it would probably make little difference and that the outcome would really be decided by Pete and Esme. My technical challenge had been incredible – both in how it had turned out, and that I'd managed to finish it at all – and my showstopper was probably the best cake I'd ever made. It tasted great, and it looked pretty good too. However, I didn't really think my decorating skills were a match for my rivals', and wouldn't have been even without the distraction of looking for Harry's killer.

'And the winner is...' Pete paused to look round at the assembled crowd, who had finally stopped gossiping about Camilla and Sheila's plan long enough for filming to take place, and at the three bakers. I grinned at both of my rivals – my friends – and we reached out and held each other's hands while we waited for the announcement, because we'd been through a lot together.

'Elaine!' announced Esme, and I was really happy for her because she deserved it, far more than I did. I felt a little bit sorry for Martin, but when I looked over at him he was smiling, and looked the most relaxed he had done all week. Maybe he'd realised that competitive baking wasn't good for his nerves.

Chapter Nineteen

'Never mind,' said Nathan, pulling me into his arms. 'You're still my star baker.'

We were standing a little way away from the crowd, who were tucking into the buffet and the showstopper cakes, which had now all been cut up, ready for everyone to try.

I shrugged – which is tricky when you're being hugged – and snuggled into him. 'I'm not really that bothered,' I said. 'I never expected to win, anyway. I'm more concerned about solving Harry Dodds's murder.'

'Indira's a blow-out,' said Nathan. 'I asked around and I think it's safe to say she probably wouldn't have worn a Catholic saint medal.'

'No, I know,' I said. 'It was always a long shot, wasn't it? But I've had a thought about Sarah Dodds...'

Nathan looked at me appraisingly. 'You have, have you? I've had one, too.'

'It was something Barbara said, about hearing it from the horse's mouth. When you checked Sarah's alibi, who did you talk to?'

'The agency she works for. But it occurred to me that they would only know what she told them – that she spent the whole day with her client.'

'You didn't speak to the client?'

'No. Which I think we need to remedy, don't you? I can make a phone call.' Nathan took out his phone. 'No time like the present.'

'Hang on.' I put out a hand to stop him. 'The *other* thought I had was about how she could've got down here, but still left her car outside the client's house, where it was sure to be seen.'

'What are you thinking?'

'Well, the client apparently has good days and bad days, don't they? Days when they can walk, and others where they're all but bedridden. I was wondering if they had a car for those good days, when they can get out on their own, and whether it's modified specifically for their disability or if anyone could drive it.'

'Sarah Dodds could've taken their car,' said Nathan thoughtfully. 'You might be onto something there…'

Nathan wandered off to make a phone call, while I

joined Mum and Daisy by the buffet. Germaine sat next to them, looking up at anyone who happened to approach the table. She was wearing the sort of expression that most people found hard to ignore, the sort that said *they don't feed me at home, please pass me a sausage.*

'I'm not falling for that one, Germaine,' I said, reaching down and making a fuss of her.

'You OK, love?' asked Mum. 'Not too disappointed about not winning?'

'No, I'm fine. Elaine deserved it much more than me. Have you tried her cake? It's amazing. So is Martin's.'

'I like yours best,' said Daisy loyally, and I hugged her.

'Thank you.' I smiled up at Tony as he joined us.

'Well, I did try to make you win...' he said, and I laughed.

'Yeah, I know. I appreciate it. But I couldn't really, could I? Not after Martin realised we were friends.'

'No, s'pose not. And I gotta admit that Elaine's cake is fantastic.'

'Better than mine?'

He grinned. 'God yeah, tons better.' I swung for him and he ducked. 'What? I'm honest, ain't I? Brought up not to lie.'

'Whatever.'

Nathan approached me, putting his phone away. 'Well *that* was interesting,' he said. 'The client, Mr Carter, says he *thinks* Sarah was there all day, but he was very ill and after she gave him his medication, he slept for most of the day.'

'So she could have slipped out? Risky, though. What if he'd woken up and called for her?'

'I thought that, too. So I asked him if any of the medication he was on causes drowsiness and he said not really, but he does sometimes suffer with insomnia and has some prescription sleeping pills.'

'Could she have given him one without him noticing?'

'Maybe. Plus he insisted on checking his medication while I was on the phone to him, and he thinks there are a couple missing. It sounds like he was in a bad way, so he may not have paid much attention to what she was giving him. Besides, he's known her for some time and he trusts her, so he probably wouldn't have questioned it anyway. And do you know how I know he trusts her?'

'How?'

'Because one day when she was visiting him her car broke down, and she had another call to get to, so...'

'So he lent her his car?'

Nathan nodded. 'Yup. I've told Matt to get onto our tech people, see if they can trace Mr Carter's car on the day of the murder.'

'How do they do that?' asked Daisy, interested. 'Do they have to look at speed cameras and that?'

'That's part of it,' said Nathan. 'But newer cars have telematics. That's things like GPS trackers, even their entertainment systems and radios, where they automatically search for local traffic news. It proves where they've been.' He turned to me. 'Whether or not it proves Sarah Dodds was in the car, though, is another matter.'

'There can't have been many other people who had access to it, certainly not on that day,' I said. 'If the client had lent it to anyone else that day, he would have told you, wouldn't he?'

'I'd have thought so. But I always like to have evidence that actually puts someone on the spot, rather than just "they probably were".'

'Something no one can argue with,' I said, nodding. I reached out and grabbed a piece of Elaine's cake – it was magnificent, I couldn't deny it – and held it up. 'Anyway, you've done your bit now. Leave it to Matt and have some more cake.'

So Nathan *did* leave it to Matt, and stayed to celebrate with me. Elaine got a bit tipsy and spent the afternoon laughing and talking to just about everybody, while her husband looked on proudly and her kids joined Daisy and Debbie's two, Matilda and George, in playing hide and seek around the tent, their hiding places instantly discovered by Germaine, who was having a marvellous time. Martin loosened up and actually chatted to me, and I realised that he'd been so wound up about winning that it had really affected his nerves. And having seen his mum – having seen that she'd not had the confidence in him to just let him compete and try to win on his own merit – I could understand it. He seemed almost like a different person now that the pressure was off.

Tony, as ever, had already made friends with everyone on the crew, and was now chatting to Shanice again. She seemed to be enjoying his flirting, but there didn't seem much point in getting too friendly as she was going to be moving on. I took Tony's charm offensive on her as a bit of fun, and a good sign that he was keeping his romantic options open. He had a big heart, a goofy smile and a daft sense of humour, and he deserved someone worthy of him.

Mum, meanwhile, was lording it up with Barbara, who did genuinely seem to enjoy her company. *Takes all sorts*, I thought, sniffily, but then I thought about Mum possibly moving out and felt a pang. She was embarrassing, she had a habit of going off at random tangents in the middle of a conversation, and the filter that stops most people saying exactly what they think without considering whether or not it was appropriate seemed to be missing from her brain; but she was warm, funny, occasionally surprisingly wise and, most of all, she was my mum. Why wouldn't Barbara like her? Tony's parents, who had come along to cheer me on and watch their son make his TV debut, gazed in awe as Mum and Barbara chatted away like they'd been besties for years, roaring with laughter and telling stories taller than the drag queen's heels. I came to the conclusion that I actually liked Barbara more than Russell, but then I supposed we had kind of accused him of murder at one point, and had then damaged his relationship with Indira (hopefully not permanently, as I really liked her) by dobbing him in about his lunchtime roll in the hay with Laura Blake.

Nathan leaned in to kiss me. 'Taking it all in?' he asked, and I smiled.

'Yes. Just thinking about how lucky I am to be here, and to have all these lovely people in my life.'

Daisy jogged over to us, Germaine at her heels. 'Is it OK if I go back to Matilda's? She's asked me and Germaine to go and play at theirs.'

'Of course, if that's OK with her mum?' I looked up as Debbie approached.

'Yeah, it's fine by me,' she said. 'Lovely to see them getting on so well, innit? She can stay for dinner and all if you like, give you two a bit of space.' She turned to Daisy. 'That's if you don't mind takeaway pizza…'

'I LOVE takeaway pizza! Mum always makes her own—' Daisy stopped and made an abrupt conversational U-turn. 'Which is lovely, of course…'

I laughed. 'Good save. Go on, have fun!'

Five minutes later Mum came over, flushed after holding court with Barbara.

'Lovely spread, innit?' she said, gesturing to the table. 'Nice party. I think I've had enough now, though.'

'That's OK, we can go…' I said, looking at Nathan, who nodded.

'No no, you stay. Brenda and Malcolm are going home soon, I thought I'd go back with them for the evening, get you used to me not being around.'

'God, Mum, don't say it like that! You're possibly moving out, not dying,' I said.

'You know what I mean. You two can have the house to yourselves,' she said, winking at Nathan, who turned bright red. Bless him. She cackled. 'I know what it's like, having to keep the noise down in the bedroom. Me and your father—'

'OK, enough! I'm not listening anymore. Off you go with the Penhaligons, have fun…'

'And you,' she said, pecking me on the cheek and tottering off. Across the car park I saw Tony waiting with his parents. He'd driven them there, and he'd have to take them all home including my mum now. Poor bugger.

'Poor bugger,' said Nathan, as Tony gave us a resigned wave and left. We both giggled. Nathan turned to me with an arched brow. 'So, Ms Parker, it looks like it's just you and me this evening. What shall we do?'

'I have a few suggestions,' I said, well, suggestively. Nathan grinned and opened his mouth to speak, but then his phone rang. He looked at the number and groaned. 'Duty calls?' I asked, and he nodded.

'Hey, Matt, what you got for me?' Nathan listened, making me lean in close to try and hear his DS's side of the conversation, but I couldn't. 'Really? That's bloody brilliant... I'd call that conclusive, wouldn't you? Call the Bristol lads, get someone over there and – what? Bugger... No, put out a call on her car reg but I reckon I know where she's heading.' Nathan disconnected the call.

'What's happened?' I asked, almost bursting.

'Lots. But the short of it is, the GPS on Mr Carter's Toyota pinged at just after 11 a.m. on the day of the murder, on the M5 just outside Exeter, and then again on the A30 at Launceston an hour later. That gives us reason enough to examine the car.'

'I told you it's always the spouse. You got enough to arrest her, or at least get her in for questioning?'

'Yes, only she's not at home, and neither is her car. Make a guess as to where she's heading,' said Nathan.

'Here, to find her necklace?'

'That's what I reckon. She might even be here already, waiting for everyone to leave. She probably wouldn't have expected the roadshow to still be here.' Nathan grinned. 'Have you ever been on a date night stake-out?'

Chapter Twenty

'You certainly know how to treat a lady.'

We were sitting in my car, parked in a shady corner of the car park, almost hidden behind some trees. We had a good view of the spot where Harry Dodds, supply teacher, sometime production assistant and unfortunate husband, had met his death, but hopefully anyone coming to search it would not have a good view of us. It was starting to get dark now, and there was rain in the air.

The rest of the roadshow had gone. It was surprising (and impressive) just how quickly they had packed up and disappeared, the only trace that they'd ever been there a tangle of tyre tracks from the production vehicles, and a Jackson Pollock-esque pattern of footprints on the churned-up lawn next to the spot where the baking tent had once stood. I'd hugged my fellow competitors and said goodbye, even promising to visit Martin's café the next time I was in Bodmin. Camilla had stiffly said her farewells to us and then begun to corral her team into packing up. She might not be around next season, but there was no doubt that she was still in charge for now.

Barbara had disappeared into the hair and make-up tent and re-emerged as Russell. He'd been somewhat taciturn in his goodbye to me, but I suppose I couldn't really blame him. At least the catering crew, on hearing our plan to stay behind on police business, had taken pity on us and left us with two insulated mugs of coffee (emblazoned with the Roadshow logo on them) and the leftovers of the buffet, wrapped in serviettes and stuffed into Tupperware.

Nathan laughed as he bit into a sausage roll. I was amazed there had been any left, what with my daughter and my dog (who were both addicted to them) being present at the buffet.

'Don't say I never take you anywhere.'

'Strictly speaking, it was me who brought *you* here, and we're in my car, so I think you still owe me a date…'

Nathan swallowed his mouthful. 'Deal. What's happening with Daisy, is she staying at Debbie's overnight?'

'No, Debbie said she'll liaise with Mum about taking her home. Mum won't stay that late at the Penhaligons', she's normally falling asleep on the sofa by nine so it'll be fine.'

'Good. It makes doing stuff like this a lot easier with your mum living with us, doesn't it?'

'Yeah, it does…' I looked at him seriously. 'Be honest, do you really not mind her living with us? You can't have imagined meeting and moving in with someone who's not only got a teenager but also her mother living with her.'

'Of course I didn't. But I meant what I said. I've always known that you come as a package. I'm not turfing anyone out just so I can move in. If your mum really wants to go, then we'll help her find somewhere nice, nearby. But I don't want her to leave on my account.'

'Did you mean that, about building an extension for her? I know it would probably be easier to just buy a bigger house together at some point, but…'

'But you love that house, because it represents you starting a new life with Daisy.' Nathan took my hand. 'I get it. I think we just need to wait and see how we all get on when I move in. We don't need to make any decisions just yet, do we?'

'Yes we do,' I said, sitting up and peering out across the rapidly darkening car park. 'We need to decide what we're going to do about *her*.' I squinted. 'If that *is* her.'

A car had just pulled up near the entrance of the car

park. I had wondered if the fact that the entrance to Boskern House was closed would stop our murderer driving in, but it was only a chain strung across the entrance, and it would have been the work of about thirty seconds to take it down, drive through, then string it up again behind them.

The car stopped, then manoeuvred until it was facing the crime scene. The headlights had been off, not wanting to attract attention, but now they flicked on; it was getting dark, and if this really was Sarah Dodds come to find her necklace – the necklace which she thought was the only thing that incriminated her – she wouldn't want to be spending hours searching through the mud for it.

The driver's door opened and a figure got out. Sarah Dodds was a statuesque woman with a powerful-looking physique, particularly compared to her slim, wiry late husband. Her work involved helping disabled clients, and I guessed that part of that included lifting them up, which required a lot of upper body strength. She looked like she would have been strong enough to smash Harry's head in with a rock, certainly if she'd taken him by surprise and from behind.

She stopped and looked around. Inside my car, we both froze: but it was dark in our corner of the car park, and she didn't see us. She began to search the wooden bridge where she'd killed Harry and left his body slumped against the railing.

'Stay in the car,' said Nathan, turning to open the door.

'But—'

'I mean it, babe. She's a killer. I don't want you getting hurt.' He climbed out of the car and slunk across the car park.

'Bugger that,' I muttered, quietly slipping out of the car as well. I wouldn't get involved, but I would get just close enough to hear what was going on…

Sarah had realised the necklace wasn't on the bridge, and had turned her attention to the nearby riverbank. I watched her skid slightly on the mud, like Tony had the day before; the day's sunshine hadn't been enough to dry it up. Nathan approached.

'Mrs Dodds!' he called, pleasantly. It was her turn to freeze now. She turned around. 'You're looking for your necklace, I assume?'

She looked shocked, and I could sense her scrabbling around for something to say. 'What – what necklace?'

'This one, the one you're wearing in your Facebook profile picture,' said Nathan, holding up his phone. We'd discovered her social media accounts while we'd been waiting for her to get to Boskern, and hadn't been able to believe our luck when we'd actually found evidence of her wearing it. 'You do realise that if that's NOT why you're here, that's even more suspicious?'

She forced a smile. 'Oh, yes, of course that's why I'm here. It belonged to my mum. I gave it to Harry when he went away, to keep him safe—'

'Didn't work very well, did it?'

'No, no it didn't. Anyway, I noticed that it wasn't amongst his things, when you lot let me have them, so I thought I'd come and look for it.'

'And it wouldn't have been easier to ask us to look for it? Or come in the daylight, like a normal person?'

'Well, I…' She trailed off helplessly and stood for a moment, just looking at him.

'Why did you kill your husband, Mrs Dodds?'

'I – I told you, I was at work—'

'We spoke to your patient. He was asleep for most of your time with him. Mr Carter is very conscientious about taking his medication and keeping track of it, so he doesn't run out. He admits he's a little obsessed with it. But when he checked earlier, there seemed to be a couple of sleeping pills missing. I'm betting those are the sleeping pills that *you* gave him, so you could sneak out without him knowing anything about it. You were very thorough. You drove over there that day and made sure you parked your car where everyone could see it. It's even on film, picked up by your patient's doorbell camera. And you left your phone at the house, so if anyone tracked it they would think you'd been there all day. But guess what the last destination on the SatNav on your patient's car was? Boskern House is in the middle of nowhere, so no wonder you needed directions. And of course the GPS technology that helped you plan the route also showed the time and date you followed it.'

'That wasn't me—' she started, but Nathan cut her off again.

'Smart watches are cool, aren't they? I've just got one of those fitness ones, but the really fancy ones sync up with your phone, or your car stereo … or someone else's car stereo, in this case. Did you sync it up when Mr Carter let you drive his car before? Big mistake. Because once it's connected, every time you get in that car it will connect again. Even without the phone it's tied to being in the car, as long as it's nearby it'll still connect. The minute you turned on the engine, your smart watch synced up with the car's entertainment system and put you behind the wheel, the morning of Harry's murder, with plenty of time to drive down here.' Nathan stared at her, but she didn't speak. 'I'll ask you again. Why did you kill your husband?'

'He told me to get out,' she said bitterly. 'He wanted a divorce, but instead of walking out on me, he wanted *me* to leave. He said he was going on the roadshow, and that when he got back he wanted me out of the house. He said it was his house, his name was on the deeds, and he didn't want me in it anymore.' She looked at Nathan, and in the beam of the car headlights I could see her eyes sparkling with unshed tears, but whether they were tears of sorrow or anger, I couldn't say. 'It might have been his house, but it was my *home*. I wasn't going to leave.'

'So you killed him.'

'I was just coming to talk to him. I found him sitting here. He was so busy playing with this stupid blonde wig he didn't even hear me coming up behind me. I didn't mean to kill him—'

'No.' Nathan spoke firmly and shook his head, but didn't raise his voice. 'No, Mrs Dodds. We've already established the lengths you went to, to hide the fact that you were down here. Why would you do that if all you wanted to do was talk? No, you planned everything very carefully. You knew you were going to murder him. We've seen your phone records. You spoke to your husband the night before he died. Did you tell him you were coming down? Did you arrange to meet him here, near the car park, so he'd be easy to find?'

Sarah didn't answer. Nathan paused, and then sighed. He stepped forward to make the arrest. Suddenly she sprang into life, leaping towards him, hands out in front of her. She shoved him as hard as he could. Nathan staggered back, and he would have been fine, but for the muddy bank they were standing on. His feet slipped out from under him and he fell backwards into the dirt.

Sarah snarled and reached down, picking up a large rock that was nearby—

'Don't beat up my boyfriend, you mad cow!' I shrieked, launching myself at her from my hiding place, just as Matt Dawson and Davey Trelawney appeared from across the car park where they'd secreted themselves earlier. They pulled Sarah Dodds away from me (which was annoying, but probably for the best) and up onto her feet, twisting her around and slamming her face-first onto the bonnet of her own car. I reached down and hauled Nathan to his feet.

Nathan recovered himself as Matt handcuffed Sarah Dodds.

'Sarah Dodds,' started Matt. 'I'm arresting you for the murder of Harry Dodds…' He added in an undertone, 'and for beating up Jodie's boyfriend.'

Nathan groaned. 'I'm never living that down, am I?'

'No, Guv. Never.'

Chapter Twenty-One

'That's the last one,' said Nathan, carrying a large box into the kitchen and plonking it onto the table. 'I didn't realise I had so much stuff. Good to see you working so hard…'

I looked up sheepishly from my phone. 'Sorry, Debbie just sent me the link to this. Look!' I passed over the phone. There was a news article displayed; a headline screaming, 'Bake Off Babs' Shock Revelation' with a picture of him and Indira, hand in hand, smiling up at us underneath it.

'He came out, then?' said Nathan. 'Good for him.'

'And her,' I said. 'I'm glad Indira forgave him. I think they look good together, don't you?'

'Like us.'

I smiled at him. 'Oh no, not as good as us…' I opened the box on the table and looked inside. 'This looks like kitchen things,' I said. 'I've probably got most of this already.' I held up a potato masher. 'Like this. I've already got three of these, for some reason.'

'We can take anything we've doubled up on down the charity shop,' he said, pulling me towards him. 'But let's not worry about unpacking now. It's my day off. Daisy's at school, your mum's out shopping, and we have the house to ourselves. I can think of better things we could be doing…'

There was a knock on the front door, which was still open, and the sound of someone clearing their throat. I hastily pulled away from him.

'Hold that thought!'

Standing on the doorstep was a well-groomed man, mid-fifties, wearing a very smart (and high-ranking, from the crown on his epaulettes) police uniform. He smiled.

'Jodie Parker?'

'Er – yes?'

'I'm sorry to interrupt, I can see you're busy. I wondered if I might have a word with you?'

'Um – okay.' I stood on the doorstep, feeling a bit dumbfounded, as Nathan came up behind me.

'Who is it, Jo—' he started, then stopped in surprise. 'Oh! Sir.'

'DCI Withers, good to see you again,' said the officer. 'Jodie, I'm Superintendent Michael Hansen. Could I come in for a moment?'

'Oh yes, of course, sorry Sir,' I said, stepping aside to let him. The superintendent laughed.

'There's no need for "Sir", Jodie, you're a civilian.'

'Force of habit, S—' I stopped myself and indicated the door to the living room, which was thankfully rather less full of boxes than the rest of the house.

Hansen led the way in and we followed, Nathan and I exchanging bemused and slightly concerned glances.

'May I?' said Hansen, indicating the sofa.

'Of course,' I said. He sat down. I sat in the chair opposite and Nathan perched on the arm.

'What can I do for you, Superintendent?' I asked, hoping I didn't sound as nervous as I felt. He smiled.

'I'm rather hoping it's what can we do for each other,' he said cryptically. 'Your fame as an investigator has spread all the way to Middlemoor, Jodie.' Middlemoor was where the headquarters of the Devon and Cornwall Constabulary were situated. As superintendent of the force, Hansen wasn't quite the top brass, but he wasn't far below them.

'Fame or infamy?' I asked, and he grinned.

'Well, yes, quite. That's why I'm here.' He settled himself more comfortably on the sofa, and I thought, *Uh-oh, this is not going to be a quick conversation. We're in trouble.* 'We're well aware that you've worked with DCI Withers on a couple of occasions as a consultant.'

I felt Nathan tense next to me. He had checked the rules and made sure that as a civilian consultant I didn't overstep any boundaries, but it was still an unorthodox thing to do.

'Nathan— DCI Withers has followed all the proper protocols,' I said quickly. 'If there's been any wrongdoing here, that would be me. I can get a little overenthusiastic at times.'

Hansen shook his head. 'No, that's fine. I'll admit that eyebrows were raised at first, but your background in the Met, and the fact that you were on the spot in these cases or had some inside knowledge of the people involved, means we can justify your involvement if we need to.' He looked at Nathan, and gave him a small but reassuring nod. 'I get it. Sometimes you need to think outside the box. As long as it doesn't prejudice a case or lead to it getting thrown out of court.'

'Has something happened, Sir?' asked Nathan. 'I wasn't aware that the CPS had had any complaints.'

'No, nothing like that. We've had one solicitor bring up Jodie's unauthorised presence at an unofficial interview, but it got thrown out because you then conducted an official one at the station, with only police personnel involved, where their client confessed to everything. It was a move of desperation, rather than a genuine complaint.' Hansen looked serious. 'That is, so far. The Dodds case involved some high-profile people, and a very popular TV show. That could have gone horribly wrong for us, and your involvement could really have blown up in our face if someone like Russell Lang or the TV company had decided to make a complaint about it. Don't worry.' He held up a hand as I opened my mouth to say something. 'That isn't about to happen. We've been able to smooth a few ruffled feathers and lay the matter to rest. Between you and me, it was less about anything you'd done and more about an upset ego. But we need to make sure it doesn't happen in the future.'

I looked at Nathan, then at Hansen with a sinking heart. 'So my detective days are over?'

'Not necessarily…' Hansen leaned forward, elbows on his knees. 'Let me level with you. Doubtless you already know this, Nathan, but we have a real recruitment problem on our hands at the moment. Our young people are leaving the area and heading upcountry, and who can blame them? There are more jobs, more opportunities and better pay in other parts of the world. The ones that are left behind have very little interest in joining the police. We've had some success recruiting officers from other parts of the country, such as yourself, older officers who are looking for somewhere nice to raise their family. But that still leaves us with a shortage.' I looked at him, wondering if he really was driving at what I thought he was. 'You have twenty years' experience in the force, Jodie. An exemplary service record. A commendation for bravery, just before you left.'

'Are you trying to recruit me?' I asked in amazement. He shrugged.

'Would you rejoin if I asked you?' I hesitated, and he shook his head. 'You don't have to answer that. I spoke to the brass at your old nick back in London, and they told me why you'd left. They also said you were one of the best coppers they had and they were sorry to see you go. So, if you did ever feel like coming back, we'd be delighted to have you. But I understand why you quit.'

'I didn't lose my nerve,' I said quickly, and then wondered why I had. The terrorist attack I'd been involved in had been the final straw, but for Daisy rather than me. I'd been fine. So why was I always so quick to tell people I hadn't lost my nerve afterwards?

'We know you didn't. Anyway, that's not what I'm proposing.' He sat back, all the better to observe my reaction, I thought. 'We'd like to put your work with Penstowan CID on a more official footing.'

I glanced at Nathan, who looked as bewildered as I felt. 'How do you mean?'

'We've talked about it…' I wasn't sure I wanted to know who 'we' were; the thought of senior-level police officers knowing who I was, let alone talking about little old me, was slightly terrifying '…and we think this is the best solution. We want to put you on a proper, permanent retainer with CID.'

'You want Jodie to join CID?' Nathan was amazed but, I thought, more than a little proud.

'In a casual capacity. Our budget for this part of the area is stretched as it is, and to employ another full-time officer with your experience, Jodie, would cost us a lot of money, although if you'd consider it we'd certainly find a way. But I'm not sure a return to full-time policing is what you want, is it?'

I thought about it. There was no denying that I did miss being a police officer. I missed being able to stick my nose in – although I still did that now, just unofficially. I missed the excitement, but working with Nathan had given me plenty of that. I didn't miss the shift work. And I didn't miss not being around for Daisy when she needed me, or that anxious look on her face every time I left for work. I did not miss that AT ALL.

'What would this "casual capacity" mean?' I asked. Nathan and Hansen exchanged grins; they knew I was on the hook.

'Exactly that. Our CID officers are pretty much

working flat out on the more common serious crime we get down here – robbery, assaults, fraud. We don't get too many murders, luckily, but when one does occur it's all hands to the pump. And sometimes there aren't enough hands. That's when you'd come in.'

'Like an auxiliary officer?' I'd worked with auxiliaries – or Special Constables, as they were known – in the Met. Some of my fellow coppers had looked down on them, sneering about them 'playing at' being police officers, but I thought they were amazing. Some of them were working as Specials while they waited to join police college, but a lot of them had other, paid jobs (often full-time), and volunteered to help us out on the beat because they wanted to help the local community, and to give something back. Not something that should be sneered at, in my opinion.

'Just like that. Except we'd pay you for hours worked, and you would be permanently seconded to CID, not on the beat. It would be a trial, to start off with, and being an auxiliary means we would be able to send you anywhere you were needed. You wouldn't necessarily end up only working with DCI Withers, or with Penstowan police. Although in practice that probably wouldn't happen very often.' He stood up. 'I'll leave you to think about it. Here.' He handed me a business card. 'Give me a call if you have any questions, or to say yes, of course.' He turned to leave, then turned back with a smile. 'I have a feeling I know what your answer will be. I hope I'm not wrong.' I glanced at Nathan, who was watching me closely, then looked at Hansen with a grin.

'I can tell you what it is right now, Sir,' I said.

Rich Cornish Fruitcake with Saffron and Orange

As I'm *constantly* telling everyone, I'm a chef, not a baker. But these days I seem to be dragged into baking more and more. I complain about it, but only because sugarcraft and cake decorating have never been my strong suit; I'm far too impatient to do all that fiddly stuff. But, as I also constantly tell everyone, my actual cakes usually taste pretty darn good, even if they occasionally look like I dropped them when I took them out of the oven.

This is one of my favourite cakes, because it ALWAYS turns out proper lush. It takes a while to make, but don't let that put you off; it's really easy, and a lot of that time is waiting for things to cool down or bake in the oven, giving you plenty of time to go off and make a cup of tea, watch a ninety-minute movie on Netflix, or maybe even solve a murder… Another bonus is you make it all in one big saucepan, so there's not a lot of washing up afterwards!

This is really just a basic fruitcake, but I've added saffron and orange juice to give it a richer flavour and Cornish-ify (totally a word) it a bit. You can leave either or both out though and it will still work a treat.

1. Put the oven on at its lowest setting and pop a **pinch of saffron** (if using) into a ramekin, and place inside to toast it slightly. DON'T LET IT BURN!

2. Add **450g/1lb dried fruit** (you can use one of those packs of mixed fruit, or sultanas, currants or whatever you prefer – I like to use sultanas and cranberries, and chopped dates might be good too), **225g/8oz soft brown sugar** and **100g/4oz butter or margarine** to a large saucepan and pour over **150ml/1/4pint water**.

3. If you're using saffron, take it out of the oven, crush it up and add to the pan. Also add **zest of 1 orange** and **1tbsp orange juice** to the pan at this point if you want to.

4. Cover the pan and bring to the boil, then let it simmer for around 10–15 minutes until the

sugar and butter are properly dissolved, and the fruit looks plump and juicy. Then leave to cool.

5. Pre-heat the oven to 150°C/300°F/gas mark 3.
6. Add **2 beaten eggs** and **225g/8oz self-raising flour** to the fruit mixture and stir well to combine, then pour into a greased and lined 20cm/8in cake tin and bake for 90 minutes. You'll know it's done when the cake begins to shrink away from the sides of the tin. If it starts to get too brown on top before it's finished cooking, pop some silver foil over it to stop it burning.
7. Leave it to cool in the tin for 5–10 minutes, then turn it out and let it cool thoroughly on a rack. Then get the kettle on and cut yourself a big slice!

Acknowledgments

Bringing a book to publication is a collaborative process, so as ever there's a *long* list of people I need to thank.

First of all, thank you to the **Great British Bake Off** for existing and inspiring me. I'm watching it as I type this (oh my God, Jürgen just dropped his vegan sausage rolls on the floor! What a nightmare!). I'm not a good enough baker to compete, so this book is probably the closest I'll ever get to a technical challenge. And I've just realised I missed a trick by not including Death by Chocolate as one of the recipes (or the murder weapon). Goddammit.

To my agent, **Lina Langlee**, and everyone at **The North Literary Agency**; I feel very lucky to have you behind me! I try not to give in to the old 'creative temperament' too often, but when I do you know exactly how to calm me down/gee me up/give me some tough love. I do occasionally need to be told to pull myself together...

To my editor, **Bethan Morgan**, and the team at **One More Chapter**; thank you for your confidence in me, and your continued support of Jodie and the Penstowan gang. We appreciate it! And we *adore* the new covers...

To my writing besties, **Carmen Radtke, Jade Bokhari, Sandy Barker, Andie Newton** and **Nina Kaye**; you are my sisters from other misters and I literally could not do this without you. I love talking to you ladies every day, our brainstorming sessions, our putting the world to rights, and our downright silliness.

To my husband **Dominic** and son **Lucas**; thank you for humouring me, making endless cups of tea, and always having my back. I love you!